An Unforgettable Rogue

"Never has a hero submitted to such sweet seduction while making it clear that he is still very much a man in charge . . . Spicy sensuality is the hallmark of this unforgettable story." —*The Romance Readers Connection*

" 'Knight In Shining Silver' Award for KISSable heroes. Bryceson 'Hawk' Wakefield is most definitely *An Unforgettable Rogue*." —*Romantic Times*

"I recommend *An Unforgettable Rogue* as an entertaining book in its own right, even more as part of the must-read Rogues Club series." —*Romance Reviews Today*

An Undeniable Rogue

"A love story that is pure joy, enchanting characters who steal your heart, a fast pace, and great storytelling." —*Romantic Times*

"An utterly charming and heartwarming marriage of convenience story. I highly recommend it to all lovers of romance." —*Romance Reviews Today*

"Awesome! To call this story incredible would be an understatement . . . Do not miss this title." —*Huntress Reviews*

"Annette Blair skillfully pens an exhilarating, humorous, and easy to read historical romance. You don't want to miss *An Undeniable Rogue*." —Jan Springer

Sex
and the
Psychic
Witch

Annette Blair

BERKLEY SENSATION, NEW YORK

THE BERKLEY PUBLISHING GROUP
Published by the Penguin Group
Penguin Group (USA) Inc.
375 Hudson Street, New York, New York 10014, USA
Penguin Group (Canada), 90 Eglinton Avenue East, Suite 700, Toronto, Ontario M4P 2Y3, Canada
(a division of Pearson Penguin Canada Inc.)
Penguin Books Ltd., 80 Strand, London WC2R 0RL, England
Penguin Group Ireland, 25 St. Stephen's Green, Dublin 2, Ireland (a division of Penguin Books Ltd.)
Penguin Group (Australia), 250 Camberwell Road, Camberwell, Victoria 3124, Australia
(a division of Pearson Australia Group Pty. Ltd.)
Penguin Books India Pvt. Ltd., 11 Community Centre, Panchsheel Park, New Delhi—110 017, India
Penguin Group (NZ), 67 Apollo Drive, Rosedale, North Shore 0745, Auckland, New Zealand
(a division of Pearson New Zealand Ltd.)
Penguin Books (South Africa) (Pty.) Ltd., 24 Sturdee Avenue, Rosebank, Johannesburg 2196,
South Africa

Penguin Books Ltd., Registered Offices: 80 Strand, London WC2R 0RL, England

This is a work of fiction. Names, characters, places, and incidents either are the product of the author's imagination or are used fictitiously, and any resemblance to actual persons, living or dead, business establishments, events, or locales is entirely coincidental. The publisher does not have any control over and does not assume any responsibility for author or third-party websites or their content.

SEX AND THE PSYCHIC WITCH

A Berkley Sensation Book / published by arrangement with the author

PRINTING HISTORY
Berkley Sensation mass-market edition / August 2007

Copyright © 2007 by Annette Blair.
Excerpt copyright © 2007 by Annette Blair.
Cover design by Rita Frangie.
Interior text design by Kristin del Rosario.

ISBN: 978-0-425-21663-7

BERKLEY® SENSATION
Berkley Sensation Books are published by The Berkley Publishing Group,
a division of Penguin Group (USA) Inc.,
375 Hudson Street, New York, New York 10014.
BERKLEY SENSATION and the "B" design are trademarks belonging to Penguin Group (USA) Inc.

PRINTED IN THE UNITED STATES OF AMERICA

10 9 8 7 6 5 4 3 2 1

With love and thanks to my three generous and delightful inspirations:

Sarah, Meghan, and Kate Malloy
Triplets Extraordinaire

For sharing a lifetime of triplet secrets
and for answering my questions
no matter where you were in the world at the time.

It seems like yesterday that you came to my door selling
cookies and I thought I was hallucinating.

Note to my readers:

Sarah, Meghan, and Kate are the inspiration
for my triplet series, not the models,
though when they raise their voices in song together,
they do raise a vibration.
And there the resemblance ends.

Chapter One

"SORRY, Dracula. That one's mine."

The costumed yard sale vampire looked up, tripped, and took a header into an appliance box of Koosh balls, taking the clothes rack—and the gown calling Harmony Cartwright's name—down with him. She thought he'd get the gown, after all, but it slipped from its hanger and floated on a phantom breeze into her hand.

Harmony helped him up. "We didn't mean to startle you."

Triplets attracted attention, but in identical minidresses, black front-lace corsets, striped stockings, and black spikes, they tended to stop traffic, even without their pointy hats. The vamp was no exception. His face as red as his lips, he firmed his spine, eyed them like freaks under glass, and moved on.

"This *is* a costume yard sale for charity," Harmony called after him. She appealed to her sisters. "It's not like I put a klutz spell on him."

"Probably thought he was hallucinating," Storm said. "We should be used to it."

"Anywhere but Salem, and we'd think *he* was weird."
Harmony hugged her psychic prize. "But I got the gown! It
wanted me. It really did."

Storm faltered. "I hope you mean that *you* wanted *it.*"

"Nope. It's meant to be mine. I don't know why yet."

"Here she goes again," Storm said turning to hug an oak
in Druidic appeal and looking toward its branches. "Help!"

Yes, Storm was making a bit of a scene, but in their
musketeer youth, when feeling like curiosities under glass
wore thin, they'd decided to give the curious something to
talk about—Storm, as it turned out, enjoyed a talent for the
outlandish.

Destiny patted the oak, apologized, and took Storm's
arm. "You're slipping, kid. I knew she was chasing psychic
bait when she missed that rare Dior handbag. Harmony, I
see stormy seas ahead for you now. Don't drag us under
with you this time, 'kay?"

Harmony gave her clairvoyant sister a hair flip with attitude. "I can swim."

Storm scoffed. "Into a swamp of eternal stench, you can
swim."

"Okay, I agree, my psychic instincts make for some
rough sailing."

"And shipwrecks," Storm added. "Remember when we
gave that widower the 'be good' letter from his dead wife?
Totally blew *his* honeymoon. And I'm pretty sure it was
your idea to chase that psychic duck across Gallows Hill."

Destiny elbowed Storm, but Harmony huffed. "An old
letter calls my name, I deliver it. Your psychic gifts get us
into trouble, too, both of you."

"I know. I love answering unspoken questions." Storm
grinned and fluffed her blonde wig. "I forgot how dressing
alike and screwing with people's minds jazzes me. It's almost as much fun as being a spike-haired Goth. Not that I
plan to start conforming."

"Don't worry," Destiny said. "I now see very rebellious roads ahead."

"More rebellious than normal?" Storm asked. "What's with the changes in our futures?"

"Holy hemlock!" Destiny reached for Harmony's bag. "I'll bet it's the gown."

Harmony grasped the bag and hurried past their vintage clothing and curio shop toward the house behind it, dodging her sister's grabby hands as she did.

Storm followed, shaking her head. "You two are acting sixteen instead of twenty-six, and for once I'm not the attention-getter."

Destiny stopped and saw the tourists watching them.

Harmony raised her chin but lowered her voice. "I'm keeping the gown. Change is good. If Dad hadn't stopped paying our college tuition and disappeared, we wouldn't have gotten kicked out of school or come looking for Nana. But he did, and we did, and though Nana was gone, and Vickie didn't even know she had half sisters, she took us in."

"And ended up with the man of her dreams," Storm added. "I'd like to think we helped."

Harmony did a double take. "That's debatable, but eight months ago, Vickie owned the Immortal Classic, and we were homeless. Now we have a home, not to mention co-ownership of the shop. I repeat: Change is good."

"Sometimes," Destiny said, giving up. "I do like running the Classic."

"You mean you like bossing us around," Storm said, "but that's okay. I find it amusing to ignore you."

Harmony climbed the steps to the kitchen door. She didn't work *in* the shop. Her psychic gift—reading old objects and their dead owners through proximity and touch—made that impossible. Warring vibes from so many objects in one place made her head spin and stomach churn. Being psychometric often felt like a curse, but sensing objects with negative vibes made her a great buyer. Customers appreciated positive-energy vintage, whether they realized it or not. "Hurry," she said. "I wanna try on the gown before you open the shop."

In her room, Harmony held the gown in the mirror before her.

Storm scoffed. "Nobody's gonna buy that ugly thing."

"I'm not *selling* it. I told you, it wants me . . . and it energizes me."

"I feel the energy force," Storm admitted. "I'm pooped just sharing it." She flopped back on the bed. "*Things* are always calling you, but you do a lot of running in the opposite direction. What's up with the gown?"

"It needed my help?" Harmony pulled the gown over her head, freed her hair from its neck, and the aged gold linen fell over her hips as if making love to her figure. But when she looked in the mirror, she saw her path disappear behind her. Oh. No way back . . . yet expectation rode the prickles attacking her limbs. Smoothing the wrinkled fabric morphed anxiety to anticipation, a good sign, since touch sharpened her psychic awareness.

"Pay attention to the signs," her sisters said, employing their personal communication device, a fine-tuned triplet telepathy.

"The owner's name was Lisette," Harmony said. "She sewed every stitch." From a lace scallop beneath her breasts, the waist slimmed then widened slightly. At knee level, vertical pleats fell from a repeat of the scallop. She smoothed a sleeve point and turned to her collection of wall mirrors. Ancient mirrors sometimes reflected images from objects with a strong sense of their owner.

Four walls of antique mirrors, and nothing. Nada. But looking back in the full-length mirror, Harmony saw, reflected from an oxidized octagon mirror, a pair of frantic hands undoing the gown's hem. She lifted the hem with an empathetic panic.

"I saw that," Storm said, and Destiny nodded.

Harmony plucked at the brittle threads. "No! Don't help. Thanks, but I'm supposed to do it myself." Harmony's lungs tightened as if the sea were trying to swallow her whole. She coughed, cleared her throat, and a gold ring fell into her hand.

She straightened, breathing easier, and held the ring palm up.

"A naked guy in a come-and-get-it pose," Storm said, describing the piece. "My kind of jewelry."

"A nude male in a full-bodied but empty embrace," Destiny murmured, taking the ring to the window. "You know . . . I think this is part of a Celtic puzzle ring. If the other half were here, the two halves, one with a man, and one with a woman, both embracing air, would have snapped together to form a ring with an embracing couple. This is a pricey find. Look at the craftsmanship."

"It's engraved," Harmony said, "with the words Love Eternal." She grasped the ring, sat on the bed, closed her eyes, and touched her fist to her brow. "Lisette was afraid," she said as the mattress gave on either side—her sisters lending their physical and extrasensory support.

As Harmony slipped the Celtic band on her wedding ring finger, a green paisley haze formed behind her eyelids, the haze writhing and hissing, racing her heart, hurting her head, until it took the form of a woman trapped in a sphere of dark discord. A flash of lightning revealed a castle behind her, then a black pit into which Harmony fell.

Her sisters called her name, but she couldn't seem to find them.

When Harmony opened her eyes, Destiny sat on the floor, cradling her. "You okay?"

"What happened?" Harmony accepted a hand up and a glass of water.

"You took a graceful slide into oblivion and scared the hell out of us," Destiny said.

"What? No Prince Charmy to kiss me awake? Bummer."

"Prince *Smarmy*, you mean." Storm handed her a painting depicting the castle from her vision, sitting high on an island in the background.

Harmony touched her sore head. "I never liked that painting."

"It reeks of bad vibes." Storm sat and held it for them to see. "Not only is this the castle from your vision, but Lili, our witch ancestor, painted it."

"Terrific," Harmony said, getting off the bed. "Exactly the kind of sweeping, psychic multiple directive I've always dreamed of getting. Not!"

"So," Storm said, "are you taking the witch-broom express?"

"To the castle? Me? I'm not going there."

"You blacked out just envisioning it," Des said. "You'd be nuts to go."

Harmony frowned. "What happened to paying attention to the signs?"

"I'm agreeing with you," Des explained. "No use looking for trouble."

"No use accepting the psychic mandate the universe just handed me?"

"*You're* the one who said no. I'm supporting your decision."

Harmony turned on her. "*You're* thinking I should go. You think Harmony against discord makes sense. I bring peace wherever I go, you're thinking." Her voice rose involuntarily. "This is blooming fate, you're thinking, damn it!"

Destiny raised a brow. "Is that what I'm thinking?"

"Screw the castle," Storm said. "It's scarier in fact than

it is in the painting or in your vision. I'm the psychic who sees and hears the present, don't forget, and I don't like the potential for either at that place."

"What do you hear?" Harmony asked.

"A wail like a death rattle."

Harmony stopped pacing. "I'll bring a gun."

"You will not!" Destiny snapped. "You'll bring your cell phone."

"I won't need a phone. You'll come if I need you."

"The police won't."

"Oh." Harmony sat beside them once more. "You think the castle's dangerous?"

Destiny sighed. "Lisette's hands were trembling."

Harmony examined their faces. "Did either of you sense anything else?"

"A dominant male." Destiny shrugged. "Hard features and a hard bod."

Storm sighed. "I got an audiovisual of a baby crying in a boat." She shrugged. "I know; I *always* hear babies crying. Who knew I'd be the sensitive one? Harmony, you're gonna play it safe and stay here, right?"

"When did I ever play it safe? And what good am I, if I don't use my psychic gifts? Psychometry! Like that'll help mankind. No, we agreed to do our best by our gifts a long time ago, so that's what I'm gonna do."

"Which is?" Her sisters asked together.

"I'm going to the castle."

"Bad choice," they said.

"Ignoring my psychic gifts is the *worst* bad choice I can make. Accepting a psychic mandate, no matter how ominous, is the least bad. I'm going. Destiny already predicted rough seas, so it's fate."

"I'll make you a charm bag." Destiny rose, not the least surprised.

Storm frowned. "You do know that Paxton Castle is haunted by a witch, right?"

"A fateful opponent. Geez, what'd I do, win the spook stakes?"

"Hardly," Destiny said. "Could be, the loser gets the castle."

"I'll take the charm bag and raise you Nana's amethyst ring . . . to protect me from psychic attack and enhance my power. For you, Storm, I'll hug every oak between here and the marina."

"Twice," Storm said, "and protect yourself with a circle of white light."

"Make that a sphere," Destiny said, "and take your wand."

Chapter Two

KING Paxton looked up from his computer screen, jarred by a sudden crisp and eerie silence, the first of his experience in this godforsaken hellhole. No construction sounds. No wailing wind. No bickering workers.

Just a goddess in the great hall.

King gave his ogling crew a fierce scowl, but they stood rooted, all gazes locked on Real-Life Barbie. And no wonder, considering the man magnet's startling effect.

Great guns, he needed his libido coming out of hibernation like he needed a root canal, but he appreciated the rare sense of peace washing over him, though its origin puzzled him. In his experience, peace and sexual attraction did not go hand in hand. And it didn't make sense to explore the anomaly or its ramifications, because he couldn't act on either. As heir to this creepy kingdom, he needed to get this castle fixed and off his hands, without interruption.

King stalked the man magnet's way, invaded her space, and towered over her—a move that had broken better men—but the goddess refused to step back or break eye contact, while the scent of a lush summer garden encircled him.

"Quite an intense, off-with-their-heads look you've got going here," the intruder said. "Drawbridge, moat, and all. Gonna put me on the rack in the dungeon?"

Damn. He had to respect a woman who could mock intimidation. "This is a construction site. You're keeping my men from doing their jobs." King gestured toward the salivating assembly.

She turned and winked at them. "Go back to work." And damned if his men didn't get to work . . . *in accord* . . . for the first time since he started this money-sucking project.

Yes, he'd inherited the bloody fortune the old pirate who built this place had amassed, but he was pissing it away by the second, here. And he did not need a showstopper . . . well, stopping the show. "This is a closed construction site, as in 'dangerous to the general population.' How'd you get past my guards?"

The goddess raised her chin. "Never underestimate the power of cleavage."

King's attraction upstaged his irritation while his blood headed south. Avoiding the rush, he turned to his crew. "My foreman will show you out."

His foreman neither moved nor blinked.

"I *said*," King repeated, eyeballing his right-hand hulk, "Curt will show you the door."

"I know where the door is, Einstein. I just used it to come in."

Curt offered his arm, but with a lethal smile, the man magnet refused and made the brick linebacker blush, her blonde hair shifting like sea waves in a salty breeze, the sight and scent embedding peace like shrapnel into the air around them.

King swore inwardly. He'd surrounded himself by yesmen and knew what to do with them. But damned if he knew what to do with the leggy blonde in red spikes, short shorts, and form-fitting Proud to Be Awesome V-neck tee, invading his castle, undermining his authority, diminishing his sanity, and refusing to budge.

Normally, he respected the use of sex appeal—under controlled conditions—and in other circumstances, he might request further . . . credentials. But her timing sucked.

He didn't need anything else getting in the way of fixing this bad-luck money pit and selling it before it caused more grief. He wished to hell he could get it off his hands as fast as he did every other high-end property he bought and restored.

Logic, good sense, and good business told him to cut free, and fast, but a secret, rebelliously undisciplined part of him—the part he struggled to keep firmly in check— wanted to embrace the legacy of the castle and find the fundamental peace inherent in its structure and location.

Peace, he'd spend his last dime to find. Hell, he was beginning to see it in this woman like a mirage, but he'd never find peace in a sexy diversion and provoking schedule glitch, blonde goddess or not. Besides, the castle's tortured past ground peace into the dust on every surface.

Everyone who walked into the place seemed to argue— the *only* reason he didn't fire his bickering crew. Dissension had conspired for generations against anyone who entered here, as if this eerie madhouse—now, suddenly and amazingly silent of the wind wailing like a ghoul— refused to cooperate.

And if that wasn't insane, King didn't know what was. Yes. Yes, he did. Insane was being magnetically—and he meant that literally—attracted to hot little miss sexy pants with attitude. Hell, she had his men drooling instead of arguing. Screw that, she had his blood making a U-turn, so the loss to his brain made him dizzy. "Out!" he shouted, pointing the way.

Make-Me Barbie folded her arms and raised a brow.

"Have it your way," King said, lifting her—ramrod

straight—off her feet and carrying her out the door, her fine ass filling the palm of one happy hand, her tight shirt riding low at its neck and high at her waist, so he couldn't help but eyeball her lush breasts while the raw silk of the skin at her waist burned his fingers and threatened to cut him off at the knees.

He moved fast, certain nothing could keep her quiet for long, not even shock. Steam rose between them where their bodies touched, the sizzle in their bold eye-to-eye causing a jolt of pure sexual energy.

Like the sea, her eyes changed color with her mood. He watched it happen. A bright aquamarine glint fit the mischievous smile she'd given his men, but when fury replaced shock, her eyes took on a stormy sea shade, more green than anything, then a muted gray blue rolled in like a fog when the heat of their connection hit her.

Their connection? He set her down with a teeth-jarring thud. "Sorry."

"Sorry?" she snapped, her latent blush ruddy. "Who do you think you are? King blooming Kong? Get your hairy, gorilla hands off me. I hate being touched."

The hell she did, but he'd forgotten to let her go. Damn. He retrieved his hands so fast, he saluted and did an about-face. Only thing to do now: retreat with mock dignity.

Safe inside the castle—a ludicrous oxymoron—King closed the iron bound door . . . on his lust and the intruder's outrage, both too perilous to consider. Aghast at the botch he'd made of showing her out, he dug deep into the cooler for a soft drink, wiped his face with an icy hand, and took a cold swig, almost relieved the sexpot was gone. But before he took another, the crew's arguments resumed as did the wind's demented wail.

King swore and turned back to his computer, but the doors squealed open behind him, and silence cut the familiar tumult to a spine shiver.

Dread and elation warred for prominence as he turned.

She was ba-ack.

He pointed her way out.

The siren in spikes folded her arms and stood her ground. "There's a For Sale sign outside." Her chin of pure stubborn came up. "I'm a prospective buyer. I'd like a tour, please."

King looked from her to his amused, newly distracted men and figured that nothing constructive would get done . . . unless he got "trouble" the hell out. He swore, anticipated her sidestep, and swept her off her feet, removing her in the way a groom carries his bride over the threshold— God help him.

He tried not to enjoy her elbow jabs to his chest, the shape of her kicking legs, or the feel of her corn silk hair beneath his arm at her back. Hell, he tried not to inhale her spellbinding scent.

He took her farther from the castle this time, set her down easy, and let her go without a commanding order. But like a horny teen high on hormones, he caught her eye and imagined a game of sex for sport, *her* on his team, and on that treacherous thought, he headed back to the castle.

"You're making a mistake," she called after him. "I can be a team player. I can even be the cheerleader. Give me an *O*."

The castle doors shut on the sight of her, cheerleading arms in the air, breasts pointing his way. King's heart raced faster and louder than the wind's newest wail. What the? *He* thinks of sex as a team sport, and *she* says she can be a team player? A cheerleader? Give me an *O* for . . . *orgasm*? He freaking wished. Talk about scary, like fate, or kismet, or . . . disaster. Sex for sport with that one would be like sailing on the *Titanic*.

Meanwhile, the wail now cut through his headache like a saber, nearly but not quite eclipsing his crew's renewed bickering. "Son of a sea witch!"

His foreman came up to him. "There's something about that woman."

"Yeah," King snapped. "She's stacked. Great rack, nice ass. Dime a dozen. What's your point?"

Curt rubbed his nose to hide his grin, and King cursed himself for showing his colors.

"The air seems to change when she comes in," Curt said. "The place feels . . . sociable. Even the wind quiets down . . . like it wants her here. And the crew? Did you see them working together for a couple'a minutes there? *Both* times?"

"Impossible." King frowned.

"Bet you a day's pay."

To add to Curt's challenge, the wind wailed louder than King remembered, even as a boy when it scared the starch out of him, until he realized that the castle, or its wind, or both, wouldn't hurt him, which it/they/she didn't . . . until he became a man.

The howl now became so strident, dust streamed from the age-ravaged ceiling, sending the crew running for cover. What kind of wind could rattle a ceiling in a structure with granite walls three feet thick?

King eyed the castle doors, swore, and went after the sexy interloper, wishing to hell he wasn't glad for the excuse to get her back, however ludicrously lame.

Chapter Three

FROM the shadow of the castle, King admired the sway of her fine ass as the goddess made her way toward the cement steps leading to the dock at their base, sunshine filtering through her blonde hair like a halo. How to get her back inside when he'd made such a point of throwing her out? She turned, hearing his footsteps, and backed away as fast as he approached.

When he picked up his pace, the seductress in scarlet ran, stopped short of heading down the steps, and he plowed into her. Afraid she'd take a tumble, he pulled her from the edge of the stairs and lost his balance.

He fell back, and she landed on top of him . . . all their contrasting parts in sync, his rising to the occasion.

"Withering witch balls," she said, raising herself on her arms and looking down at him. "Killing me is not the answer, and neither is groping my—" She reared back and scrambled off him. "*That's* not the answer, either!"

He got up as quick as she did. "Uh, sorry," he said. "I'm

a man. It's a reflex. What can I say? It has nothing to do with you."

"Gee, thanks."

"Well, it does, because you're . . . you're . . . bootylicious?"

"You just keep the compliments coming, don't'cha?"

He raised his hands. "I can't seem to stop myself."

"Your big mouth, clumsy gorilla feet, and that loose cannon you keep in your pants should be registered as lethal weapons."

King coughed to hide his amusement, as foreign as a fishbone in his throat, which didn't keep him from admiring the angry rise and fall of her breasts.

The small skiff motoring toward Salem seemed to make the mad, bad, and furious-to-behold lady in red take out her cell phone and walk around, checking for a signal, which gave him a fine view of her curvaceous lines from every angle.

"I can't get a blooming signal!" She clamped the phone shut—her narrowed eyes telling him she'd rather clamp it on something meaty . . . like his loose cannon.

"Sorry." He shook his head. "No signal on the island."

"Can I use your landline then?"

"Generators supply electricity but no phone lines from the mainland. The Paxtons liked it that way. Tells you something about them, doesn't it?"

"Screw the Paxtons."

Screw this Paxton.

"*That* was my ride home." She pointed toward the retreating boat. "The ghoulish howl you had going there must have scared Captain Jerk away."

He'd never heard the wail outside. "You heard it out here?"

"You got that straight. Scared the birds from the trees. Hey, forget the wail, I'm stranded, slam it. How am I supposed to get home?"

"You have a weird vocabulary."

"Negative words invite negativity into your life, so I try to be positive."

"Withering witch balls?" he asked.

"Oh, that's harmless. It's like suffering succotash. Succotash can't suffer, and witch balls can't wither."

"Okaay," King said. "Slam it?"

"Basketball term."

"Screw! You said screw." He had her now.

"I like to screw. Screwing is good. Feels good. It's positive."

Trying not to hyperventilate, King rubbed his chest. He didn't know what to make of her. Part of him wanted to screw—as in get the hell out—and the other part wanted to screw—as in get the hell in . . . *her*. "Glad we got that straight."

"Now, about my ride home?"

"Right. I'll take you in my helicopter later tonight, or you can catch the five o'clock water taxi back to Salem with the construction crew from hell."

"Why don't I just swim back?"

"Or you could swim back. Don't bite any sharks on the way."

"I'll take the crew, thanks."

King tested the bristle on his chin, and like a horn dog cadet after maneuvers, he wished he'd shaved that morning. Great guns; he didn't even know her, and she'd dragged him into a kinetic minefield of heat-seeking testosterone ready to explode on contact.

She sat on an outcropping of rock overlooking Salem Harbor, crossed her legs, dangled one red high heel, and improved the view tenfold. After running her fingers through her hair to push it from her face, she looked back at him. "Why did you chase me, anyway?"

"You ran, so I chased."

"I ran *because* you chased. Are you nuts?"

"I'll have to plead the fifth on that, especially since my foreman thinks you're a calming influence on the crew *and* the wail. Come back inside long enough to prove him wrong."

"Hell no. You just threw me out. Twice. Besides, you've got yourself a lose/lose situation."

"Come again?"

"Don't I wish."

King stilled. Since she admittedly like to screw, she must mean . . . Nah, she couldn't. God, he needed a woman. Any woman . . . except this one. She was a nutcase . . . who could bring him peace? "What do you mean, a lose/lose situation?"

"You're bound to lose that bet. Rather than humiliate you, I'll just sit here and wait for my ride home."

"For seven hours?"

"Rather the deep blue sea than the devil."

Just what he needed, a sultry brat with attitude pursing her full, sassy, kissable lips his way. He'd never seen a face that looked both so innocent and seductive at the same time.

King went over and hefted her back into his arms. No hardship there. Carrying her over the threshold was starting to grow on him . . . which meant he should toss her like a live grenade.

She looked him in the eye. "I *said*, I hate being touched."

"Sure you do. That's why you're fighting me, right?"

She resisted on cue, a token struggle at best, a seduction at worst, or was it the other way around? King got into the sport of her letting him manage her until her every curve and hollow were imprinted on his sensual memory banks, not to mention his physical ones. She wanted inside, and damned if he didn't want her there. No. He wanted details about her sudden appearance . . . and her vital statistics . . . and *he* wanted inside . . . her.

The hell he did!

He dropped her like a hot dish—exactly what she was—and when she hit the pallet of foam insulation, she bounced and swore.

"You're a regular hellcat," he said, rubbing his thigh where she'd kicked him. "I think I'm gonna bruise."

She shot to her feet. "Too bad; I was going for blood." She swiped her blonde waves from her eyes, and like a Salem sorceress, she brought him under her spell—him and every other man—her breasts heaving as she pulled air into her lungs.

"Hey," he said, tearing his gaze away. "It's quiet. Damned if the ghoulish wail hasn't stopped. Curt was right. Go figure. No arguing crew. No wailing wind."

"Wailing *wind*?" Like the feline that got the cream, the hellcat grinned, nearly knocking him on his figurative ass. "Oh, that wasn't the wind," she said, too smug for his peace. "Did you think that was the wind? No, no, no, no, no. That's one mighty pissed-off ghost. I hear she was quite the witch in her day."

King laughed. His men didn't.

He extended his hand, despite the warning in his head, but he couldn't seem to help himself. "King Paxton, and you are?"

"It *is* King? Are you kidding me? But not Kong, right?"

His men broke into smiles, but King snapped his fingers, and they went back to work. He gave the brat his fiercest I'm-gonna-fire-your-ass scowl, because this frightening sense of peace he felt around her invited him to let down his guard. "And you are?" he repeated, a little louder, a lot more determined.

"Real scared." She gave him a flirtatious wink, and he wondered what color her eyes turned in passion.

"Name?" he snapped like a ranking cadet high on his own importance.

She clicked her heels and saluted. "Cartwright, Harmony, sir."

"At ease." King unclenched his fists, once, twice, three calming times, exercising his hands to relax them. "Harmony, is it? As in musical, melodious, sweet, pleasant, peace—not peaceful. No way."

"Give yourself a salute, soldier, or is that anatomically impossible?"

King turned toward the crew, almost hoping they'd argue again, or the wind would wail, or a wall would fall in, anything. For the first time in his life, he sought the castle's personal brand of torture, but no go. "You're *not* kidding," he said. "That wail hasn't stopped in a hundred years."

She gave a half nod. "I seem to have a knack for calming people, pets . . . entities, as it turns out. It's a gift, but don't let it go to your head. Pick me up, again, and I'll deck you."

"Is that any way to be positive?"

"I'm *positive* I'll deck you."

"That's better." King picked up a blueprint, instead of her. A calming effect, his ass, and yet . . . She'd been both calming and tormenting him since she walked in. She was no ordinary goddess. This one packed a warhead that could disarm even *him*—peace—if his "harmonious" crew and the blessed sound of silence were any indication. But anyone who could disarm his self-protective instincts became the enemy. Without his defenses, he'd never have endured his family, military school, or his own stupid mistakes.

He was a survivor, to the death, but he had a feeling this woman could jeopardize even *his* killer instincts.

He tossed the print back on the makeshift plywood table and wished he could kick a sawhorse to ease his frustration. "I need to know who you are. And I presume you have a reason for being here." King tried to ignore the challenge the peacemaker presented, sexual and otherwise. "After all, you didn't take a water taxi out here by accident."

He caught her disturbing withdrawal, her long ginger lashes at half-mast, her eyes the smoky blue gray of doubt.

She bit her bottom lip as if . . . seeking a plausible excuse. He could almost see the lie forming.

"Um . . . vintage clothes," she said in a rush. "Got any lying around the castle?"

He'd never heard a worse excuse for a fake accidental meeting. "Bullcrap."

"Oh, oh, you just invited a bunch of poop down on you."

He gave her a look. "Methinks its name is Harmony."

"No, people love old clothes. Some collect them. Some use them for costumes. I sell them."

Hell, she was making it up as she went along.

King went back to his laptop and took a sip from his empty foam coffee cup. Crushing it with his embarrassment, he shot a basket in one and decided to play the scented sex-pot's way, to see if he could wrap his mind around her tactics . . . or himself around her.

"I've got rooms of old clothes," he said, pretending to ignore her for his computer. Hiding from her, was he? Hell, he was gonna need a shrink after an hour in her company. "You're stuck here anyway," he said, typing nonsense in his spreadsheet, "so you might as well look around upstairs and see what you can find. Go ahead. The place is nothing if not sound. Just stay up there until I come for you. Contrary to what you've seen, a construction site is dangerous."

"Good Goddess!" she said. "I have a castle to pillage?"

King raised his head and caught a smile that could melt glass.

"That's it!" Short-circuiting, and forfeiting whatever wits he had left, he indicated that she should precede him up the circular stone stairs, out of hearing and sight of his men. At the landing to the balcony above the great hall, he stopped to press the elevator button. He hadn't wanted his men to see them get on the elevator downstairs. Too cozy, which he didn't intend. He intended to get the truth out of her.

She peeked toward the balcony. "One more flight to the

living quarters?" she asked. Oblivious to his fury? Or pretending to be?

She preceded him into the elevator, and he pressed Five for the tower.

"Retro elevator," she said, tracing the diamond shape of the gated door. "Turn of the century? The twentieth century, I mean?"

"Good guess," he said. Halfway up, he hit Stop.

"Hey, we're between floors."

He pinned her to the wall, one arm on each side of her head. "You pillage, and I plunder? Is that your game?"

She frowned, her confusion real enough. "I beg your pardon?"

Confused as well, King forged on, stubbornly entrenching himself. "You are *way* out of your league, here. I don't know which one of my ex-friends is playing matchmaker this time, but I'm not in the market."

"You sure think a lot of yourself, *Your Heinieness*." Her deep curtsy made him feel like a horse's ass, as she intended.

He gave her a hand up, and held on too long, but she didn't pull away. One or both of them stepped closer. He wasn't sure which, but he did know that he wanted to kiss her . . .

Out of the question.

With an apology on the tip of his tongue, her ring caught his eye and he became transfixed. He ran a thumb over it. "Where did you get this?"

She pulled away, flipping her hair, hitting him in the face with corn silk and giving him a peppermint high.

His body went on red alert. All systems go.

"What do you care?" she snapped. "You're *not* in the market."

Chapter Four

HARMONY had suspected that the ring might be her ticket to fulfilling her psychic mandate, and judging by her host's shock, she might be right. "Are we getting out of the elevator?"

Paxton backed against the control panel, denying her access, and slipped his hands into the pockets of his classy black slacks. "That's up to you."

She shivered at the hottie's frosty demeanor; talk about a contradiction. His square, unforgiving chin, and his soft-worn tee, as black as his hair—despite the dusty construction site—made him look like Satan come to call.

Granted, the negative energy in this place had long ago created a type of karmic quicksand, the kind that sucked you under before you could call for help, but her presence had calmed some of it, so why was he so upset?

She had a psychic job to do, whatever it was, yet her host seemed to be doing his best to stop her. She couldn't tell him the real reason she was here, a lie of omission she probably sensed. Between the two of them, there were enough karmic vibes and raging pheromones to hamper anybody's endeavors, never mind a mandate as nebulous as hers.

The pheromones, she couldn't help. A physical sexual pull was just that, and theirs carried enough energy to light New York. She'd deal with that later . . . or not.

She did, however, need to understand his karmic vibes. "I realize you're a Paxton," Harmony said, "but how closely are you connected to this place?"

"I own it, lucky sucker that I am."

When she attempted to circumvent him and hit the Down button, Paxton took her wrist in a grasp she found both gentle and stimulating. Now she was more turned on. No. That couldn't be right. She hated being touched, except by her sisters . . . and, apparently, by Brass Ass McGrumpy.

Slam it! He'd breached her protective circle of light, and she hadn't realized it. She'd forgotten about keeping herself protected, *or* her sphere of white light remained intact, and she didn't *need* protecting from this guy.

As she watched, Paxton's luminous whiskey eyes probed hers . . . and didn't she want to give him . . . *everything* he wanted. His gaze touched her physically, stroking her brow, her lips, parting them . . .

Harmony struggled from her sensual stupor. She knew better than to meet a man on a spiritual plane. Yet this didn't seem to be the same man. Had she dreamed his ego trip of a short while ago, his certainty that this was a setup? Because now he was simply annoyed . . . and horny . . . and curious . . . and horny . . . no ego involved.

Given his captivating gaze, not to mention his charisma and his body sculpted by a master, she could see why unwelcome setups might plague him. She also understood why he ran. Women chased him. Not the other way around. Sometimes he let them catch him, and when he did, he used them—for sex, nothing more.

Not a one had ever touched his heart. Sex for sport, as

he'd thought outside. Wait! She'd heard his thoughts? Her heart skipped a beat. *Oh, oh.*

News flash—she could *read* him.

Hot flash—mutual-attraction city going up. High-rise under construction. Hold on to your underwear.

Good Goddess, she was sensually, sexually, and most important, cosmically hot-wired to the hunky tight-ass. If she let her emotional barriers down, she was screwed . . . literally.

Why *didn't* that sound as bad as it should?

She might ordinarily think about jumping his bones, but under the circumstances, in the midst of her psychic mandate, she shouldn't even consider it. Should she?

Um, yeah. He was the best prospect she'd had in . . . Withering witch balls, he was the best prospect she'd *ever* had.

Warning! When flying into the teeth of a cosmic sexual attraction, mistakes . . . of cosmic proportions . . . could be made.

Slow down, she told herself. *No knee-jerk reactions here. Take a deep breath. Think. And try to make some blooming sense of this.*

Why, of all the people she came across, could she read *him*?

She usually read people who owned the old objects into which she came in contact—dead people. Long dead. So why could she read this living, breathing hunk of hundred-proof testosterone, this earth god who filled his molded black T-shirt like a workout model?

"You own the place alone, right?" she asked, to be sure. "No partners or siblings co-own it with you?"

"That would be too easy," he said. "I'd love to pawn the nightmare off on a relative. There isn't a one of them who doesn't deserve it."

Her suspicions were getting the better of her. "Did you spend a lot of time here as a *very* young child?"

"If you must know, I was born here."

Holy astral plane! "Why not in a hospital?"

"I arrived early in what the record books call the hundred-hour snowstorm, February 26, 1969. Storm surges of hurricane proportions. Couldn't get my mother to the mainland, but what does that have to do with—"

His beeper went off. "My foreman needs me." Paxton hit the elevator's Down button and stopped on the second floor. Before he got out, he turned to her. "Stay."

"Woof," she replied, as she stepped on the landing to watch him run down the stairs, admiring his loose-limbed, pantherlike gait, his butt as tight and fine as his pecs. Hot and hunky Hurricane Paxton, whose spirit and ownership so permeated this ancient stronghold that he became her very own psychic pot of gold.

When he'd released her wrist to leave, she was surprised she'd let him hold it for so long, but now she felt bereft, foolish her, and reading him became difficult, which shouldn't surprise her. Proximity always shed light on a psychometric's impressions, and touch clarified them. Touch brought images, scents, sounds, and emotions into focus. Positive vibes uplifted her. Negative vibes depressed and sometimes made her ill.

For *that* reason, the only physical contact she allowed and trusted were her sisters' . . . until King blooming Kong.

In a castle overflowing with negativity, *he* had touched her. And not only had she allowed it, she'd welcomed and wallowed in the skin-on-skin contact. Like water in the desert, she'd welcomed it.

Who knew she'd been so parched?

She hated being touched. She hated being carried, and she particularly hated having her space invaded—her father had said she was a horror of a screaming baby—but when Paxton took her outside, then back in again, she had to force herself to stop being passive by pretending to fight him.

His touch warmed her. To cinders, it could warm her. If he put his mind and man brain into it, who could tell what kind of inferno they could create.

Wha'd'ya know, her psychic gift had led her to a horny hunk with a lockbox of lifetime secrets and assessing Jesus eyes . . . a man as instantly and magnetically hot for her as she was for him, though he'd never admit it, not to himself, and especially not to her.

She'd seen a hint of the real man in the wild ebony curl on his brow and in the unexpected laugh lines around his eyes—a seductive and challenging surprise.

Men like him starred in a lifetime of sexual fantasies—hers and every other woman's. He was that one unreachable, potently sexual male whose stone-encased heart and self-erected wall flashed Not Emotionally Available in neon . . . the beast every woman dreamed of taming.

Not five minutes later, he carried himself up the stairs in a rigid stance that proved he'd gotten his emotions in check. A drill sergeant under orders had replaced the man unnerved by a connection he sensed but couldn't name. But on the inside, he seethed with a heat she had a surprising urge to match, a sharp sexual intensity, which he managed admirably to hide—from everyone except her—so it came off as disdain to the room at large.

"Who are you, really?" he asked, a question she'd considered asking when she encountered the brick wall around his heart.

Harmony shivered and crossed her arms. Reading him did not count among the most placid of abilities in her psychic life journey. "I told you. My name is Harmony Cartwright. My sisters and I own the Immortal Classic Vintage Clothing and Curio Shop on Pickering Wharf in Salem. I'm the buyer. Old castle, old clothes, right? What's the harm in asking? Do I still get to look around?"

He wanted to say no on principle, as a means of self-protection, she knew, but his ego despised human weakness, especially his own. He read her shirt again and something in the words, Proud to Be Awesome, made him frown.

Reading her breasts distracted him, which annoyed him. And though she should probably be afraid of the way she could read him, she liked that he spent time thinking about what he'd like to do to, and with, her.

Hot damn, they were in lust—mutual lust—which she knew, and he didn't. Which she'd like to explore, and he'd fight. Oh, the possibilities.

Because of his stubbornness, and because she'd revved his libido to a high-octane purr, she knew he was going to let her stay. Hot, and getting hotter, the sergeant suffered from a raging case of unwanted lust, yet his body kept co-operating.

Enjoying her ability to bring him to his knees—figuratively speaking, un-blooming-fortunately—Harmony grinned inwardly, but she shouldn't let her power go to her head. Because, in addition to his high-alert lust, Paxton was confused, annoyed, and determined to deny the sexual pull and halt it midsizzle.

Like she'd let him work the sizzle anyway, she thought, admiring his fight. Glory, if only she had the time to tame him.

As determined as him—and sorely tempted to jump his bones on general principle, if only to show her mettle—*she* at least understood that the gown and ring, or something connected to them, had fused this scorching, if temporary, psychic connection between them.

She knew she had to put distance between them, or one of them was gonna catch fire and consume the other. "See you later," she said, running up a set of tower-circling stairs, smiling because she experienced his aftershocks as he stood where she'd left him, poleaxed and reeling.

The space she put between them, with each subsequent level she reached, lessened her ability to sense his emotions.

Each landing appeared to lead to a different set of living quarters, as if the tower was the axis around which the castle had originally been built, which, architecturally speaking, didn't seem possible, but what did she know?

Harmony started her journey of discovery at the top. Finding vintage clothes would be serendipity compared to her psychic mandate, which might affect King Paxton himself.

Whatever her purpose, she intended to make the journey count.

She took a few false starts onto several floors, or wings—hard to tell which. The older wings were quite nautical in design. No surprise when the place was purported to have been built by a sea captain, the man after whom the former Paxton Wharf had been named.

From what she saw, the castle appeared to have been redecorated by subsequent generations and modernized to a fault—the fault being the utter destruction, in some areas, of a truly remarkable piece of history and architecture.

Ultimately, Harmony returned to the third floor and what appeared to be the most originally intact wing of the structure so far. She followed her psychic instincts and stopped in a black and red bedchamber that filled her with as great a sense of purpose as negativity. It must have belonged to the witch of Paxton Castle, a woman, judging by its furnishings.

One aspect, however, confused her. Not the furnishings but the red damask walls bearing at least a dozen picture frames, all empty.

Every object she touched, clasped, or held to her brow exuded a potently negative force, seething and perilous.

The ghost of Paxton Castle could very well be the strongest negative entity Harmony had ever encountered.

Chapter Five

THOUGH negative and powerful, the Paxton Castle witch posed no threat, a surprise, when antagonism seemed to be the witch's calling card. Then again, Harmony sensed that love might once have resided in this place, if only for a time.

The red and black decor was as eclectic and contradictory as the witch herself, and despite the cryptic picture frames, it revealed a surprising love of art. No mate to Harmony's ring hid in the ancient Chinese black lacquer chest, atop which sat a tiered tabletop étagère displaying a dolphin collection, crafted in onyx, jade, ivory, and such.

Harmony touched the cool onyx. She collected dolphins, too, though hers were made of silicone and required batteries, which she could just imagine explaining to a nineteenth-century ghost.

Notable among the Paxton collection were a bronze dolphin holding a nautilus shell, a rosewood trio cavorting in a stylized water splash, and a malachite mermaid driving a dolphin chariot. The mermaid, as usual, controlled the dolphin, which made Harmony hope that she, with her mermaid totem, would wield a natural power over an entity with a dolphin totem. Perhaps an overly optimistic bit of magickal speculation, but it gave her at least a sense of control.

Harmony turned to the room at large. Even the carved mahogany rocker in the corner bore carved dolphin arms, and now that she thought about it, didn't the castle's heavy double doors each sport a dolphin door knocker?

To the Celtics, the dolphin symbolized water energy. It must take a great deal of power to raise the kind of wail this ghost had raised on a daily basis for years. *Could* the ghost be drawing energy, even now, from the sea around them?

A ghost with an unlimited supply of energy boggled the mind. Harmony hoped she was wrong, because if her psychic mandate meant dealing with the witch in particular, Harmony herself would be in for some rough seas . . . as Destiny predicted, slam it.

With a sigh of acceptance, Harmony looked for clues to her psychic goal, any number of possibilities having already surfaced. She needed to find the other half of the ring, and perhaps she was meant to protect the castle, but *from* the ghost, or *for* the ghost? Protect the Paxtons, or the workers? So many possibilities. So little time. And perhaps she hadn't come close to sensing her purpose yet.

Meeting the witch might help.

In the drawer of the black lacquer bedside table by the matching four-poster, Harmony found a bone buttonhook with a strong sense of its owner. Holding it, she sat on the bed and understood that the hook had been crafted for the entity, who seemed as confused as Harmony. Maybe the ghost had been wandering in aimless frustration for a hundred years, which would be enough to make anybody wail.

All this paranormal confusion should make her objective clear. Not!

Withering witch balls, she was glad she'd tucked the

charm bag between her breasts. Covering it, she asked for guidance.

She replaced the buttonhook and drew with her finger a Celtic peace knot in the dust on the bedside table—offering a peace pipe to the entity, without pipe, smoke, or entity.

No sooner had she done so than an icy draft drifted into the room as if awaiting her invitation. Smelling of decaying lilacs too long in the vase, the icy draft moved insidiously around her, as if to examine her from every angle, its cold breath nipping at her face, her ears, the back of her neck.

Harmony shivered and covered the ring, swallowing a knot of unease.

The cool air receded from her face, as if the entity stepped away, and as it did, the glass in the frame directly across from Harmony frosted over and cracked.

Warmth claimed her then, for less than a beat, until a chill ran down her left arm. The ring got so cold, it almost hurt to wear, but Harmony made a stubborn fist to keep it there. She sensed that if she lost the ring, she'd fail in her psychic purpose. Maybe the ring was more of a psychic get-out-of-jail-free card.

"I wish I'd worn a coat," Harmony said, shivering, showing the entity she accepted her presence while injecting a note of reality into unreality. She opened the lacquered chest. "I hope you don't mind if I borrow some of your things to keep warm. Besides, I'd better start looking for vintage clothes, or the tyrant who owns this place is going to throw me out."

Harmony wrapped a quilted mulberry dressing gown nearly twice around herself, tied the sash, and raised the hood. Painted silk scarves served as neck warmers. She traded her spikes for a pair of fur boots that might be Eskimo, pulled on a pair of hideous yellow green leather gloves, and rubbed her hands together. "Now, where can I find some vintage gowns? Oh, too late. Our host is coming."

Harmony stood almost at attention as she sensed Paxton on the other side of the closed door. Funny, she didn't remember closing it.

It opened before either of them reached it, both too far away to have managed it. Harmony hummed the theme song from *The Twilight Zone* so Paxton could hear it, the open door a proclamation from the hereafter that he failed to acknowledge.

He came in and focused on her clothes. "Who do the fashion police monitor? Because I think you've been taken captive by the enemy."

Harmony looked down at her mukluks, gaudy gloves, and antiquated dressing gown. "I'm a work in progress?"

"Aren't we all? Who were you talking to?"

"The ghost."

"There is no ghost," he said, and the door behind him slammed with a resounding echo. "Whatever," he added. "Did *she* dress you for Halloween?"

"Then it *is* a woman?"

"How the hell do I know?" Paxton raised Harmony's temperature with his assessing gaze and interest alone, while hot licks of desire crept along her spine, radiating to her breasts, her inner thighs—and to the places where he was going with his lips in his imagination. *Glory!*

Like a deer in headlights, she stood motionless and dumb as a box of frogs, while King Paxton had his imaginary way with her, and she—in his mind—reveled in it and asked, no, *begged* for more. As she climaxed in his fantasy, she gasped, bringing them both back with a start, and she wondered which of them was more surprised.

Paxton wiped his brow with the back of a hand, while his ginormous erection tried to break free of its zipper. She looked up and caught him watching her watch him. "You find this outfit a turn-on?" she asked, taking her question toward but not too close to the truth.

"What can I say? I've been out of commission for a long time."

"Looks like everything works great."

"Oh, it does."

"Tested it, have you?"

His laugh lines deepened. "Do you always say what's on your mind?"

"Hardly ever," she said. "This place has a weird effect on me."

"Neither do I, obviously, though some things speak louder than words."

"Very loud." She watched his erection become manageable, but who wanted that? Not her.

"Keep watching," he said, cupping the back of his neck, "and it'll never—"

"Oh! Sorry." She backed into an armoire and hit her crazy bone. "Ouch." She rubbed her elbow, surprised they weren't both smoking a cigarette—not that she smoked, but the correlation seemed appropriate.

He turned her to face a standing mirror, corroded, but reflective enough to give her a jolt at the sight of herself. She turned back to him with a hand on her hip. "I call this look 'homeless on a budget' or 'scare today, circus tomorrow.' Wha'd'ya think?"

He tied one of her neck shawls on top of her head like bunny ears, and that small bit of personal attention turned her on. "Hard man, hard bod," Destiny had said, and here he stood in the flesh, every muscle clearly outlined beneath a hundred-dollar tee that felt like butter. Oops, when had she put her hand on his chest?

She took it back, fast, but the imprint of his pecs warmed her palm.

"All you need is a red nose," he said, "and the circus it is."

She wiggled her nose. "Are you sure it's not already red?"

He cupped it between his hands, blessing it with a warmth that spread like jelly on hot toast, until she felt the heat at her center.

Downplaying her sexual reaction, she crossed her eyes to watch his hands.

Sir Galahad looked up, stifled a hitching cough, and gasped like he'd swallowed a chicken bone.

She tried giving him the Heimlich, which made him cough more. "No more," he gasped, pulling away. "I can't."

"Are you laughing at me?"

"Never. I—" A last cough before he caught his breath. "I don't . . . laugh."

She came into psychic contact with the real him then, the man whose need to laugh scared the military starch right out of him, the man who worked very hard to keep his no-emotions-allowed wall erected.

Screw the wall. From him, she'd like a more gigundous erection—several, if you please, nightly for a month at least—then maybe she could concentrate on his psychological problems. She was only here for the day, though she felt as if it was the right place . . . for longer than that.

The dichotomy between the real and the psychic was hard to shake. Unnerving, too. "It's blooming cold in here." She pulled her tattered lapels together. This outfit is called self-preservation," she said. Like his wall. "You know a little something about that."

He went from human to robot in sixty seconds. An emotional systems freeze out.

She felt the chill and practically heard his wall lock in place. "You're a hard one," she said.

The lines around his mouth relaxed, but not much. "As you saw. I could be hard again . . . if you wanted me to be."

Yay team! "No kidding?" The possibilities thrilled her as she eyed the evidence. He was halfway there, already. *Come on, boy. Sit up. There you go. Now beg.*

He watched her and finally clued in to the fact that theirs was a mutual attraction, and warmed the entire room with a newly vigilant and assessing once-over.

"I think I'm having a hot flash," she said, fanning her face with a hand.

"That would make two of us." But he'd never give in, and it was all she could do not to argue with the thoughts in his head.

They stepped apart and looked for places to put their hands, and before she knew how it happened, they were all over each other. Where he touched, she blossomed, even through the robe. Lightning flashed, but only in her mind, and her limbs, and deep at her center—surges of pure electricity. Paxton felt them, too.

He opened his mouth over hers, devouring her as if he'd been starved, and she became his very happy meal. He kissed like a professional, not that she'd ever kissed a professional, but she recognized experience when it Frenched her.

He'd barely started undoing her sash when he groaned in frustration and fell against the wall at his back. Head down, hands on his knees, he shook his head, and by the time he straightened, she'd retied her robe.

He'd regained his sanity.

She wished she could reclaim hers.

He cleared his throat. "So . . . are those the clothes you want to buy? Because we have better. Vintage ladies' underclothes two floors up."

"How do you know?"

"I found them when I was a boy."

"By accident, of course."

"Absolutely." His laugh lines appeared again, nothing more, but the transformation was a heart-stopper. "I was thirteen. What say you try them on next?" He took her hand, as if he did it every day. "Come on." He pulled one way, she pulled the other. He let go first.

"Doesn't seem prudent right now," though something rebellious in her would follow him anywhere. "I haven't started looking for vintage *clothes* yet."

"Fifty men downstairs would take one look at you and say you have."

"Your ghost froze me out, I tell you."

Paxton saw the picture frame with its ice-cracked glass. "I don't have a ghost," he said as he straightened it.

Oh man, a picture-straightener . . . with an ego, walled-off emotions, and a powerful finger-snap. *Him*, she wanted to get in the sack? Which just went to prove that sex appeal was stronger than good judgment. "If the castle has a ghost, you have a ghost. We both know she's real. You must've seen more proof of the otherworldly than a piece of cracked glass and a conveniently open door over the course of your life."

"There *is* you," he said. "You're the most otherworldly thing I've come across. Did you zoom down from another planet?"

"No, seriously."

"You think I'm kidding? You scare me."

"Focus on the question. Do you have any idea who the ghost could be?"

Paxton untied her bunny ears—as if doing so would undo his lapse into humanity—and put a hard space between them. "There is no ghost."

"You're in denial, Hurricane Boy. I know you have a suspect."

Paxton took in the room, the empty frames, and sighed. "Only one person lived out her life here. She died in that bed—Augusta 'Gussie' Paxton. My mother used to say that Gussie never left. 'Unfinished business,' Mom said."

"You had a mother? You *didn't* get shot from a cannon during a twenty-one gun salute and land at attention?"

"Old habits. Military school. It's textbook. I've tried to escape it."

"Escape it? You embrace it. No, let me rephrase that. You hide behind it."

Paxton moved closer—too tall, too close, not close enough. "You don't know anything about me," he said towering over her, which didn't seem possible, because she was nearly as tall as him.

Not to be outdone, outmaneuvered, or bullied, Harmony moved in as well. A sheet of paper wouldn't fit between them. If it did, it'd catch fire. "You, sir, have a steel rod shoved up your ass. When you issue a command, I get an uncontrollable urge to salute. You need someone to loosen you up, take the starch out of you, melt the steel rod, and teach you to be spontaneous. I'm sorely tempted to take the job."

"Give it your best shot, Witch Whisperer."

"There's a challenge I can't refuse. Don't worry, pulling down your walls won't hurt a bit."

"You leave my walls where they a—I don't have walls. Loosening up is one thing; giving up control is another, and I won't." Paxton snatched at the doorknob behind him, and it came off in his hand.

On the opposite side of the door, the knob's mate hit the floor and bounced—an echoing reminder of his stupidity— an unnaturally lengthy echoing reminder. Gussie must be helping it bounce.

Paxton threw the crystal doorknob on the bed. It rolled off and bounced as well—like a rubber ball, it bounced— and he growled.

Harmony imagined the growl deep in his throat during sex, him deep inside her, and . . . Withering witch balls, she needed to get a grip.

"Do it again," she said when the knob stopped bouncing.

"You really piss me off, you know that!"

Harmony raised her chin. "So why did you come looking for me?"

"Hell if I remember. Oh yes. I was wor—I thought you might need protecting. Hah!" He charged the door with his shoulder.

It splintered and slammed open with a resounding crack.

Paxton straightened, slipped his hands in his pockets, and left, whistling.

Hot. He looked hot walking away. Damn it. He looked hot going and coming. Oh man, she really wanted to watch him coming.

"I'm gonna unstarch you, Ramrod," she called after him, "whether you want me to or not!"

Chapter Six

HARMONY thought Paxton was beginning to seem human. But she wasn't here to pick up men, or she didn't think she was. Who knew?

Harmony turned back to the room. "Okay, Gussie. Vintage clothes; lead the way."

A door on the far side of the room opened and Harmony stepped into a cedar dressing room containing sheet-covered racks of something that might very well be vintage clothes.

"Thanks, Gussie." *I think. Hmm, wha'd'ya know?* Gussie liked her. Oh, oh. A friendly but negative ghost might be a ruse to get the ring, or whatever the heck had kept the poor thing wailing for a century.

When the air warmed, Harmony figured Gussie retired to replenish her energy, and she shed her layers. She wished she could read her dead hostess the way she read her bigger-than-life host. Then again, there was a lot about Paxton she couldn't read. Hell, his walls had walls, which she was gonna pull down, brick by sexy brick.

In a dressing room lit by electrified dolphin gaslights, Harmony caught the faint aroma of herbs in addition to the cedar. An amazing dressing table called to her. The top wore a playful spray of red tulips, with stems growing up its legs and leaves flowing around its mirror. Once upon a time Gussie had had a playful side.

Harmony felt cold air on the back of her neck again, smelled the dead lilacs, and saw a woman in the mirror behind her—Gussie, forty years old, maybe, and expressionless, wearing a purple crepe gown, diamond necklace and earrings, and a dolphin brooch. She looked . . . lost, or she felt lost, or lonely, and angry, and she wanted . . . out? Then she was gone.

In Gussie's day, purple had been the purgatory color between the black dress of mourning and the release from mourning colors. Was that what she meant by wanting out? Or did she want out of the castle?

Not a little jarred by the encounter, Harmony looked through the dressing table drawers for the other half of the ring with no luck. But she did find Gussie's grimoire and leafed through it. Finding no spells of import, she lifted a couple of sheets from the clothes racks.

In recent years—well, maybe not terribly recent—someone had put the dresses and gowns on padded wooden hangers and covered them with linen sheets. The gowns were plentiful and awesome. Harmony wished time wasn't an issue.

Several old trunks held accessories, nightclothes, and bed linens, and between the layers, dried sprigs of southernwood, or garderobe, kept the moths away while lavender kept the linens smelling fresh. Most were in decent shape because of the conservation attempts and low temperatures. But the place wasn't air-conditioned.

Harmony followed the draft to a glass-fronted corner curio full of jewelry, trinkets, and scrimshaw, some with dolphins, but no Celtic rings. Feeling along the outer edges of the cupboard, she found a trip latch. The curio swung out as a whole, leaving a gaping entrance to a dank and chilly tunnel with a ray of natural light at the far end.

She followed it, ignoring the occasional squeal and clickety-click of teeny toenails, the owners of which she refused to identify. If she ever came this way again, she was bringing reinforcements.

The scent of brine told Harmony she was headed toward the sea. A red lacquer door opened to an overfurnished, overlarge, formal Victorian parlor, with Oriental rugs and enough treasures to make an antiques dealer salivate.

She cut through the musty parlor. She'd explore here later, but right now, she was called toward a door behind a small tapestry—as seduced toward it as she'd been by the gold linen yard sale gown.

The door opened to a tower room—octagon, with seven more doors inside, each a different bright color, the walls between painted with clown faces, all eerie and unique.

The sights, colors, and scents of . . . cotton candy and candy apples . . . fascinated her. But Gussie's energy ran rampant here, despite the room's masquerade as a toy room with sweet scents to seduce.

The toys stood abandoned, sad, silent, solitary, sinister. Harmony propped the door open with a heavy, cast-iron tricycle before she went inside.

A wooden box, about seven by seven feet square, centered the room, its painted sides showing a colorful sea floor, dolphins and a mermaid swimming above it. Harmony touched the mermaid's face and could have sworn it was Lisette. She closed her eyes as she kept her hand on the depiction, and saw Lisette wearing the gold linen gown and kicking her way up from the depths of the sea.

Harmony coughed like when she'd undone the hem, as if the sea was trying to swallow her whole. Whisking her hand from the image, she caught her breath and calmed.

Lisette had not drowned, or the dress would never have come into her possession.

Relieved and holding her chest, Harmony turned to the room at large. An antique wicker doll carriage, or perambulator, remained pristine, as did a regiment of life-sized windup toy soldiers, arranged in rows and standing at attention, bayonet rifles at the ready.

In a life-sized red mechanical fortune-telling box, a wooden marionette gypsy wore too much makeup.

Welcome to nightmare alley. Next stop: psychotherapy.

This place was neither for children nor for the faint of heart. Harmony knew it in her bones, and she'd better control her unease, or her sisters would come running.

Before she could calm, her left arm got cold, and the Celtic ring went icy again. Harmony closed her hand to keep the ring on and stepped away from the frigid source, until she backed into the giant mermaid box, accidentally elbowing a crank on its side. The nudge was all it took, and the crank began to turn, gain speed, and spin out of control.

Music filled the air, movie music, like when an ax murderer waits at the bottom of the dark stairs for the heroine to come down in her nightgown.

Harmony's heart went into overdrive, and the box popped open.

She screamed, then the face of the giant jack-in-the-box lunged her way.

Something hit the back of her knees, and she turned, her arm raised in self-defense, but it was just the doll carriage . . . with a headless doll inside.

The sinister music slowed, and Jack went limp, bent over double, and stared into her eyes, his smile garish.

The dappled gray hobby horse started rocking, then the windup soldiers took to marching in place, and the fortune-teller dipped a wooden eyelid in a macabre wink.

Harmony ran . . . straight into Paxton's arms. She

screamed while he tried to hold her and didn't stop until he kissed her.

She fell into the kiss to erase the horror and because it felt so blooming good to be safe. "Oh," she said, coming up for air. "It's you."

"How many men do you kiss with that much passion?"

"I haven't kissed a man in three years."

"Liar. You kissed me an hour ago."

"Yeah, well, I'm up to my ass in alligators, so forgive me if it slipped my mind. How long have you been standing there?"

He gazed furtively about the room. "Long enough to need a shrink?"

"That makes two of us. I have to go home now."

Pulling her along, Paxton stepped into the room with the same morbid curiosity that had kept her glued to the floor in the midst of the nightmare, his arm so hard around her shoulder, she couldn't tell who was protecting who. He looked down at her. "You're not going anywhere. You've already proved you're not easy to get rid of. I mean—"

She elbowed him. "You're right. I don't give up easily. My staying power has been tested and honed. And I've seen my share of ghostly activities, but this about blew—"

"Enough with the ghost, already. You probably tripped some old switch. Nicodemus Paxton, the old pirate who built this place, was into eerie midway horror house tricks. You should see the funhouse mirror room upstairs. I'm telling you, we don't have a ghost."

The tricycle she'd used to hold the door open rolled into her line of vision, and Harmony ran to catch the door, but it slammed shut and clicked, as if it locked. Around the room in turn, came one click after another. Eight doors. Eight clicks.

Harmony tried the door to be sure. "Locked." She fell against it and watched Paxton, across the room, trying one of the others. "Don't bother," she said. "She locked them all."

"She, who?"

"The ghost."

"There . . . is . . . no . . . ghost."

The lights went out, throwing the room into a pit as black as the one into which she'd fallen when she passed out at home.

Except this time, she was awake.

Chapter Seven

TRAPPED, and at the blind mercy of terrorizing toys, panic gripped Harmony with a ghostly hand. "King, I can't see you. Talk to me."

"I'm here." His voice like a blessing echoed in the darkness. "Keep talking so I can find you."

"Uh, okay . . . my shirt. You hate it, but I have snarky and suggestive ones that you'd hate more, like—"

Paxton's searching hands found her . . . breast first. "Oh I don't know," he said. "This one is starting to . . . grow on me."

A flirting brass-ass technocrat whose walls went down with the lights. What *couldn't* she do with one of those? She grinned into the darkness as he lingered and found her other breast—and now that he had both hands full, and his touch could hardly be called accidental, she raised a brow. "What are you doing?"

He stopped fondling, but his hands remained where they were while her breasts peaked and swelled to better fill them.

Paxton cleared his throat. "I'm . . . reading your shirt . . . by Braille. I wanted to be sure this was really you . . . not a ghost."

"It's really, *really* me."

He fingered a nubbin. "And you're really, really happy to see me." The banked amusement in his voice failed to hide his intense sexual interest. "You stopped talking," he said, his voice soft.

The heat from his touch warmed her to her core. "I uh . . . forgot what I was saying?"

"Suggestive shirts," he prodded.

"Right. Two come to mind: Fast Girls Finish First, and Bad Girls Finish Often."

"I find both inspiring, but I'm glad you didn't walk into the great hall wearing one of them. I would've had a mutiny. I know, because I don't give a damn about the project right now, and I'm the freaking boss."

"Positive words, please. You're the aroused boss. Aroused is good, and it's positive."

"In that case, I'm a *very* good boss." He licked her ear.

Harmony tilted her head so he could nibble at will, his warm breath and roaming lips and hands sending shivering shock waves though her system. He brought her close, as if she needed warming.

She needed cooling, but who was she to quibble?

She'd been too long without a man when Brass Ass Mc-Shaft seemed the warm and cuddly type.

Cuddly being a momentary lapse, as McShaft pinned her against the wall in a me-man/you-woman move, cupped her head in his hands, opened his mouth over hers, and silenced her good sense. One big hand sleeked from her shoulder to the small of her back, where he pressed her flat against him.

Harmony about melted when her warm and willing center met his hard, probing man brain, and the darkness became her friend. No light needed to feel, touch, taste, as he incited a series of trembling minishocks, arousing an answering need in her to return the pleasure. In addition to the gift of his firm muscles and firmer rod, he tasted of spice, cinnamon, and coffee—exotic and arousing—and he dominated the kiss with a world of experience.

This man didn't just kiss; he made love with his mouth in the way an ice cream addict approached a fresh cone, delighting in that first lick of cool and creamy froth, wallowing in every subsequent, satisfying tongue swirl, the ultimate in sweet, sensual pleasure that ended in a burst of satisfaction. An exercise to gratify a deep, abiding hunger. And while Paxton's tongue made a sensual dessert of her mouth, spirals of need licked along Harmony's inner thighs, tonguing her higher, so high, she whimpered and flowered in ready welcome.

With the onslaught of desire, she worshipped his mouth in return with a zeal she'd never experienced. Paxton's tongue should be registered as a lethal weapon. What kind of man made you wet your panties with his tongue . . . *in your mouth*? She nearly came at the thought.

This man. The King of Paxton Castle.

"You know what we're doing?" he asked, his voice jarring in a world of mounting pleasure.

"Doing?" she repeated. "Oh. Losing our minds?" *Our clothes, next,* she hoped, *our grips on reality, please.*

Paxton sighed against her ear as if he heard her treacherous thoughts, which would be seriously scary.

"There *is* a lot of mind loss, mind bending, and mind blowing going on," he said. "But I wanted to make sure you were with me. I'm not alone feeling this . . . this . . . instant and overwhelming . . . draw, pull—"

"Magnetic attraction?" she suggested.

"Exactly. I needed to be sure you were aware and on the same page as I am. Getting hit upside the head with an industrial-sized magnet is rarely mutual and often harmful."

"Oh, it's mutual." Just to prove it, and because she

wanted to, Harmony slipped her hands beneath his shirt, appreciating the increased pace of his heart and the catch in his breath. His skin and its nap of chest hair were softer than his shirt, the silkiest she'd ever run her fingers through—Egyptian-cotton soft—and so hot it should come with a warning label. Warning: Might Cause a Fiery Swell of Orgasmic Insanity.

Paxton's sigh turned her to liquid honey as she resumed her tactile exploration and regularly scheduled sexcathalon—a gold-medal hands-and-mouth competition, fired by endurance and determination—a race they both wanted to win.

He slid both his hands down her back to cup her bottom and pull her up into his arms. Instinctively, she wound her legs around him, and he turned them so he leaned on the wall and slid them down to the floor, where she straddled him.

"I don't care why the lights went out," he said, "this is absolutely—"

Harmony fingered his man nips to hard little pebbles so he stopped talking. "It is amazing, but haven't you figured Gussie out by now?"

"Gussie?"

"Every time you deny her existence, she does something to prove she's here."

Chuckling, Paxton slid his hands beneath her shirt and stopped. "What do you have between your breasts? It feels like a . . . pouch."

"It's a sachet of perfumed herbs," she said, telling the truth.

He unhooked her bra in half a beat. "You know," he said. "If the ghost does exist, this is the nicest thing she's ever done for me. I've never been happier about anyth—"

The lights came on with a flash that half blinded them, and with the light came clarity of mind.

They couldn't look each other in the eye, but they

retrieved their hands so fast, their fingers tangled. A second later, Harmony stood to dust herself off and give Paxton time to stand and lose his boner. The locks clicked, eight in a row. "The doors are open," she said.

"If the ghost exists," Paxton said, turning her way, "she's a mean old bat." He shouted as if in pain, lurched, and knocked her on the floor.

"Hey!" she snapped.

"Sorry." Paxton bent to give her a hand up, but straightened with a shout, before he could.

"Did you throw your back out?" Harmony rose on her own, watching Paxton turn to look behind him, and as he did, she saw the cause of his discomfort. A huge honking splinter, and not just any splinter.

One life-sized toy soldier's rifle was missing its bayonet.

"What is it?" Paxton asked, trying without success to see his own backside.

"I really hate to tell you this, but you've been shot in the ass by a wooden soldier."

Chapter Eight

"A *toy* soldier? That's impossible," Paxton snapped.

"No. That's Gussie trying to prove she's here." Harmony walked around him, assessing the damage. "You know, judging by its placement, if you hadn't turned to me when you did, she might have shot you in your man brain."

Paxton paled, and Harmony put her arm around him. "Is there a nurse on the construction site?"

"There's a first aid kit. Curt usually takes care of scrapes and bruises, but I'll be damned if I want him knowing about this."

"Too embarrassing?"

"Too close to feeding your ghost stories. I don't want a mutiny, however close I got to abandoning ship for a weird spell there."

"You gonna yank that bayonet out of your butt yourself, or are you gonna walk around like that and refuse treatment like a real man?"

"You're enjoying this!"

"Hey, it's not every day a military man lets a toy soldier shoot him where the sun don't—"

"Never mind. I need treatment. What did you say earlier? Rather the deep blue sea than the devil?"

"Hah. I suppose I'm the deep blue sea?"

"You got it in one, babe."

"Call me babe again, and I'll stick something sharp in the other cheek."

"Point—ouch—taken. I apologize. Harmony . . . Crap, I can't believe I'm asking you this, but would you please remove this bayonet from my backside?"

"Okay, here goes." She rubbed her hands together and circled him.

"Wait!" he shouted, pulling his ass from her reach with a groan. "Not like that!"

"Like what then? Does it hurt bad?"

"It's just a splinter."

"Yeah?" She went to the life-sized wooden soldier with the missing bayonet. "He did it," she said, pointing. Then she measured the length of the bayonet on another rifle, and turned to Paxton, her hands at the same spread. "Your splinter is . . . *this* . . . big."

"This is *not* a fish story to tell your friends," he snapped.

"Spoilsport. Your splinter's a foot long, McBullseye. Hurts more just knowing it, doesn't it?"

"Could you stop enjoying this and get the first aid kit? Don't tell Curt why you need it. I'd never live it down."

"Okay, but you're a little pale. Why don't I help you lie on your stomach on one of the sofas in the formal parlor while you wait?"

He walked slowly and painfully to the sofa, and she helped him lie down, while he cursed the castle and his family tree in general.

Harmony towered over him. "Wanna pull down your slacks to let the air get at it until I come back?"

"Cartwright . . ."

"I'm going, I'm going." Spooked over the toy room horror show, but more so by their magnetic-libido kissing fest, Harmony ran through the tunnel and down the stairs, slowing as she turned to the construction site so no one would be suspicious. She managed a nebulous request, as if she needed the first aid kit for herself.

Curt, being a man, probably thought, Woman trouble—yikes! and handed it over without question.

By the time she got back to Paxton, he had recovered his manly pride, if not his manly stance. "Okay, tough guy," she said, sitting beside him, thigh to thigh. "Have no fear, your nurse is here. Oooh, nice ass."

"Harmony, I'm warning you—"

"Sheesh. You're no fun when you're a pain in the ass. Oh, sorry. No pun intended. Shall *I* pull down your slacks, or do you want to do the honors?"

He looked back at her. "Shouldn't you take out the splinter first?"

"If you want me to." She cleared her throat and looked around the formal parlor. "Wanna bite down on the family saber while I do? If not, I have a topical anesthetic in here that'll make removing it much less painful."

"Cut the sarcasm. Are there scissors in the first aid kit?"

"Yep."

Paxton rested his cheek on the sofa arm. "Cut my slacks out of the way. I have spares upstairs. I'll change after."

"Going commando are we?"

He looked back at her. "Are we?"

She raised a brow. "One of us could be."

"Which one of us?" he wanted to know.

"I'm just screwing with your man brain. Boxers or tighty whities?"

"Cut the slacks, and you'll find out what to cut next . . . if anything. I can't believe I'm putting my ass in your hands."

"Such fine words; such unromantic circumstances."

"You want romance? Get that stick out of my butt."

"That's romantic, all right. But which stick? The *wooden* one or the steel rod? Because I gotta tell you that I think you'll need a major attitude adjustment, and even then, surgery might be required to remove—"

"Shut . . . up!"

"Okay, playtime's over. Geez, are you touchy. Wow, your slacks cut like butter. That's quality. Ooh, yum, black silk." She knuckled the fabric of his underwear. "But I can't tell if they're boxers or briefs. What a waste."

"My briefs are a waste?"

She looked up. "Yeah . . . those too." She continued cutting. "Having your ass in a sling is the real waste," she mumbled.

He craned his neck to see her face. "What?"

"This whole scenario is a sad waste—the sofa, the ambience, your bare ass. I could fantasize all three into a much better situation."

"C'mere." He crooked a finger, and she leaned down so far, she practically lay beside him. Not even the sofa's aged musk nor the brackish scent of low tide at this end of the building calmed her raging hormones.

Paxton caught the under-wave of her natural pageboy and tucked a thick curl behind her ear. The slide of his fingers along her earlobe radiated to her breasts, budded her nipples, and brought her to flower.

She could go to bed with this man, which was saying something. She was particular. Not liking to be touched did that to a woman.

"Go ahead, distract me from the pain," he whispered, his lips so close she could meet them. "Tell me your fantasy."

Fantasy? Oh yeah. Well, at least he had a playful side, even if it was only sex play. She wanted the real thing, not the fantasy, but her seducer was too skewered to play the kind of game her body craved after his sensual onslaught.

She wanted to be impaled . . . by him. "Much good you do me like that," she said.

"You're all heart, Cartwright."

"I try." She turned her mournful sigh into a sexy one. "Okay, here's the fantasy . . . I'm thinking your chest is as exposed as your ass—"

"Your word choice sorely lacks fantasy quality. As a matter of fact, it's flip and annoying."

"Sorry," she whispered and blew in his ear. "I'll try to be dulcet and seductive in tone." She sat up and turned her attention to his tush.

"Without sarcasm," he suggested, resting his forehead on the sofa arm.

"Fine. In my mind, I'm stripping you naked, slow and easy, one piece of clothing at a time, and I'm kissing every bit of skin I expose, licking you inch by salty inch." She picked up the spray can of topical anesthetic. "Then, because I want that hot rod where it belongs, I stand and take off my panties, one side, then the other . . . and you reach up and—" She sprayed his butt.

Paxton yelped.

"I didn't touch you."

"That was as cold as your heart."

"You must've made one tough soldier, buster."

"I never joined the military."

"Don't military school grads usually go on to join one branch of the service or another?"

"I didn't graduate."

"You didn't quit. You'd rather be shot than quit. What happened?"

Paxton heaved a sigh. "I was expelled, if you must know. Ouch! Cripes!"

"Splinter's out!"

"You could've warned me."

"I wanted to surprise you so you wouldn't . . . ah . . . clench. Maybe I should bruise some southernwood from

Gussie's witch garden and spread it on your ass. Her grimoire says that southernwood 'draws forth splinters and thorns from the flesh.' It makes a good worm medicine, too."

"I wonder how many people she shot with those bayonets, if she had to grow her own remedy." Paxton touched his temple. "Look at me, talking like there is a—"

"Don't say it. You can't afford another hole in your—"

He looked back at her. "Being tended by you is like playing ice hockey bare-assed."

"Or like being seduced with no payoff?"

Paxton slammed his forehead against the sofa arm several frustrated times.

Chapter Nine

*
 * *
* * *
* *

"NOW we have to get you back on the job as if nothing happened." Harmony cleaned and disinfected Paxton's wound, applied an antibiotic ointment, and covered it with a bandage. All set." She palmed, stroked, and slapped his perfect, undamaged cheek. "Soft as a newborn peach," she said, sliding a roving finger lower, lower . . . but stopping short of giving him—and herself—the sexual jolt his tense body expected.

When she leaned toward him, his expression expectant, he looked shocked to see her. Releasing his breath in a whoosh, his body went limp, except for the tic in his locked jaw muscle.

"You okay?" she asked.

He narrowed his eyes. "*Why* did you do that?"

"Hey, you see a fine piece of a . . . art, and you wanna touch. I'd ask if I took any of the starch out of you, but—" She sat back to admire his backside, and lower. "But from this angle, you seem generously starched."

His eyes were no less intense when he looked back at her. "I mean, why did you stop?"

"I'd never take advantage of a wounded man."

"My luck. How about I lie on my side and give you full permission to take advantage?"

"I think you're delirious."

"I *am*. What would you do if I copped a feel of your backside?"

"What did I do when you copped a feel of my boobs?"

With a head tilt, he granted her the point. "I think you purred."

And she damn near came, if only he knew.

He leveraged himself on his side, his zipper tented with his slacks so loose, and he pulled her down against him. "You're trouble, Cartwright." He made another meal of her lips, nibbling her top lip, then her bottom, and when she opened her mouth to return the favor, he Frenched her and surged against her with the energy of a bull out for stud, his man brain primed and thinking *hard*.

"Wow," she said, coming up for air. "Wounding your pride didn't hurt your kissing skills. You're still good at it."

"Thank you, but I can't take all the credit. An equally greedy partner helps," he said, swooping in for another, cupping her bottom, and pulling her pulsing center against his pulsing rod.

When they took to rocking against each other, and Harmony thought she was gonna come just like that, Paxton pushed her away, and she nearly slipped off the sofa.

He saved her and held her, his brow against hers, while he caught his breath. Brow to brow, breath to breath, Harmony tried not to cry, or scream, or rant, or deck him, just for the fun of it.

King sighed. "Help me, will you?" he asked, words she suspected he'd never strung together before. "Another minute," he said, "and I would have been up to my . . . man brain . . . in trouble."

"Your point?" she snapped.

"We'd be sorry. Me for taking advantage, and you for letting me."

Harmony mocked him with a laugh. "That was *mutual*!" She shoved a finger into his chest so he winced. "Look, you brass-ass humanzee. I'm a big girl, responsible for my own sex life and my own orgasms. I'm not some throwback to the dark ages. If I were staying longer, you'd need protecting from me. I'd get you in the sack, sooner or later, and you'd plucking love it. The name's Harmony. Remember it, because you'd be screaming it in ecstasy under other circumstances. Now shut up before you piss me off."

She helped him stand, and he was too shocked not to lean on her. She held his pants together in the back, and by the time he took over, he had himself in control, which couldn't be said for her.

"Harmony?" He put an arm around her shoulder to turn her his way. "For the record, I thought if I took advantage of you, you'd 'deck me' or 'strike me with a sharp object in my good cheek.'"

Harmony wilted. "I'm sorry. I have been sending mixed signals. Not intentionally, and not that I haven't gotten a boatload of those, myself, today. So let's say we forgive each other and start fresh? The statement I just made stands. This is the new millennium, Paxton, and I'm the queen of my own sex life. Got it?"

She'd gotten through, she saw. He looked at her in a new and more enlightened way, as if she—as a sex partner and a proponent of the spontaneous—might be his equal. An obviously new concept for him. "Thank you," he said. "For a proud-to-be-awesome seductress, you make a good nurse."

Okay, he'd changed the subject, but she loved a challenge. "My sisters and I practically raised each other. We're good at scraped knees and such."

"There are more like you?"

"You have no idea. Scary thought, isn't it? But that's not the point."

"There was a point to this?"

"There was a point to the toys. A message."

Confusion furrowed his brow. "Which is?"

Harmony huffed. "Gussie was *toying* with me to show me she could. Then you rescued me and we joined forces, so to speak, so Gussie toyed with us both. Ergo, a bayonet landed too close to your man brain for comfort."

Paxton winced. "I'm not a cliché. I stopped using my 'man brain,' as you call it, when I was in high school."

"You wore it out?"

"No, I used it for nefarious purposes and got myself screwed in every possible way."

"Even so, you don't live like a monk, because the way you kiss—"

"I'm a sane man with a strong sense of self-preservation . . . and a healthy libido. I choose carefully, *nearly* to the point of celibacy."

"And yet, you just put your ass in my hands."

"I must have been in shock."

"You could have gone to a hospital."

"They'd have put me on the psych ward if I told them how it happened."

"Whatever." Harmony looked toward the toy room. "Warning taken, Gussie," she called.

"I'm going up to change," Paxton said. "Want me to walk you as far as the cedar dressing room?"

"No thanks. This parlor's like a museum. I'd like to look around for a while. Gussie's too tired to cause any dire mischief. Besides, this parlor is nowhere near as negative as the toy room, plus Gussie likes *me*."

"I'll come back for you after I've changed and checked on the crew. Don't go back to the toy room."

"I'm not crazy."

"See, that's where our opinions differ." He limped away.

The formal parlor emitted an unusual vibe. Harmony was used to different people's vibes warring for prominence in her mind, but strangely enough, the only warring energy in this room, whatever Harmony touched, belonged to Gussie. Glory, the poor witch even fought with herself.

After the toy room, Harmony understood her better. Mad, sad, and belligerent, Gussie had lived and died to wreak havoc. She caused discord and fed on it, either for fun or to set herself up as both controller and arbitrator, which meant that she had probably been universally disliked, even in life. But why? And while wreaking havoc might have satisfied her in life, nothing seemed to satisfy her in death, so what did she really want?

That new but familiar cold draft and decaying lilac scent entrapped and danced around Harmony while the answer filled her mind: *Vindication.* "Oh boy." The scorned, mad, dead witch, who for some reason liked her, or thought she could use her, wanted vindication.

Vindication from what? And who had scorned her? Two more vague pieces to an indefinable puzzle.

Harmony thought she should get her twitchy witchy self out, and fast. But despite the psychotic ghost and because of the psychic mandate demanding to be fulfilled, she needed to explore the castle, its treasure of vintage clothes, and its owner, not necessarily in that order. To that end, she wandered the formal parlor, sat on a piano stool with dolphin feet, and played "Chopsticks." She opened every drawer, searching for the other half of her ring or another clue. Sensing Gussie, she sat in a Queen Anne chair beside a long wall covered by an equally long tapestry.

The chair, or the area surrounding it, vibrated with Gussie's energy—not simply her malevolent ghostly energy like in the toy room, but her true spirit, as it might have been in life, some of it powerfully *positive*.

Pay dirt. Gussie had frequented this area in good times

and bad, and the sum of her energy seemed to boil down to this one wall.

The strains of Brahms's "Lullaby" reached Harmony, and she turned to see the piano keys moving, with no one playing. If Gussie was playing, the hopeful vibes were out of character. Yet Harmony believed the music was a sign that she should continue, that she was on the right track.

She pushed furniture aside and slipped behind the tapestry, but she found no hidden latch, door, safe, staircase, or tunnel along its length, nothing but an oddly textured surface that reminded her of brushstrokes. Harmony pulled a corner of the tapestry aside to reveal a wall that looked like a dirty canvas, its vibes muted by a strong force.

Gussie puzzled her almost as much as Paxton, the kick-ass kisser, who was returning now to get her.

As Harmony combed her hair with her fingers, Paxton closed the distance between them, his thoughts focused on corn silk that smelled of peppermint—her hair! She felt his yearning and his dogged determination to ignore her from now on, though he'd slipped several sensational times.

Aw, how nice. He thought she was sensational.

In other circumstances, *she'd* work him hard, and he wouldn't be able to ignore her. She liked her effect on him as much as she hated it, yet he kept returning for more. He believed he should have stayed on the construction site, yet he'd headed her way instead, annoyed with himself over his attraction and his weakness in following his sexual inclinations where she was concerned.

Too bad she couldn't tell him the truth, that when she fulfilled her purpose—whatever that was—their connection would be severed.

A clock struck three, and she realized the day had passed too fast. She couldn't possibly examine and evaluate the clothes in the cedar dressing room in one day, never mind in the rooms she hadn't explored. Neither could she solve the puzzle of her psychic goal.

The closer Paxton got, the stronger and deeper Gussie's hatred became. For a minute Harmony hated him as well, but she fought the encroaching negative vibes.

"Boy are you in trouble," she said as Paxton came closer. "Gussie hates your guts. Did you know that?"

"All my relatives hate my guts. Your point?"

Chapter Ten

DETERMINED to get Hellcat Harmony to hang around for a few extra hours, King followed her back through the tunnel toward its termination in the cedar dressing room.

She'd had a nasty look on her face for him when he got to the parlor. Odd that. A few times today, she'd reminded him of a small wildcat—a lynx or a bobcat—graceful, beautiful, disarming, a feline who could close in with stealth and feed off you before you knew how deadly she was.

She hadn't felt deadly when he was driving himself crazy kissing her in the toy room. He'd disarmed *her*, not the other way around. Not that she'd fought him.

Neither had she fought the sexual pull when she was bandaging his wound and frustrating the hell out of him with her teasing. Everything that happened between them this afternoon would make keeping her at a safe distance more difficult. But keeping his distance would be safer than the unwanted fantasy she inspired of the two of them together. Very together. Very bad.

What they'd shared, which had seemed fine for a day out of time, now endangered the scheme forming in his mind. Okay, the scheme his men had just planted, and not gently, in his mind—damn them and damn her. But that arrangement would only work if he could keep his distance. Not easy when she could seduce him with a look.

Before he took steps to put the scheme in motion, however, he needed to know the enigmatic interloper better, and the best way to do that would be to keep her around for a few more hours, after the crew left, no construction issues to distract them.

Back in the dressing room, he gave her some space.

"Something's stuck in your craw," she said. "You wanna tell me what?"

"Your acuity is alarming, but if you must know, I almost did have a mutiny, because of your ghost stories. My workers *all* want to quit, and that's the first time they've ever agreed on *anything*, thank you very much." King tested his five o'clock shadow and examined the wildcat's flawless features. Full lips, pouty, kissable—eminently kissable, he now knew. Hair of spun gold, eyes as big as saucers, aquamarine, and *deceptively* innocent. "Call me crazy," he said, "but I'm determined to complete castle restorations, despite Paxton generational failures to do so . . . and despite the fact that you think I'm being hampered by a ghost."

"I *think*? Have you sat on your punctured butt in the last hour?"

"All right, so maybe I'm beginning to suspect you're right. So what? I still have to finish the job I started."

"Which is?"

"To get this hellish place off my hands and sell it to the highest bidder."

The familiar wail came from so close beside them, he jumped almost as high as the sexpot, which hurt like the devil. Pissed by his startled surprise, and by the pain in his ass, he took Harmony's hand to lead her from harm's way.

In Gussie's room, she pulled him up short. "Wha'd'ya know, there's a gentleman hiding behind those invisible fatigues, but *I* hardly need protecting."

"You're slipping, oh mighty mediator. That wail just now sounded more like a war cry than a peace offering, and did you already forget the toy room? Peacemaker, my . . . ass."

"Now you're just being mean." Her full lips at rest fell into a natural pout, but when she all-out tried, like now, he wanted to make a meal of her, starting with her mouth, and ending with her mouth, but stopping at some amazing places in between.

"Unkind, perhaps," he said, pulling himself from his fantasies, "but honest and practical, too. I have no choice. Getting this place off my hands is serious business."

"More serious than you know. You heard Gussie's wail of protest. She wants you to keep the castle in the family, and I think she has some serious persuasion in mind."

"What do you care?"

"I . . . it's complicated," Harmony said, sounding to him like she was hiding something, then she bit her lip for a pensive, and seductive, minute. "I thought I heard in Salem that the castle *can't* leave your family," she added.

"Legally, it can, and local gossip never gave my family anything but grief, so your sources are as suspect as your motive for being here." King took down the empty picture frame with the cracked glass and waved it under the hellcat's nose. "Off-loading this albatross, lock, stock, and bad luck, is good business. Excellent business."

"For who?"

"Me. My heirs—the next generation of Paxtons, and the generations who come after them."

"Since you told me you stopped thinking with your man brain—which, if you ask me, is a blatant misrepresentation of the facts—I didn't expect you to produce any heirs."

"You know nothing about me."

"You did mention celibacy."

"In the present tense, and nearly so."

"So the future's up for grabs? Pardon the pun."

"No, damn it."

Her eyes got so big and deep, he could fall in and die happy. "You already have an heir!" She spoke with such certainty, the hair at his nape stood and saluted.

Chapter Eleven

"YOU'RE fishing," King said, a weak defense at best. Who was she to say he had heirs?

"No, I'm using the sense I was born with, and it says there's no reason for you to sell this place, because you have heirs who'd want it."

"Your intuition is faulty. This is hardly a profit-making proposition."

"You're avoiding the subject of heirs, but that aside, homes are for living in not for making a profit."

"There you go. My point exactly. Generations have tried and *failed* to live here. They worked to make this castle a home, part of Paxton family life and legacy, but misfortune dogged them the way it dogs me. Spending time here caused my ancestors physical and emotional harm. Husbands and wives—whole families—left, alienated from the castle and from each other. Many of them separated, never to reunite."

Harmony nodded as if she knew the reason why.

"What?" King asked.

"Gussie likes to stir things up, and not in a good way. She can be downright malevolent, if you get on her bad side, which you obviously have. Keep that in mind when you think about signing on the dotted line."

"If you say so." King tried to guess at the hellcat's game. He doubted she had a vintage clothing store. Her motives were something he needed to discover. "Feel free to stick around for a few more hours," he said. "You lost time tending my . . . wound, and I appreciate it, but you haven't had much of a chance to look for vintage clothes."

He went back into the dressing room to check the clothes racks for pillaging and plundering. "Looks like you barely got started. This is a small piece of the castle's vintage-clothing pie," he said. "What's a few more hours? I could get you to the Beverly Airport by nine, then to Salem by ten."

"I . . . it's a tempting offer, but—"

He knew she'd decline. She didn't want him to see there was no vintage clothing store. You know what; he could prove that right now. He took a random gown off the rack, whipped the sheet off it, and held it up. "What do you call this?"

"A beaded flapper dress, circa 1920. Why?"

"Value?"

"Today? Or when it was new? I'd need to examine it for condition and maker to give you a fair price for the vintage market. Is this a test?"

"Yes." King replaced the flapper number and showed her a navy gown. "On sight, tell me what you know about this one."

The hellcat grinned, and the devil in him rose to attention.

"That's a Worth," she said. "Designed and produced in Paris. It cost big bucks around 1860, and it costs big bucks vintage, just because it's sturdy enough to stay on that hanger. How'm I doing?"

King checked the label, saw she was right, and shoved the dress back on the rack.

"Hey, take it easy. I definitely want that one."

"But you said it was big bucks."

"I'll give you a *supplier's* fair price. I have a market for it. You don't. A successful businessman like you knows we both have to make a profit."

King cursed beneath his breath. "You passed."

"With only two dresses? Are you kidding? My sister Vickie was harder on me when she was teaching me about vintage clothing and accessories. Test me some more. This is fun."

"Okay." He led her to the cabinet that closed off the tunnel to the east wing. "Name the geegaws in the cabinet."

Her eyes actually twinkled. "That's a sterling vinaigrette geegaw, a buttonhook geegaw, a fan geegaw."

"Enough with the sass."

As if to prove she didn't have it in her to obey, she removed the stick she'd called a fan from the bottom shelf, and with a flick of her wrist, it became a fan after all. She covered her face with it to flirt with her eyes—very effective—then she gazed demurely down.

If he didn't know better, he'd think she was checking out his package, the thought giving her something bigger to contemplate. Damn, she had an effect on him.

King coughed with a rare shot of embarrassment, denied the warning in his head, and turned back to the case. He pointed to several more mysterious women's accessories from the last century.

"Tussy-mussy," she said, "a tiny vase for flowers that women wore on their dresses. That's a jewelry casket; it opens at that latch. See?" She grinned like every straight-A student he'd ever hated. "The shoe is a snuff box."

"Please. The shoe's a knickknack."

"It's a snuff box shaped like a shoe." She took it from the case, opened the top, and shoved it under his nose. "Smell."

King reared back, sneezed, and pulled out his handkerchief.

She laughed, a sound he liked too much.

"You win," he said.

"What do I win?" asked the enchantress, giddy with success.

"You win a few more hours to go through the castle, and my belief in your knowledge of vintage clothes, if not my belief in your shop."

She shrugged. "Like it matters. A few more hours to search would help, but staying here alone with you doesn't seem prudent. Nothing personal."

"I kiss you senseless and bare my ass to you, and you're afraid to stay alone with me?"

"I rest my case."

"You make me sound like a pervert."

"If the bare ass doesn't fit, try the Braille boob-reading."

"Hey, there were extenuating circumstances, which you damned well know."

She patted his chest. "I'm screwing with your mind again. But staying alone at night with a man I don't know, in a castle I don't know, with attacking toys . . . Nah."

"Wise girl." He'd be wise to let her go home with the crew for the same reasons, not to mention his out-of-character, out-of-control attraction. "We wouldn't be alone," he said, despite his good intentions. "I have a live-in cook. Her husband's the head gardener. The guards you charmed with your . . . cleavage, was it? They live here as well."

He'd found the peacemaker's Achilles' heel, judging by her look of interest. His libido did a happy dance while his common sense shook its sad head. "Tell you what," King said, "after the construction crew leaves, you can meet the residents and tell them we're working late tonight. That way, you can pillage and plunder while I finish my work. Deal?"

She extended her hand. "Deal."

King shook it, and ducked.

Harmony looked down at him with a furrowed brow. "What was that about?"

"Hell if I know. When I kissed you, I got shot in the ass. For shaking your hand, I expected nothing less than a goose egg the size of Rhode Island."

"It's true," she said. "Gussie would rather we weren't in accord, because discord is her MO, but she expended a lot of energy in the toy room, so I don't expect we'll hear from her for a while."

"You really believe that?"

"A ghost needs time to regain her energy, like a man after sex."

"You're a laugh a minute, you know that?"

"I got a million of 'em."

"Spare me."

"How can you doubt my sincerity after today? There's proof of Gussie all over the castle."

"What proof?"

"For one thing, nobody has ever finished refurbishing this monstrosity. What makes you think you can succeed where your ancestors failed?"

"I can handle the accidents, the arguing, and wailing— unless you're here so I don't have to. I'm stronger and more determined than my ancestors. I have the killer instincts to get the job done."

"Do you expect to find buyers with killer instincts to live here?"

King reared back. "Now you're just being mean."

"Me? I'm being a realist. Look at your butt. Oh, sorry, that's anatomically impossible. Sit on it then and tell me you don't believe Gussie can stop you. She *won't* let you finish restoration, never mind letting you sell the place to strangers. She doesn't even like *you* here."

"So why doesn't she mind you?" King asked. "Crap,

listen to me, talking as if she actually exists. Besides, she *doesn't* like you. Look how she scared you today."

"She toyed with me. She *wounded* you."

"Nevertheless," he said, "she—*it*—whatever—was quiet today for the first time in a century."

"You know the reason for that, right?"

"None that I'll admit to . . . in the event of a sanity hearing."

"Fine, don't admit it, but if I stay, you'll at least know you're safe for the evening. Whether you know it or not, you need protecting."

"The hell I do!" He touched his throbbing butt. "Well. Good job so far." Half of him wanted to pretend he needed the annoying brat so she'd minister to him again—he guessed that was his man-brain half. But the real-brain half—the military-trained businessman with no heart—knew he'd best stay rank-on stubborn and keep a safe distance where the sexpot peacemaker and his overactive libido were concerned.

Unfortunately, for the sake of getting the place finished, he needed to chance keeping the seductress around. "So you're staying after the men go tonight," he confirmed. "You want to; you know you do. So you will, right?"

"To keep you from getting brained, yeah."

"Something tells me," King admitted, "that I'm more than likely to get brained by you."

"There is that."

Chapter Twelve

HARMONY had enjoyed her evening at the castle, but she was on her way home, now, mission *not* accomplished. Done. Finis.

She'd seen enough signs from Gussie to know she *should* go back, but time had run out, so what excuse would she give when she showed up tomorrow?

Paxton started his jet-powered Eurocopter and winked. "I always watch out for flying brooms here," he said. "Kidding. They're not bad in the summer, but come October, you can't get airspace around here."

Harmony smiled at his joke and wondered what he'd think if he knew he'd made a witch joke to a witch. They'd had a good evening, her searching for vintage clothes, and him doing paperwork. And they were more attracted to each other than they'd been earlier. How weird was that? If she wasn't reading his mind, she'd never believe it.

He looked powerful and commanding, controlling his helicopter, his pride and joy obvious; he became one with the beast as they rose straight up and off the island.

Darkness had set in by then, and the lights of Salem beckoned, though they'd fly over it to the Beverly Airport and take a car back.

"We're cruising at about a hundred and twenty-five miles an hour," Paxton said, but Harmony was so enthralled with watching him, she wasn't inclined toward chitchat. He enjoyed flying so much that his defenses were down. He didn't worry about putting up walls in the sky. He liked her sitting beside him, and he admitted as much to himself.

His mind was full of the two of them spending time at the castle, and not purely for keeping Gussie quiet. Over the course of the flight, he relived their every embrace, and by the time they landed at the Beverly Airport, she was as aroused and ready as him. He'd conjured up some pretty impure thoughts about getting her back in his arms.

She was pretty sure he was the first man whose *mind* intrigued and seduced her. But why was he thinking about her at the castle in the future?

She guessed she should try to draw him out. Give him a reason to get her back there.

A short while later, as he led her to a black stretch limo, Harmony sensed a need to take the lead, because his walls were going up again. He helped her into the backseat, got in beside her, and his driver shut the door.

"I did a lot of searching during those few extra hours tonight," she said, "and I found some prime vintage gowns."

"Good. Head for Salem, Ed," Paxton told his driver. "Pickering Wharf." He turned back to her. "I got a lot done, myself, probably because I wallowed in the rare quiet. I liked the castle tonight for the first time in years."

"Your men could have accomplished a lot, if they'd stayed as late as we did."

"Ever since I met you," Paxton said, "I've had the strangest feeling that you can read my mind. You're brilliant, you know. I could use somebody like you on my team."

"I thought I pissed you off."

"Oh, you do, but listen. You're right. The men could have gotten a lot done tonight. They worked like gangbusters in the quiet peace today. No arguments, which never happened before. Not when my grandfather rebuilt the east wing or his father added the west, or when my father added the boathouse."

"Who added the mismatched addition that makes one side of the castle look like a drunken sailor rambling toward the sea?"

"Nicodemus, Gussie's husband. But he had a method to his madness. A landmass once connected Paxton Island to Marblehead, and an old steam train carried the family back and forth from the mainland."

"That's hard to imagine."

"The engine and parlor car are in the east wing. The toy room leads to the train shed. I would have showed it to you, if I hadn't gotten—" He looked at his driver. "Distracted."

Paxton's wink gave her a sense of intimacy. He asked Ed to lower the privacy window, and she shivered like a teen on her first date. When he took her hand, Harmony wondered if he'd try to read her by Braille again. "Let me get to the point," he said. "I have a business proposition for you."

That sounded sexy. *Not!*

"If I could keep the men working harmoniously for as many hours as we worked today, I could finish the restoration and sell the place before summer's end."

"Providing Gussie lets you."

"Precisely, which is why I'd like to offer you a live-in job at the castle."

Live in? He'd hit her with dumb surprise. How could she have missed the live-in part?

But she hadn't missed it; she'd wallowed in it, fantasizing along with him, not realizing that the best way to live the fantasy was to live together.

"With you in residence," he explained, "my crew could work every day instead of arguing. The men are always up for overtime pay, and longer hours would make them happier than getting along."

The thought made her heart skip a beat. "Live in?"

He wasn't revealing all his motives. He wanted to know more about her ring, and, okay, about her, too. His men believed she appeased the ghost, and they'd threatened to quit if he *didn't* hire her, which annoyed the hell out of him, but at least he didn't take that out on her. She intrigued him and—her favorite incentive—she'd jump-started his recently dormant libido. Yay. "So you want me to be, like, your secretary or something?"

"No, it's a much easier job than that. I want you to hang around. Go through the clothes and geegaws, catalog and price them. Buy what you want and tell me what to charge for the rest." He squeezed her hand. "All you have to do is show up and treasure-hunt every day. Piece of cake." He shook his head. "Damned if I don't feel as if I'm hiring a witch doctor."

"A witch peacemaker, you mean."

"Do I?"

"You betcha. A ghost tamer."

"Okaay."

"And my wages?"

"Hungry, are you?"

Reading his own libidinous take on the question, she raised a brow. "As hungry as you."

He spontaneously defrosted, masking his ruddy flush with a brusque cough. She'd almost made him forget his men had forced him into this, which he would always resent, which meant her job might not be as easy as he tried to make out.

"Wages?" she repeated.

"I don't know what to call your job to put a price on it."

"I'll be keeping your construction crew working. What do you pay your foreman?"

"Curt's job is way more complicated, so how about I pay you fifteen dollars an hour, and you name your price for the clothes you want?"

"Fifteen an hour for twenty-four hours a day? Because I'll be keeping Gussie quiet twenty-four/seven . . . if I take the job."

"Rob me blind, why don't you."

"I'm just saying . . ."

"Let's say I don't pay you while you sleep eight hours a night."

As serendipitous as the chance to buy his vintage clothes, the extra pay would help her and her sisters expand the store, plus she could work on her psychic mandate at the same time. "Done," she said. "About the vintage clothes? Suppose I want them all? If I take the job."

"You have no idea how many there are. It could take you months to find them all."

Was he dangling a castle full of vintage clothes like a carrot before her? Because, frankly, dangling himself would be enough. Oh, the eye candy in that vision. Swoon.

"Here's the deal," she said, thrilled, but trying to be practical. "Fifteen dollars an hour for sixteen hours a day, it is, but if you ever snap your fingers at me the way you snap them at your men, my claws will come out."

Amusement deepened his laugh lines, though she could hardly call his look a smile. "I like a woman with claws. Bring 'em on, Hellcat."

A psychic mandate with all the trimmings *and* a hungry panther, too. "I have only one stipulation, providing I take the job. I'm not sleeping on one of those moldy old mattresses."

"There's a newly remodeled suite on the fourth floor with fresh bedding and all the conveniences."

"Bathroom? Shower? TV? Tub? Doors that lock?"

"Everything except regular TV and cable, but it's got a flat screen and a great collection of movies."

"Now that I think about it, locks wouldn't keep Gussie out, anyway. Hey, I'm not sleeping alone in the castle with a negative ghost witch."

"I'll stay as long as you do. I sleep there half the time, anyway."

"Are you suggesting we share a suite?"

"It would up the odds," he said. "Two against Gussie."

"That's true, but she hates you. For me, that would be like sharing a suite with ghost bait."

"Gee, thanks."

Harmony sat forward and knocked on the privacy window, so it rolled down. "Driver, take the next right. Wharf Street. My house is the big Victorian with the wraparound porch."

The limo came to a stop, and Harmony still hadn't accepted the job, because she didn't want Paxton to see how eager she was.

He told his driver to wait, got out, and saw the shop. "The Immortal Classic Vintage Clothing and Curio Shop," he said and looked back in the car. "My apologies."

He came around and held her door open.

"As you see, I live and work here," she said, glad to prove him wrong, though she did have other motives for going to the castle, but she had no reason to split hairs. "I live behind the shop," she said pointing the way.

At the kitchen door, he took her key and unlocked it for her. She thanked him but stayed on the stoop. "I'll think about your offer," she said, "and you'll know tomorrow, one way or the other."

She read the consideration he gave to her lips, which didn't surprise her, but she also saw his intent to keep things strictly business between them—a *big* disappointment. She liked him, even if she'd only known him for a day. She would always know where she stood and what challenges she would face with King Paxton.

"We start work early," he said as he went down the

steps, stopped, and turned back to her. "Harmony, about sleeping arrangements. If you take the job, you should know that the suite—"

"I don't want to work for you," she said.

Paxton came up a step. "I'm sorry to hear that."

"I don't want to be your employee. I'd rather be your equal. If I go to sort your vintage clothes and keep your ghost quiet, I go as an independent contractor."

Paxton's shoulders relaxed. "That can be arranged. Same figure, on a per diem basis?"

Harmony gave a half nod. "I'll sign a contract."

"I'll have one ready, in case you decide to take the job. But . . ." His gaze veered once more to her Proud to Be Awesome T-shirt. "You should know that I dislike clothes that make a literal statement."

"I'll keep that in mind." She opened the door.

Chapter Thirteen

"I want every literal-statement shirt you can find," Harmony told her sisters as they helped her drag her suitcases up from the basement the next morning. "As long as they're tight and V-neck."

"That about sums up all our shirts," Destiny said. "You want the suggestive ones?"

"Especially the suggestive ones."

"This sucks," Storm said. "Des, tell her that going back to that place is chancy."

Destiny looked thoughtful. "There are chances . . . and there are chances."

"That's a lot of blooming cryptic help," Storm snapped.

Harmony handed the rebel a suitcase to fill. "That's Destiny."

"How witchy is the ghost?" Storm piled in the shirts. "Is she as scary as me?"

"Scarier. She hovers over the castle running roughshod over anyone who steps inside. Hang around long enough, and you become as negative as she is . . . unless I'm there."

"And the guy who offered you the job?"

"Thinks he's the center of the universe. A brass-ass technocrat who barely looked up when I went inside. Then he stalks my way like a loose-limbed panther, despite the finest steel rod money can buy shoved up his ass."

Storm chuckled. "Hey, you're starting to sound bitchin', like me."

"Thanks. He wears clothes as black as his hair and more expensive than our van." Harmony pulled out her sock drawer. "His eyes are clear and whiskey bright, and his voice . . ." touched her everywhere, made her shiver and— "He's closed to emotion, but I can read him, because he's attached to the castle. He'll be a challenge." One she couldn't wait to tackle. "He's not happy about having me around. He thinks I'm trouble." She raised the shirt she'd set aside: Here Comes Trouble. "I'm wearing this to work today."

Storm touched her heart. "I'm so proud."

Trouble ahead, Harmony's sensible side shouted. Free-spirit psychic witches didn't mesh well with tight-assed technocrats. But she didn't care. If she was gonna get burned, let the smoldering begin.

"You know how, when we meet a new guy, we nail his potential after two minutes, no first date required? Well this guy's got true potential, if I can loosen him up. Anybody mind if I take the toys from that obsession party we gave? I've got a hard nut to crack."

"As long as you don't really crack his nuts."

"Guess that depends on his performance. Besides, someone has to teach him to be spontaneous. He's way too controlled. I plan to enjoy removing that steel rod from his spine."

"And that's the only rod you have designs on, right?" Des laughed. "As if we didn't know."

"She's gonna melt his brass ass," Storm said. "When can we meet him?"

Harmony wasn't ready to tell Paxton that blondes like her came in a three-pack. "You'll know when it's time. Rent a boat, but don't leave it by the cement steps. There's a landing on the west side, with a small Gothic door not far away. I'll unlock it when I know you're coming. Let's play three musketeers when you get there; use the 'power of three as one' before Gussie suspects I'm not alone. Wear matching outfits, and bring one for me. Storm, don't forget your blonde wig."

Des sat on one of Harmony's suitcases to zip it. "So do you know why you were sent there?"

"At least part of it is to persuade Paxton to keep the castle in the family. I think another part is to set the castle free of Gussie—or to set Gussie free of the castle. I sense there's more, but I'm still working on instinct. Your job, while I'm playing ghost tamer, is to think about ways for us to help Gussie move on."

"Be careful," Des said. "It's a plus that you can quiet her, but it's frightening as well. You're polar opposites. I don't want you getting hurt. She might be stronger than you."

"I think she is. But you'll know if I need you. I'm not worried, so you shouldn't be." Gussie was not only stronger than her, she was quite possibly stronger than the three of them together—which she wouldn't tell her sisters—especially if she read the dolphin symbolism correctly, and the sea provided her with an unlimited energy source.

It was all quite scary, but Harmony felt useful for the first time in her life, and she'd deal with whatever unimagined ghostly manifestation jumped out at her . . . when it jumped.

She grinned. Besides, Paxton Castle contained some mighty powerful perks, and one of them was King-sized . . . she hoped.

Chapter Fourteen

HE didn't need Harmony. Didn't need anybody. He hoped she *didn't* take the job. King paced the construction site the morning after offering her the job, while the wind—or Gussie, if the sexy nutcase was to be believed—wailed as loud as a bloodthirsty banshee.

Earlier, two of his men got into such a heated argument, they'd beat the crap out of each other, and he'd had to put them in the chopper and take them to Boston to get stitched up. He'd expected Harmony to be here waiting by the time he got back.

One o'clock. She wasn't coming, then.

If she didn't take the job, he didn't know how he'd finish restoration without someone getting hurt. Gussie was on the rampage today. Worse than ever.

King wished he could walk away and leave the place to rot, Gussie along with it. But all his life, he'd harbored a foolish, nagging need to restore his godforsaken heritage and bring it back to glory.

How plucking stupid was he? He rubbed the back of his

neck. Look at him, substituting ridiculous, barely positive words for barely negative ones. What was wrong with the real word, anyway? He was positive he liked to do it, and he'd tell miss sexy two shoes so, if she ever showed. Maybe he'd let her fulfill her threat and "pluck" the starch out of him.

If she didn't come, he'd never finish. Too bad. This would make a great home for someone who liked ghosts. Some people went nuts over that kind of thing. He wasn't one of them. Besides, he'd bet Gussie only wailed with a Paxton in residence, not that she'd stopped when he went to Boston that morning. According to his men, she'd wailed louder.

Where was the sexpot? What if she didn't take the job? Maybe if he raised her wages . . . Damn his men for forcing his hand and making him offer the job to her in the first place. And damn him for liking the idea of having her around.

He wondered how cohabitating would have worked out for them. Probably best he didn't know. She'd freak if she ever saw the suite. She might quit on the spot, though she was anything but a quitter. An hour in her company, and he'd learned that lesson.

He'd dreamed about her last night. Hot . . . hot, hot, hot. A sensual, cold-shower-required, damned-near wet dream. Bad . . . bad, bad, bad. You'd think he was thirteen again.

God, he wanted to take her to bed.

If she showed, he'd be *forced* to build a second suite. He couldn't afford to lower his guard and give in to an attraction he suspected—feared, hoped, prayed—could be cataclysmic. Getting mixed up with a woman that seductive could only lead to trouble. Especially one as crazy as this one. Around her, crazy was contagious. Better she should stay in Salem.

King went outside, crossed the old bridge over the sludge moat—soon to be a rose garden—and stopped at the top of the steps to the boat dock. With a hand over his eyes, he gazed toward Salem. Sailboats, yes. Water taxis, no. Where the hell was she?

He walked the perimeter of the castle, every lopsided, stone-set, mismatched wing, and stopped to gaze toward Marblehead. He'd thought he could count on Harmony . . . after one day. Great guns, his fantasies about her ranked right up there with dragons, unicorns, and flying pigs.

Relieved she hadn't taken him up on his offer, he went back inside through the kitchen to tell cook there *wouldn't* be two for dinner. He'd restore the castle without Harmony. His men would get along or get out.

A crash sent him running to the great hall, where he found a free-for-all fistfight. No holds barred. Swearing and cussing, and . . . silence.

The wind stopped wailing. The men stopped fighting, looked surprised, and broke their choke holds. A couple stanched the flow of blood or wiped sweat from their brows. A few bent over, hands on knees, to catch their breaths. Only one thing they had in common. They were all smiling.

A goddess in the great hall.

Harmony Cartwright in the flesh, trailed by guards and gardeners, two-fisted luggage bearers all, putting a mountain of suitcases down around her . . . and going back for more? "How the hell many suitcases did you bring?"

"Enough." Counter to his request, Harmony's tight royal blue V-neck tee said, Here Comes Trouble. She faced his crew, shifted her hips, raised her arms, and said, "Here I am, you lucky boys."

They cheered and applauded, and she took a bow.

King gritted his teeth at her rebellious shirt and late arrival. He shouldn't be happy to see trouble. "It's about time," he said. "Look at this mess. My men have been fighting all morning."

"You think it's easy to find three water taxis at one

time? I wasn't leaving my luggage on the dock for the next taxi, like the first driver suggested." She held up three fingers. "Three, at one time."

"Curt," King said, taking Harmony's arm. "Open the cooler and take a break before going back to work. When the men have rested, have a dozen of them bring Miss Cartwright's bags up to the suite." *All thirty-three plucking mismatched pieces.*

"Planning to stay for the millennium?" he asked her. "Or did you bring empty suitcases to carry your vintage clothes home in?"

"Heck no. I'll get them home later. I brought the essentials—clothes, shoes, toiletries, makeup. There's no Shoppers Heaven next door, you know."

"Hey, boss," Curt said. "What do you want me to do with the cats?"

King turned, wondering if Curt got punched in the head during the brawl. "What cats?"

"My cats," Harmony said.

"You brought cats? Are you out of your mind?"

"They're sweet cats."

"No cats."

"Hey, I came to live with mice, I brought cats. They go, I go."

"How many?"

"Tigerstar and her kittens, Gingertigger, Caramello, and Warlock. They're too young to be away from her. Do we stay or do we go? Think about it. We'll wait outside for your answer." Trouble in blue spikes picked up her cat carrier and let the castle doors slam behind her.

Gussie wailed fit to wake the dead—her blooming peers, damn it!

His men pretended to work as he went to the door and opened it.

Free from their crate, three bouncing baby felines chased butterflies, their tails, and each other, while the brat lounged on the castle steps, filing her nails—white nails crowned by rainbows.

With her head tilted toward the water, her blonde hair curled under her chin and covered her face on his side. Sexy. Man-hardening. He should know. Legs that went on forever, catching some rays, kicking his libido into high gear, overriding the sanest fury he'd ever experienced.

"Cartwright," he said, jerking a thumb over his shoulder.

She stood, as graceful as the queen of . . . the castle . . . and when she and her quartet of felines came back in, those cats held their chins as high as the sexpot did.

"My castle is your castle," King said with visionary dread.

Chapter Fifteen

RAISING the bar on her determination to take the starch out of Paxton, the first thing Harmony did after arriving— as soon as the opportunity presented itself—was find Paxton's briefcase and replace his dull silver paper clips with pink penis paper clips. A small victory, but a start.

Penis paper clips might not unstarch him for good, but he might actually crack a smile.

After that, she spent the afternoon in the west wing's nautical library searching for any mention of her ring, Gussie, or Lisette in Nicodemus Paxton's ship's logs.

Perusing them, she saw that Nicodemus spent years at sea, bringing Gussie gifts from all over the world on the rare occasions he came home. Harmony sensed he'd never completely given Gussie his heart, while his life, he'd given to the sea. Oh, he brought toys home in hopes of a family, but they never had one, which helped explain Gussie's discontent. On the other hand, if he rarely came home, no wonder they didn't have children. Sheesh.

Harmony brought one of the logs upstairs that night as

she followed Gilda the deaf cook up to the suite she'd yet to see.

"The boss said to tell you he's flying to the mainland for supplies," Gilda shouted at the landing. "Won't be back till late."

"Thanks," Harmony replied as loud, wondering why Paxton had kept his distance all day, outside or off-site, which could be her imagination, since she was jumpy about their living arrangements.

Harmony went in first and stopped dead. "All the conveniences?" Her hands on her hips, she surveyed the room. "It doesn't even have walls. It's a blooming dormitory!"

Gilda nodded. "Cots, in case of a storm or a late work night."

Great, Harmony thought. She might get to share with the whole crew. Lucky blooming her.

"Boss man owns the bed, so choose your cot, and I'll make it up."

Harmony took her bedding from Gilda. "*I'll* make up the one farthest away from him."

"I might be seventy, but I'm not dead," Gilda shouted close to Harmony's ear, as if whispering. "I'd take the cot closest to boss man."

"Not me. He called this a suite. I was gonna put the feisty feline four in their carrier for the night so they wouldn't pester him," she yelled, "but to hell with that! They were cooped up all morning waiting for the boats, weren't you, babies?" She cuddled Gingertigger. "As far as I'm concerned, King Kong deserves no such consideration. Have at him, psycho cats."

Gilda shook her head. "You're really gonna stay?"

Harmony realized this was an unorthodox situation, but besides fulfilling her psychic mandate, she was too curious about Gussie to quit, plus she had some added monetary, and hunky, incentives. "Of course I am. You're only a bell pull away, you said. You do hear the bell, right?"

Gilda chuckled. "I hear it."

"Fine. I'm staying, and I'm gonna give boss man what he deserves."

Harmony intended to explore the mutual attraction she and Paxton were cooking up—over an open flame, they were cooking—but Gilda didn't need to know that. She thanked Gilda and made up a cot as far away from Paxton as she could get . . . temporarily. This is where she was meant to be. She touched her ring and thought about sharing the room with the hunk. She liked the idea of two against Gussie. Plus there was the psycho-cat entertainment factor.

She needed to protect the room from Gussie first, so she swept it from east to west, a ritual sweeping away of evil. She sprinkled salt, sage, angelica, and lavender around the room's perimeters and lit corner candles for protection, peace, harmony, and blessings. Opening the window, she waved her wand and began her chant:

> *"On this beautiful night in June,*
> *By the power and light of the moon,*
> *This room I protect and bless*
> *From those with harm to address.*
>
> *No evil through this door to seep*
> *Into bodies, hearts, minds, in sleep.*
>
> *Guard night and day*
> *Negativity, keep at bay*
> *And none shall it harm*
> *Hear my will, bide this charm.*
>
> *So mote it be.*
> *So mote it be."*

Harmony sighed, feeling good about being here.

The remodeled bathroom did have all the conveniences,

she discovered a short while later. She changed into a pair of boxers with Storm's ratty old Plays Well with Others tee, but she left some long johns by her cot in case of a ghostly, ice-age wake-up call.

By the time she settled in, Tigerstar and her hyperactive kittens had installed themselves on the royal blue satin bedspread of Paxton's manly antique four-poster. Harmony fell asleep smiling.

She heard him come into the room, and she pretended to be asleep as he went to and from the bathroom, preparing for bed.

He swore, and something shattered. Harmony peeked and saw Tigerstar riding his shoulders. That cat could leap, and she'd scared the dickens out of him. Harmony bit her lip against a laugh.

Paxton picked up the broken pieces of . . . an alarm clock, maybe, while Tigerstar used him as a climbing wall when he sat on the bed. Up down. Back and around. A paw in the face. A drawstring chase. Across his lap. A claw to the groin. A pain in the loins.

"Son of a bitch!" King shot to his feet.

Harmony buried her face in her pillow so she wouldn't giggle. That man was not going to get any sleep tonight.

He went to the bed, whispered to the kittens, and petted them, the sneak. He *liked* cats. "You're frisky little things, if you're anything like your mama—your cat mama," he said, "not the pretty lady who brought you here to screw with me, so let's fool her and be friends."

The double-crosser.

Harmony rolled over to face away from him as Paxton came her way. She did not want him to know she was awake.

"Let's go, Trouble with a capital *T*," he said as he scooped her up and carried her to his bed.

Huh?

Did he think she was gonna sleep with him?

Chapter Sixteen

HARMONY rode the roller coaster of Paxton's bare arms while he turned down the blankets on his bed and set her down beside Tigerstar and her kittens. Was he toying with her? She could go for some mutual toying with . . .

Testing the sexual waters, she rolled over, as if in her sleep, trapped him, caught him around the neck, and brought his face to hers.

She might have initiated the kiss, but he took over with gusto. Heat purled through her in rolling waves, bringing her to life and making her hungry for a whole lot more. Withering witch balls, but the man could kiss.

She moaned, and so did he, then he sat beside her to cradle her in his arms and bring the kiss to another level, raising her up, readying her for anything. When he stopped, out of the blue, she whimpered.

"Yeah," he said. "I know exactly how you feel."

He walked away, and she got a quick profile of a mighty fine boner. He sat on the cot she'd vacated, scrubbed his face with both hands, turned out the light, removed his sweats, and lay down, his hands behind his head.

The scent of him filled his bed. Bailey's Irish Cream, spicy aftershave, and a hint of cinnamon coffee. She inhaled and got hot. She turned her face into his pillow and nearly came. He'd slept there last night . . . and dreamed of her.

She turned to watch him in moonlight. His sexual energy was high, his fantasies clear. He wanted to read her by Braille again, without her shirt. Ooh! He wanted her breast in his mouth. He turned her way. He'd like to see her move, see her cute little ass in the air.

Harmony turned on her stomach and raised her knees a bit.

Paxton raised himself on an elbow, as if he couldn't believe she'd acted out his fantasy. Great, now he was gonna test his power of suggestion.

She tried to block his thoughts, but she was too blooming curious and terribly turned on. Great. Sure, she'd brought her dolphin vibrators, but what good would they do her with him in the same room?

He imagined her getting out of bed and "strutting" to his cot, removing her clothes, piece by slow piece. She stripped him naked and took his man brain into her mouth, then she climbed on and rode him like a blooming bucking bronco while he lay there and let *her* do all the work!

"Geez!" she said, sitting up. "I'm a witch, not a call girl."

He jumped and shouted at the same time, which pretty much woke her to her big-mouthed stupidity.

"What?" He threw off his covers and charged her bed, his boner a sight in moonlight. "What did you say?"

"Put some clothes on," she snapped.

He growled. "Forget the clothes."

"The theme for the night," she mumbled as she pulled the covers to her chin. "Did I tell you that I talk in my sleep? It's insane, the things I say."

"Did you say you're a call girl or a witch?"

"If we weren't sleeping in a blooming dormitory, you wouldn't have heard—"

"Harmony." His low-toned warning meant she was treading water in that swamp of eternal stink again. Besides, he rarely, if ever, used her name.

And what could she use for a defense? Tell him not to *fantasize*? *That* would get her out of trouble. Not.

Fortunately, the cats came to her rescue as if they sensed her need. Gingertigger stretched out on her head like a hat. Caramello sprawled across her chest, and Warlock curled up at the apex of her legs, which she was forced to spread. Figures, the only male cat in the bunch, and he liked her crotch.

But Paxton liked cats, so she felt reasonably safe answering. "Well," she said. "I'm *not* a call girl."

"Why would you say such a thing?" he asked.

"Because I'm not."

"Not that. You practically—"

"What?" she asked. "I practically what? I said I talk in my sleep." And she sure hoped she'd remember to do it again, so he'd believe her.

"Are you a witch?"

"Withering witch balls, do you have to ask straight-out?"

"Do you have to use *withering* and *balls* in the same sentence? The combo makes me nervous as a . . . cat. And of course I have to ask straight-out. What other way is there to ask?"

"You could beat around the bush a little?"

"Give you some wiggle room, you mean?"

Damn. He knew her pretty well. "Something like that. Because, sometimes it's . . . You know, Paxton, you're practically naked. Great pecs, by the way."

"Only the pecs are great?"

"Well, no actually, I'm seriously impressed by your dic—"

"Wait a minute," he said. "No changing the subject. You're not overdressed either, by the way. Plays Well with Others, my ass. Now, if the shirt said Great Rac—never mind. There's no such thing as a witch."

"Like there's no such thing as a ghost? Your left butt cheek says different. How can you come from Salem and not believe? Did you never step into that city? It's full of witches who think they're . . . witches."

"Are you?"

"Absolutely certain that witches exist. Yes."

"Do you think you're one of them?"

She sighed heavily. "There are some things I can't deny, and that's one of them. I'm a witch."

"Why didn't you tell me? That's a helluva thing to keep from an employer."

"You're not my employer. I'm an outside contractor, remember? So, in what religion were you raised?"

"A Methodist. What difference does that make?"

"Did you introduce yourself to me by saying, 'Hi, I'm King Paxton, and I'm a Methodist'?"

"Of course not."

"Well, I don't say, 'Hi, I'm Harmony Cartwright, and I'm a witch.'"

"It's not the same thing."

"It most certainly is. Are you always this negative, or is it only when you're here at the castle?"

"What the hell are you talking about?"

"I figured since Gussie spreads negative like frosting, you'd been iced."

"Yet you're a regular Pollyanna. Are you immune because you're the same?"

Harmony laughed. "Hello! Gussie and I are polar opposites. My *gift* is peace and her *curse* is strife. There are different kinds of witches, like there are different kinds of Methodists. Some break the law, some don't. Some do good, some do evil. I'm a white witch. I believe that anything I do, good or bad, comes back to me times three, so I try to do good. I live and let live, give and take fairly, and harm none."

"I take it Gussie's not a white witch?"

"I don't blooming think so."

"Are you a hocus-pocus witch, with spells and stuff?"

"I can make your penis grow."

Chapter Seventeen

HARMONY figured Paxton needed to know about her witchcraft, but he wasn't ready, yet, to hear that she was psychic. Her efforts to loosen him up had worked to a point, but this *would* set him back a bit. She sighed. "I'm a hereditary Pictish witch. My family's roots are in the Druidic and Celtic traditions. My ancestors come from Scotland. Pictish means *picture* or *tattoo*. The Picts are a tattooed people."

"Are you?"

"I just said I was."

"Are you tattooed?" he clarified.

"Uh, yeah. Are you?"

"Sure. Where's yours?"

"Oh no you don't," she said. "Twenty-four hours after meeting is a bit soon for the 'you show me yours, and I'll show you mine' routine. We've already toppled the lust-at-first-sight boundary. I'm not ready for any more boundary-testing at the moment."

"Tomorrow, then?" He frowned. "It's hard to focus seriously on someone wearing live fur accessories. Your cats are distracting."

"Your penis is distracting."

He sat on the cot near the bed. "*Are* you?"

"Distracted? Yes."

"Hold that thought. Are you going to show me your tattoo tomorrow?"

"Tattoos, plural, but that's only a few hours away, and I'm tired." She snuggled lower into his cushy bed and turned on her side to face him, while her purring accessories readjusted themselves. She closed her eyes. "Night."

"You saw my ass after half a day," he grumbled.

"Dumb luck."

Paxton strolled like a lazy panther back to his cot. "You never answered my question."

"I did, too."

"You missed one. Are you a *hocus-pocus* witch?"

"Look, I'm a little tired. Tomorrow I'll turn you into a toad, okay?"

"Now why would you want to go and do that?"

She sat up. "Oh, I don't know. In appreciation for this gorgeous *suite*, maybe? Funny when I asked you for details, I never doubted it had *walls*! You have protective walls all around you, but you have none around your bed. What does that say about you?"

"Walls. Right." Paxton yawned. "Night."

"Warthog," she accused, settling in and closing her eyes, though she found it difficult to sleep in a strange bed with a vital, virile man across the room. And his scent so infused the bedding that some of his sensual fantasies were creeping into her mind without any need to read his thoughts. Maybe she should try counting . . . warthogs.

"Argh! Ouch! Attack cat!"

Harmony opened one eye. Tigerstar stood on Paxton's

chest staring down at him, her claws likely pricking his flesh a bit.

"Harmony?" Paxton called softly. "Harmony?" he whispered.

Every time he spoke, she knew Tigerstar dug in her claws. "You should be proud," Harmony finally said. "She likes you. She hasn't been that friendly since she fell in love with my Scottish brother-in-law. That cat's got a real thing for good-looking men. I wish I had a camera. You'd make a great scene for a cartoon strip."

"Help," he whispered.

"All right. Walls or not, if you let yourself relax, Star will pull in her claws."

"Does that go for you, too? Ouch!"

Paxton lowered his head to his pillow and took a visible breath. In out, in out, he breathed. Harmony saw him relaxing. Inevitably, he sighed in relief. "It worked. I guess you know your pet."

"She's not mine. She's my sister Vickie's, and she won't hurt you. You're safe, though I can't say the same for the castle's mouse population."

"She's not moving," Paxton said, "and her eyes glitter in the dark, and they're two different colors. She's weirding me out over here. Is she going to watch me from up there all night?"

"Nah, she'll have to nurse my hat and muff soon."

As if Tigerstar heard, she jumped off Paxton.

He sighed with audible relief. "Witches use cats for spells right? Can Tigerstar turn me into a toad, or worse, a mouse, when she gives me that glitter stare of hers? Or am I mixing up my fairy tales?"

"Witchcraft is not a fairy tale."

"Right. Sorry."

One by one, Tigerstar picked up her kittens and jumped off her bed to go and deposit them on Paxton's chest.

"Uh, does she think she's gonna nurse them on my . . . yep, she does."

Harmony tried really, really hard not to laugh. "You must be very comfortable, and Star must love you deeply."

"I . . . think I'm gonna build the five of you a separate room."

"Yesterday, I would have considered that a good idea." Harmony raised her head to rest it on her hand. "But now I think this is cozy. Besides, we're two against 'you know who,' like you said."

"We can't say her name?"

"The existing walls have ears," Harmony replied. "Nuff said."

Paxton groaned, which was the last thing Harmony remembered, until fifteen minutes later, or so it seemed, when the sound of multiple motorboats woke her. Then she heard the joking construction crew approaching the castle. "What time is it?" she asked.

"Grr, growl, grumble," Paxton said, already sitting on the edge of his cot scrubbing his hands over his whiskers, looking morning-snuggle soft and sleep-mussed kissable.

"Ah, a morning person," she said. "You look like hell."

"Gee thanks." He did a double take. "You look good enough to—"

"Thanks!" She got up and ran for the bathroom, turning to him in the doorway and raising both arms. "Ta da! I'm first!"

Gingertigger took a flying leap from the floor to his chest and knocked him back on his cot. "You know what I hate more than anything?" he said, staring up at the ceiling. "Wise-ass brats and flying cats in the morning." Gingertigger licked his nose.

Harmony closed the bathroom door on a chuckle.

"Living with you and your kamikaze cats is like being married without the perks," he grumbled as he passed the bathroom door. "I have a meeting today," he yelled, then she heard him walking down the hall. Good, the place must have another bathroom somewhere. Served him right for telling her the dorm was a suite.

After she showered, put on her makeup, and dressed, she saw that he'd made up his cot with military precision. She'd almost forgotten about the obsessive picture-straightening flaw in his personality.

Just to drive him nuts, she unmade his cot, corner by corner, and placed the kittens in the curl of his blankets. She petted Tigerstar as the cat jumped up to join her family. "Show your kids how to be mousers today," she said, scratching behind Star's ear. "If you can't find any mice, there'll be kitty munchies in the kitchen. Litter's that way." She pointed. "Aunt Harmony has to go to work now." She kissed each kitten on the head, turned to leave, and came face-to-face with Paxton.

"They're cats, not people," he said. "You think they understood your instructions? *Aunt* Harmony?"

"Three of them belong to my sisters. Caramello, the caramel and marshmallow swirl, is Destiny's. Warlock, the pure black, belongs to Storm. And Gingertigger, the orange and black striped, is mine." Harmony wondered if Paxton had looked this good last night, and if so, why hadn't she shown him her tattoos? That kiss had been sexy as all hell.

They remembered at the same time, every taste and texture. Harmony stepped away from his heat, but Paxton had no such intention. What had they done, switched places?

He examined her shirt and her nips got hard. "How May I Ignore You?" he read, his laugh lines deepening. The man didn't even need to smile to turn her on. His breath warmed her as he nuzzled her ear and whispered, "Let's see if you *can* ignore me."

"What is this, freaky Tuesday?" she asked as his embrace made her feel safe and cherished. His hand at her back pulled her into a sphere of protection, his bare chest upping the intimacy factor.

His parted lips came slowly for hers, heightening her anticipation.

No swooping in to steal a kiss. This morning, Paxton savored. The touch of his lips barely there, like fluttering butterfly wings, he prodded her upper lip to separate it from her lower, then he teased her lower with his upper, the two of them sharing breaths. This was taking kissing to a new level, raising the bar on her expectations, and her appreciation and desire, to the point that . . . she could really learn to care for this guy.

After kissing him and reading his fantasies last night, she'd had some pretty erotic dreams—of him in that bed alone, hot . . . of the two of them there together, hotter—and yet her dreams were nothing compared to being in his arms at this moment.

Losing all sense of self, Harmony fell into the kiss with ease, knuckling his rugged back with one hand while sliding the other up his centerfold chest. Sifting through his chest hair, she found a nipple and took to curling the hair around it until it pebbled like her own, while her favorite steel rod got harder, too, as it prodded her ready center.

She got greedy with the kiss. She couldn't wait a second more, and Paxton groaned and became as ravenous, their tongues mating, the two of them arching to get closer.

Harmony moved her hips to abrade his erection, taking a good deal of satisfaction in their complementing rhythm, but she wanted more, which he surely had to give, because Paxton was hard and thick with plenty of giving power.

He lifted her off her feet, laid her on the bed, and slid over her, taking up where she left off, his purpose clear, to graze her aching center with the treasure in his unsnapped jeans.

Harmony wanted to release, fondle, and torture the

standing soldier. She wanted it inside her, until they both came their brains out.

Someone coughed. King stilled.

Harmony looked toward the door.

"Well," said a scraggly stud muffin voyeur. "I didn't know the place had gone coed, or I would have come up sooner."

Harmony expected Paxton to come out of his sexual haze, but he returned to nibbling her mouth. "Go away, Aiden," he said between nibbles.

"Yeah." Harmony licked her parted lips. "Bye, Aiden." She pulled Paxton's head back down for another kiss, so he had no choice but to cooperate.

The intruder chuckled, and Storm's kitten followed him out the door.

"I—" King slipped a hand beneath her shirt to place it flat on her midriff. "have—" He kissed the corners of her mouth, "a—"

"Breast in your hand." Harmony placed his palm over an aching breast, arching so he'd do something amazing with it, which he did, then he lifted her shirt, unhooked her bra . . . and saw her tattoo. He fingered the pale aqua triquetra, symbol of three, in a heart, low on her right breast near her cleavage.

"It's a Celtic design. Pretty, isn't it?"

As if captivated by it, Paxton brought his mouth close, closer, and he kissed it. When he was finished adoring her tattoo with his lips, he breathed on her nip, warmed it, and let it cool. "I'm gonna be late for my own meet—" He reared back. "Hey, witch. Am I under a spell?"

Disgust turned Harmony to ice. "The Denialator strikes again!" She shoved him away with so much force, he fell back and hit his head on the footboard.

"Good!" She pulled down her shirt and jumped from the bed. "Meeting," she said. "Downstairs. Now!"

She went in the bathroom and slammed the door.

Chapter Eighteen

KING went downstairs, determined to get his meeting over with so he could get the castle finished and the witch—the sexy one invading his home, bed, and dreams—out and away from his short-circuiting libido as quickly as possible. Was it only yesterday that he'd climbed the walls, impatient for her arrival? He was a sick son of a bitch.

He found his antiques restorer and architect in the wide balcony area overlooking construction in the great hall.

"Good morning, you lucky dcvil, you," Aiden said, petting the black cat nuzzling his neck.

"Be careful," King said. "Insanity runs in that cat's family."

"Look at you." Aiden shook his head. "The reliable, uncreased, ultraperfect King Paxton—all creased and wearing what? Yesterday's clothes? And late for your own meeting." Aiden slapped him on the back. "I'm proud of you, old boy."

King stepped from his friend's mocking congratulations. "I don't need your patronizing jokes right now."

"Hey, who better to help shove a stopper in your search for perfection than one of your oldest friends who happens to be one of the most imperfect men on God's green earth?"

King turned his back on Aiden to greet his more serious friend. "Morgan, good to see you. I'm sure Aiden filled you in on the torrid scene he walked in on upstairs, though he should have been filling you in on the restoration project, which is why we're here. Did you bring the plans for the altered design?"

Morgan tapped the unrolled architectural drawings on the table.

The devil cat jumped from Aiden's arms to the plans as the seductive witch strolled in and removed it to join its siblings on the floor. "Paxton," she said, her screwball cats hopping around her gorgeous legs like popcorn. "Introduce me to your friends."

"This is a business meeting," King said, eyeing the tight pink bare-midriff tee that proclaimed, I've Upped My Standards. Up Yours.

King fisted his hands, less at the insult than at her shorter-than-short black skirt, with those spikes, whose cross-straps tied halfway up her endless legs.

"Did you two have a lovers' quarrel?" Aiden asked, rocking on his heels, eyeing them, and catching a cat mid-catapult.

His friend's comment cut too close to the surface for King's peace, yet not close enough.

"The lady's shirt tells me somebody didn't finish what *he* started." Aiden shook his head in a pitying way. "King, old boy, couldn't you have loosened up for once and *forgotten* about work?"

King wanted to clock him.

"Hi, I'm Harmony Cartwright." The hellcat cut Aiden's sarcasm by shaking his hand. "I can't believe Warlock likes you. He's very picky about his people."

Aiden picked up the cat to look it in the eye. "Hello there, Warlock. Nice to make your acquaintance. Are you and your mistress new residents of the asylum?"

"Ramrod, here, hired me." Harmony elbowed him, and King wanted to elbow her right back. "I'm the witch whisperer in residence," she added.

"Ramrod," Aiden said with a bark of laughter. "Good call."

"Hello," Morgan said, shaking her hand. "You can't be a witch whisperer, because witches don't exist, except in people's minds."

"And yet, Paxton's unreal resident witch shut the hell up when I walked in, or haven't you noticed? Ramrod here is keeping me around for the duration. And you are . . . his fraternal twin?"

Morgan stiffened. "I'm sorry. I'm Morgan Jarvis."

"I'm sorry you're Morgan Jarvis, too."

Morgan recovered quickly. "I'm the architect on this job and a paranormal debunker in my spare time."

"Withering witch balls!" The hellcat said. "Then we should get along *just* fine." Harmony and Aiden laughed, and King wanted to take a header off the balcony. He needed a shower and a good night's sleep, but first, he needed to slake his lust with the witch, if lust this powerful could be slaked.

"I sense that you're not just business associates," Harmony told Aiden. "You're too free with the insults, plus you invaded his . . . *suite*."

"Actually," Aiden said. "King and I went to military school together."

"No way. Did you get thrown out together, too?"

"Ah, no. King did that by himself. I actually graduated."

King frowned. "By the skin of his teeth."

"Hmm. If King got thrown out and you finished, how come he's the straitlaced tight ass, and you're the scraggly stud muffin? I'd think you'd be the opposite."

"Oh, I like this one," Aiden said, hugging her and not letting go, the bastard. "She's a keeper."

Harmony raised a brow his way, which made King want to pull her from Aiden's clutches.

"Morgan, do you and Paxton hail back to college, or something? You're old friends, too, right?"

"And she's perceptive as well." Aiden slid his hand from her shoulder to her waist, and if it landed on her ass, King was going to—

"Since senior year of high school," Morgan said. "But I'm curious about your perception, Miss Cartwright. You classified my friends as tight ass and stud muffin, but you didn't classify me?"

"You defy classification, Mr. Jarvis. What *are* you hiding?"

Aiden got out of firing range to play with the catapulting kitten squad.

"I assure you, Miss Cartwright, that I—"

"Oh I believe you have a degree in architecture, and some kind of paranormal gripe, but there's more to you than you're willing to admit."

Morgan adjusted his cuffs. "No classification for me, I guess. I'm disappointed."

"No, you're not, but if it's any consolation, the rest of the world doesn't think what you're hiding is as bad as you do."

Caramello flew into Morgan's arms as if to prove Harmony right. "What is this?" Morgan asked. "Adopt-a-cat day?"

"You've got me," Harmony said. "They're not people cats, but they're all over the three of you."

"Fine with me," Morgan said, petting Caramello.

"I do have a description for you, after all," Harmony said. "Morgan the mystic."

He frowned. "I can't be a mystic. I'm a debunker."

Harmony nodded. "You're right. I was going for alliteration, but let me clarify. I should have said Morgan the spiritualist."

Aiden's head came up, but King thought their serious friend held his own, considering.

Morgan shrugged. "However confused you are, Miss Cartwright, I do feel at peace with your try."

"Harmony has that effect on people . . . and ghosts," King said.

"And a keen sense of their flaws, I think." Aiden ate her up with his look, damn him.

"By the way, Harmony, we always called him Morgan the Miserable," Aiden said.

"Works for me. Hey, I don't suppose you two would consider trying to talk Ramrod, here, into keeping the castle?"

Morgan tapped the designs on the table. "Too late. He's already accepted an offer, and the clock is ticking for him to finish, or he'll lose it. That's why we're here."

"Watch out, King!" Harmony shouted, throwing herself at him so they both flew and landed on his sore butt, as a ceiling beam swung in and broke through the wall where he'd been standing.

"Son of a sea witch!"

Aiden and Morgan caught the beam to steady it and keep it from swinging back like a pendulum.

Harmony got up and leaned over the railing. "Everybody okay down there?"

"Yeah," Curt said. "The winch snapped. Everybody okay up there?"

"We're fine," she said.

King rose and tried to ignore his throbbing butt.

"I don't know why," Morgan said. "But all the accidents in this place happen around you, King."

"They do?" Harmony asked. "That's odd . . . or not."

Aiden touched her arm. "Why *isn't* it odd?"

"You won't want to hear this, but my theory is that Gussie—Ramrod's witch ancestor who's haunting the place—doesn't want the castle to leave the family."

That shut his friends up. King gave her a look that he hoped shouted, "Out!" and she got the message. "It was nice meeting you both," she said. "I'll leave you to your meeting." She tried to swipe his briefcase, but King caught her arm, stopped her in her tracks, and crooked his hand for her to give it back. "I need that."

"Oh, sure," she said, handing it over. "Well, I'm glad Aiden and Morgan both have a good sense of humor. You should consider growing one in the next two minutes." She turned to his friends. "You need to know that Ramrod challenged me to try to take the starch out of him. Bye." She waved. "I'm off to keep the imaginary ghost quiet."

"Harmony," Aiden called after her. "Care to have dinner with me sometime?"

King watched the hussy's gaze flit from his former friend to him and back. "I'd love to," she said. "Thank you, Aiden." And with that, she disappeared.

King figured his heart rate had risen because of his near accident, not because Harmony agreed to date Aiden.

"Damn," King said, "I forgot to thank her for saving my life." He looked at Aiden. "No matter. I'll thank her tonight . . . in bed."

Chapter Nineteen

HARMONY intended to pay Paxton back for leaving her hot, wet, and aching this morning. *He* might think the great paper clip switch was enough—though she'd yet to hear his thoughts on that—but he had no idea what he was in for.

She'd hung around on the balcony landing long enough this morning to hear his friends' laughter when Paxton found the paper clips. Who knew he wouldn't be alone when he did?

At any rate, Paxton had thrown the paper clips away, but Aiden gave him hell and rescued them to keep as a memento. That must have gone over big with Paxton. He'd been jealous from the minute Aiden put his arm around her. She'd enjoyed that. Problem was, she hadn't seen Paxton all day, and she didn't really know how he felt about her attempt to unstarch him. Had he been stewing? she wondered as she moved his bedding to the cot beside hers.

Maybe he'd forgive her when he saw where he was sleeping.

Fifteen minutes later, he came upstairs as if nothing was wrong and sat beside her on the bed. "Thank you for saving me from the swinging beam this morning. I might have been seriously hurt. I'm sorry I didn't thank you right away. I think I was in shock."

And green with envy, she thought. "You're welcome. I'm here to keep Gussie in line, after all. I told you I'd protect you."

He petted Gingertigger. "Don't start that again."

"Start what?"

"Cut the innocent act," he said. "Innocent fits you like lace on a porcupine. Look, I have another meeting here tomorrow morning . . . with my bankers . . . and as much as Aiden and Morgan enjoyed your leggy attention and penis paper clips, *don't* introduce yourself to my bankers. And please, Harmony, no penis erasers, pencils, or anything that only you could imagine planting, and no shirt—"

"You want me to go topless for the bankers? Sure. You think it'll help?"

Paxton took Gingertigger off his shoulder. "No shirt with a suggestive message on it. Great guns, do you joke about everything?"

"Laughing at life's realities makes them bearable. You should try it sometime. You, McBullseye, have to learn to be spontaneous."

"After I meet with my bankers, okay? Did you bring anything to wear that doesn't have a message on it? A dress maybe?"

"Of course I did."

"Wear it, damn it."

"Are you sure?"

"Sure? I insist. You'll get a bonus if you wear your dress tomorrow morning."

"Can't argue with that. Why don't you meet with your bankers in the formal parlor? It really shows off what the castle has to offer."

Paxton scrunched his nose like something smelled bad. "It's old and dusty."

"It's safer than the gallery, where deadly beams are being raised."

"Good point. I'll meet with them in the dining room."

"Ooh, I haven't seen the dining room yet."

"You will *not* see it tomorrow morning. Got it?"

"Then why do I have to wear a dress?"

"In case."

Paxton stood and crossed his arms to grab his shirt at the waist, but Gingertigger returned to his shoulder a nanosecond before he pulled it up. With a howl, her captive cat rolled over Paxton's head and down his face.

"Ouch! Son of a—" Paxton caught the fighting shirt ball in one arm and touched his cheek with a finger. "Blood. Great. A scratched face should impress the bankers. Do all witches have kamikaze cats?" Paxton asked. "Or did you put a spell on yours just for me?"

Gingertigger popped from the neck of his shirt and took a flying leap into her arms. Harmony cuddled her shivering kitten with its paws around her neck. "Poor baby. You're trembling. Did the nasty man scare you?"

Paxton rolled his eyes, balled his shirt, and tossed it toward the empty cot at the far end of the room. That's when he noticed for the first time that the cot on the other side of her bed was made. "Did Gilda do that?"

Harmony continued to nuzzle her kitten. "I did it."

"You want me to sleep there?"

She glanced up at him. "I'm scared?"

Paxton shook his head. "Not buying it. It's a new form of torture, like penis paper clips," he said, shaking his head. "Why? Why in front of my friends?"

"Better than in front of the bankers, right?"

"Right." He went toward the bathroom.

"Take a shower," she yelled as he shut the door.

He popped his head out. "Come again?"

"If you play your cards right."

"A trap," he said, shutting the door. Behind it, his voice sounded like a mumbled hodgepodge of gripes and grumbling, but the shower did go on.

Harmony changed into her mermaid pajamas—sports bra and capri bottoms—and grabbed her overnight bag of obsession party goodies.

Paxton came out, jeans unzipped, toweling his thick, black, wavy hair, and caught her sorting through her free-the-uptight-stud candy.

"What the hell?" He picked up a pack of Dicklit gum, shook his head, and tossed it back in the box. "I'm about to be sacrificed on the altar of spontaneity, aren't I?"

"You said I could give it my best shot."

"I said you could try to take the starch out of me. I didn't know I was signing my own insanity warrant. Who knew you'd resort to torture tactics?" He was fishing around in her overnight bag before she could stop him, and he came up with one of her dolphins. "Whoa."

"Give me that."

He held it away from her and grabbed the straps of her bag with his other hand.

"Paxton!"

He dumped the bag on the bed. "What do we have here?"

Harmony held her cat in front of her face, and Paxton chuckled. But because she wanted to see him laugh, she lowered Gingertigger to her lap.

"This beats Gussie's collection of dolphins hands down." Paxton wiggled his brows. "Battery powered, right? You have hidden depths, Cartwright. Give me the scoop. What have we got here? And don't say vibrators. I got that by myself."

Thinking about it, Harmony figured this turn of events might help with her payback for his badly timed desertion this morning. She sighed. "Okay, this one's a crystal tickler.

Pretty basic. Best when I'm already halfway there. I call him Chuck." She turned it on to tease Paxton.

He pulled away from its spell. "Chuck?"

"Sure, Chuck likes to—"

"Got it!"

"Good. This one's a ten-speed waterproof. Talk about bath-time fun. I usually light scented candles, put on soft music, turn on the jets, relax and . . . you know . . . take my time while I take Ryder out for a . . . ride."

Paxton was getting harder by the minute, while she was enjoying the hell out of herself.

"Now the tall guy here, he's Lance, the big guns." She turned Lance on and watched Paxton's pupils dilate. "Lance has a textured tip, for a *deep*, soothing massage. He's also got five rows of pearls, see? For the G-spot. And multiple speeds, for multiple . . . everything, and as if all that magick isn't enough, this little dolphin up front, Lance Junior, he does a happy dance in a very happy place."

Harmony leaned against her pillows as if she'd just enjoyed all three, bent a knee, and selected a large chocolate penis from her goodie box. She held it up, examined it from every angle, licked it slowly up one side and down the other . . . and she bit off its head.

Paxton shouted and clenched his thighs. "Son of a . . . witch . . . bitch, I meant bitch—I can't even watch you chew." He went to hide out at his dresser and use his hairbrush, but he kept peeking in the mirror to see if she'd finished. "You're like a . . . a sexual cannibal."

Harmony laughed. "This is what *spontaneous* is all about. Come to think of it, you were spontaneous when you stole my goodie bag. Aren't you glad you did? Wasn't that fun?"

King mumbled something beneath his breath about his self-destructive behavior.

When he turned back to her, she flaunted a peckermint blow pop, which she licked with great attention to detail, sucking on the head and enjoying it immensely. She took it deep into her mouth and pulled it out slowly, and while she did, Paxton grew taut and separated his zipper bit by bit.

Like a deer in headlights, he stood watching her, mesmerized, while she made a blatant and luscious meal of her treat.

Her ploy was backfiring, though. She got hotter as he got harder. Not screwing him screwed her, and not in a good way. She put the blow pop down, opened a bag of mini gummy penises, and bit a few in half to cool down. When she finished, she crumpled the package and threw it across the room. Then she stood, threw back her covers, climbed into her bed, and turned off the lamp.

Paxton had not moved.

"Night," she said, rolling to her side.

It took a full minute, maybe two, before he walked over to his cot, slipped out of his jeans, and lay down . . . naked . . . on top of the covers . . . his man brain pointing heavenward . . . as if pleading for release.

She wished she'd kept her eyes shut, except that she wouldn't have missed the sight of him like that for the world. Heat, admiration, and something more—caring and concern for this particular man—washed over her. She'd never seen anything or anyone as beautiful in her life. She could adore his body for hours. She could eat *him* with a spoon. She wouldn't even need chocolate sauce. Ramrod McHunk looked gourmet yummy au natural.

Withering witch balls, she couldn't be falling for the cranky, bossy, brass-assed, loose-limbed panther. Could she?

Harmony flipped to her back, kicked off the covers, and listened to the waves crashing on the shore, while a salty breeze wafted in through the open window to cool her fevered skin, but not enough.

Only Paxton could cool her enough to satisfy her.

He moved, and she nearly came, she'd been so focused on the fantasy.

He rolled to his side, but she didn't know which, because she refused to look and come face-to-face with him.

When he placed a gentle palm on her belly, above her pajamas, her stomach jumped as if she'd never been touched by a man before, though to be fair, no one like him had ever come her way.

She felt the heat of his fingers hot against her skin, branding her, his hand huge, his thumb at her navel, his little finger pressing a bit closer to the center of her need. Dear Goddess, she was ready to come with his palm on her belly. She didn't say a word, couldn't speak. Didn't know what to say, anyway.

He kept his hand there . . . forever. She wondered if he could sense her rising need, like heat lightning zephering through her body.

He was driving her crazy. She didn't want him to take his hand away, but she *did* want him to move it . . . an inch or six south.

He palmed her northward, instead, up to her waist in long, slow strokes, causing static surges of electricity with the tips of his fingers. He went as far as the crest of her breasts, and with every new slide of his palm, he'd stop and . . . drive her crazy!

At her breasts, he splayed his fingers so far apart, he managed not to graze her nipples, though they arched and hardened for his touch.

He must know; her heartbeat must be giving her away.

Paxton sighed as he caressed her neck, cupped her face, and combed his fingers through the hair behind her ear. He fingered her earlobe and touched her lips.

She parted them so he could trace each separately. She licked every finger that came her way, which made him pause for a beat each time, as if each tongue touch was a new surprise.

He made his way to her breasts again, this time finding and gently rolling a budding nipple between his fingers, too gently. A tease of the first order. Any more gently, and she'd come. She moaned and felt the tension in his fingertips. He was feeling the same.

She should have worn a cami and bikini set so he could slip his hand beneath, but no. She thought she was gonna be smart and toy with him. Hah!

His palm glided softly across her belly now, slow, slower, approaching her center, so wet with wanting he'd know, just touching her over her capris.

When he finally touched that spot, he stopped and toyed with her, stroked her with just the one finger, a flutter against her nether lips, barely. She was too constrained by her blooming spandex capris to open to him. More than anything, she craved the silk of Paxton's flesh against hers.

She'd never been more frustrated or more aroused in her life. She was gonna die of a slow burn.

With barely a touch, he was taking her higher than she thought she could go without a climax. A slow rise like none she'd known. A tease to the death, and just when her climax seemed imminent, when no word had been spoken between them, she turned his way, looked into his eyes, frank and hungry, and saw that he held his cock in his other hand.

Watching him come made her climax. Never had she been so turned on, brought so high, or reached such satisfaction . . . without touching her partner.

Harmony lay spent, Paxton cupping her throbbing center, laying claim to her orgasm in the same way he laid claim to his own.

Embarrassed, titillated, their gazes met and mated, made promises, went drowsy, said good night.

Sated, exhausted, Harmony closed her eyes.

"After I rest a minute," Paxton promised. "I'm gonna do that with my tongue."

Chapter Twenty

KING woke around midnight with a raging boner and a hand between Harmony's legs. He removed it, and she whimpered, but she stopped when he began working his hand beneath the waistband of her bottoms, and when he reached her, she purred, spread her legs, and doubled the size of his cock.

Last night he'd set out to make her pant after him like a mare in heat. And now they were both hooked. He grazed the very edges of her nether lips with a finger, and he felt her welcoming heat, slick and ready, open and willing. He found her swollen nubbin, flicked it, and she gasped, then he all-out invaded her. One finger, two; slow at first, then faster, in and out, his thumb working her clit, her moans making him ready to come as she climaxed—in her sleep, the brat—without waking to give as good as she got.

He wanted to make her come again, until she woke and understood what he was doing, until she jumped his bones and put him out of his misery.

She was a ready one, and he was a randy one, getting thicker and harder in the palm of his own hand.

He worked her and raised her again, until her wailing climax woke her to her surroundings, to his busy hand, and she sat up, pulled off her top, slicked off her bottoms, and spread her legs for him, and he mastered the queen of the multiple orgasm.

She might set a new record. He lost count. His hand began to cramp, but he didn't complain, didn't give up, and kept her coming. When her legs collapsed and he thought she would fall asleep, she pushed at his chest so he fell back, and she rolled on her belly. Still in her own bed, she reached for him and palmed her way down his chest, torturing him the same way he'd tortured her.

King tried to relax and let her take her sweet, sultry time, as he'd taken his at first with her, but he was so primed, he half expected to embarrass himself before she got to the point of the matter.

At his waist, she stopped and skipped the important part. Damn her for copying his torture tactics. She grazed him from his knees to his thighs, and he thought he'd die of need.

She slid a finger over his balls to the base of his cock, slid two up his shaft, and when she rubbed the droplet at the tip of his dick over the head, she raised him off the cot; then she finally, finally, closed her hand around him.

"This," she said, "is gorgeous. I'll never forget the sight of you making yourself come." She put everything into working him and making it happen again, in her own sweet time, and he bent to her will.

He floated daringly close to heaven while trying to stay beneath the clouds to ride the wind of perfect pleasure. Her skin against his, the pressure and perfection in her movement, her tenderness and attention to what raised him up and lowered him to rest, were incredible.

King struggled to ride her hurricane-strength winds, but bliss caught him unaware and shattered him into more pieces than he could reclaim. He was afraid that like Humpty Dumpty, he'd never be put together again. Not in the same way, at least. Not so the attention of other women would satisfy.

"Sleep," Harmony said, holding his soft, happy cock. "And thank you."

King woke to construction sounds, and by the slant of the sun, he knew they'd overslept, but who cared?

"Did you lock that door?" Harmony asked, sliding her hand around his morning boner and leading him toward another roaring climax.

"I locked it."

"No banker's gonna come in and—"

"The bankers!" King jumped from his cot. "I have a meeting in six minutes."

Harmony flopped back on the bed, but she had him so primed, washing his cock finished the job. More than anything, he wanted to finish inside her. But he needed this meeting. "Damn it."

Before he left, he checked his briefcase for paper clip imposters and took a last look at Harmony, sleeping naked in his bed, exhausted from all the orgasms he'd given her during the night.

He did not want to leave this room, but he had no choice.

Lucky for him, the water taxi was running late, so he stood on the dock waiting to greet the bankers. Everything was set to go smoothly. But they found the crew tearing the dining room apart. *Now*, they had to get efficient? With the bankers waiting and watching, King clumsily moved them, his paperwork, and architectural drawings to the formal parlor.

He didn't get far into his smooth-talking, never-fail, rah-rah, big success speech before the bankers shook their heads. "I'm sorry, Paxton," the older of the two said. "Though *you* might see this place as an asset, we see it as a liability. It is worth millions, but only to the buyer who'll pay that much for a pile of frozen rocks come winter. Anybody with castle cash buys in Mexico or on the islands these days."

"I have a buyer—"

"You're not likely to meet his deadline, and you've got your own slowdowns to blame."

Damn you, Gussie, King thought. Since *his* money was tied up in long-term investments, King needed a break, the right words to change their minds, a diversion, something . . .

And something came along . . .

Tigerstar and her kamikaze kittens catapulted into the room, chasing each other and stopping to hiss at empty chairs. Harmony came in behind them wearing red spikes and a white strapless sundress with a pattern of cutout flowers, her red bra and panties visible in the cutouts. "I apologize for intruding," she said. "I didn't think you were meeting in here." She turned to go. "Tigerstar, bring the kids."

"Harmony, wait," King said, rising. "Gentlemen, let me introduce you to my right-hand . . . girl, Harmony Cartwright." He sat when she extended her right hand, because his body knew it too intimately. "Join us," he said.

As if she read the trouble he was in, Harmony unleashed her sex appeal and dealt it in spades. She oozed charm and complimented the bankers on their refined taste in clothes and investments. "Paxton Castle includes Nicodemus Paxton's extensive nautical library," she said. "He's the historical shipbuilder and sea captain for whom the old Paxton Wharf in Salem was named." She slid a ship's log across the table for them to peruse.

"As you can see from his entries, Nicodemus brought art treasures here from all over the world. Our extensive collection of Oriental artifacts is priceless and filled with one-of-a-kind pieces. In addition, we house an original steam engine and a midway funhouse exhibit and toy room. Besides making a unique museum, the castle would make a fine upscale hotel."

She chuckled. "Unfortunately, or fortunately, the moat is being turned into a rose garden, but who can resist a stone castle with a drawbridge these days? The garden walks and nature trails are natural. There's even a witch garden out behind the kitchen, if you can believe it. And who doesn't like to stay in a hotel with a ghost or two, especially the ghost of a *witch* so near Salem?" Harmony turned to him. "You did tell them about Gussie, didn't you?"

"Uh, no," King said, ready to strangle her.

"I'm sorry, gentlemen," she said. "Mr. Paxton was saving the best for last, and I spoiled it."

The bankers were salivating, and King was in shock.

Gingertigger landed on his shoulder and licked his ear. The kitten weighed less than her psycho mother, so her sudden weight hadn't startled him, and being appreciated right now, even by a kitten, felt good.

Caramello and Warlock curled up in Harmony's lap, and Tigerstar stood close by, her back arched, hissing toward the ceiling

"We also thought sailboat tours would add to the getaway ambiance of the island," Harmony said. "Plus private suites could be built at the lighthouse and windmill, but of course that would be at the discretion of the buyer. All the big hotel chains—"

Tigerstar backstepped and hissed louder, dancing cautiously around.

Harmony's ideas were brilliant and resourceful, and the bankers thought so, too. "This is not a moldy old castle," she said. "It has the potential to be a huge, money-making enterprise. After all, it's a private island close to one of the most famous historic sites in the world."

The bankers talked deal, but Harmony laughed at the rate of interest they offered and tried to get it lowered!

Something started to hum, and as the hum got louder, Tigerstar danced and hissed, and the chandelier began to rattle.

King panicked and Harmony took the bankers, one on each arm, to escort them from the room, but before she got them out, the chandelier fell and landed at his feet.

"Abra-candelabra!" Harmony said, making a joke, but the bankers nixed the loan, anyway.

On the dock a few minutes later—after the bankers agreed to revisit the loan further into castle restoration—he and Harmony waved them off.

"I'm sorry. I tried to get them out of there faster. I knew Gussie would make you pay for trying to get a loan to finish and sell the place. I didn't want them to see the roof or walls fall in."

"Surprise," King said. "They saw the chandelier fall, instead."

"I'm sorry you didn't get your loan. What happens now?"

He thought about that for a minute. "I apply to another bank, or I try selling without restoring the place."

"Or you restore it little by little, with your own money, in your own time."

He quirked a brow. "I'm not a man who likes to wait, but I'm sorry I doubted what you said about our resident wailer. I just wish I knew what to do about her. Listen to her howling in there."

"Did you see how fast the bankers walked after she started?"

King rubbed the back of his neck. "She's really a problem."

"I know," Harmony said, "but we can't talk about her here. I've been researching ghosts, and she's as likely to roam the grounds as the house. Do you have any bicycles so we can get away for a while and talk privately?"

"Any preferences? We have all kinds."

"You choose. I'll go change into some play clothes."

"That dress sure in hell makes me want to play."

"Stop using negative words. It sure in *heaven* makes you want to play, which surprises me, because I thought you'd be ticked off when I showed up wearing it."

"Oh I was, until I saw how you handled the bankers. They had already refused me, you know."

"And I nearly changed their minds? See." She raised her chin. "I'm almost good for something."

"You're aces, Orgasmatron. You set a world record last night. I had to put liniment on my hand this morning." He flexed it and winced.

"If you had actually *slept* with me . . . you'd need liniment on your pecker." She ran toward the door he'd nearly kept her from entering the other day, and, now, just being near her made him wonder why he'd tried to keep her out.

"Get the bikes," she said, "and something to snack on. I'll be right back."

"I could snack on you," he called, and the gardeners applauded.

What the hell was wrong with him? He'd never made such an inappropriate statement out loud in his life. He blamed Harmony for unstarching him, but he might as well accept the inevitable. She had him by the balls, and, for now, he liked it that way. He went to get the bikes.

Bicycles and bananas. That's what he had waiting for her when she came back. She wore short shorts and a black hoodie, and she threw a hoodie his way.

"What the hell are those?" she asked, eyeing the bicycles.

"Mine is an 1869 English Velocipede, or a boneshaker as they were not so fondly called. And yours is an 1889 Lady's Rover. The amazing selling point on yours was that the central bar had been removed to allow for your long, cumbersome skirts."

"Get a life. What's with the bananas? You got a monkey on the island?"

"You said to bring a snack."

She shrugged and got on her bike. "I guess fruit's better than cookies. Not. Hey, my bike has tires, and yours doesn't."

"No kidding," he said, peddling his ass off behind her.

"Peddle fast," she said, "because the louder Gussie wails, the lower our odds are of getting away."

The wail caught up with them at the bottom of the hill, and so did the sound of Curt shouting their names. Before clearing a wooded area, King grabbed a tree branch and dragged it behind his bike to erase their tracks. His military school pranks had finally paid off.

Harmony led the way, because King liked watching her backside as she pedaled in those spandex shorts. Tough, riding a bike with a boner.

"What's this?" Harmony asked when she saw the fence blocking the entrance to the old cave.

"I honestly don't know. As a kid, I was always told it was dangerous and forbidden, and to stay away."

"I find it hard to believe that you obeyed."

"I never lucked out with disobedience in this particular spot. Probably the only forbidden place on the island I missed, though."

"It's a great island. I adore the peach roses by the front doors, the trellised wisteria, the stone walls covered with ivy, the wildflower woods." She shrugged. "I guess I love the whole place."

That threw him, because deep down, he felt the same way.

"Shall we see what's in here?" She pulled the rotting fence from the entry with one tug. They walked their bikes inside and slid the fence back in place. To hide the bikes, they walked them deep into the cave, choosing the brighter tunnels as they went. When the ground got rocky, they grabbed the bananas, abandoned the bikes, and went on.

Harmony was curious, maybe a little too curious.

"I think we've gone a bit too far," King said, "and taken a few too many turns. We need to find our way back, don't forget."

"I know the way. I'm wondering why it keeps getting lighter in here. Watch, we'll come out somewhere else on the island. Yikes!"

Whoosh. She disappeared into the earth, as if she'd taken an express elevator to hell.

"Harmony!" King took a cautious step to the side, so he could rescue her, not follow, and whoosh, he took a slippery slide on his sore ass, until he came to a hard stop in a bright, icy, underground . . . palace?

"Isn't this gorgeous?" Harmony marveled at the stalagmites and stalactites. "Talk about your phallic symbols. Oh look, that one's bent. Do you think this is the center of the earth?"

"That was some tumble," King said. "Did you land on your head?"

She grinned. "It was energizing, like taking an icy water slide straight to—"

"Never-Get-Out Land?"

Chapter Twenty-one

KING put an arm around her to keep her warm, but her shiver ran straight through him. "I didn't mean to scare you," he said, "but we can't leave the same way we came."

"It's so beautiful; it's worth falling down an icy rabbit hole for. Like a cathedral, but more spiritual, don't you think? Mother Earth at her finest. The colors of the chemicals in the limestone deposits are amazing, but look at that."

She went to a tall, jagged, concave surface on one wall. "Good Goddess, these jags are amethyst crystals. Did you ever see anything so gorgeous?"

King took a handful off the floor. "Look, broken crystals. Some of them are good-sized."

"I collect crystals. These are powerful." Harmony put loose crystals in her pockets. "Amethysts have a vibrational frequency that protects its wearers from external negative energy. Can you think of anything better to carry around in the castle? Oh, and the crystals you *find* are more powerful than the ones you buy."

King touched the wall of crystals and closed his eyes. "I feel the power."

"Mock all you want. I know what I'm talking about. These will help slow Gussie down. They should also come in handy when we figure out how to send her on her way."

"We can do that?"

"We came biking to talk about getting rid of her. Maybe the Goddess sent us down here for a reason."

"So we could freeze our asses off?"

"It's bright over at that end, but it's also cloudy, or steamy." Harmony shivered.

King unzipped his hoodie. "You can't tell at first glance, but I think there's an underground pool over there."

She accepted his hoodie, held it together in the front like a cape, and collected amethysts for his pockets. "Is the steam rising from the water because it's like a hot bath? Or is that a mirage? Think we could warm up and swim toward the light? Does this feel like a near-death experience? Suppose we died. Who picks priceless gems off the ground on earth?" She shivered again. "If we are on earth, are we stealing?"

He put an arm around her. "We're alive, and I own the island. They're my amethysts. Take all you want."

"Whew. Good. Let's go for a swim and get warm."

"Don't plan on the water being too *warm*." He went to the pool. "Steam simply means the water's warmer than the air. Now take off your clothes."

"I beg your pardon, but I'm too blooming cold already, thanks, especially if that isn't a *hot* spa."

"I can't believe you're being prudish, after last night."

"I'm not. I just don't feature being rescued naked."

"If we *can't* get out by following the light, we'll be glad to have dry clothes to put on when we get back."

Harmony perked up. "And if there *is* a way out, we can come back for our clothes before we take it, right?"

"Whatever you say." First, he wanted her naked in the

hopefully warm water. He was primed thinking about it. Hell, finding their way out could wait. He wanted to find his way inside in the worst way, especially now that he knew how hot she was. He'd bet he could have her willing and begging in two seconds.

"Begging? You blooming wish. I can't believe you want to play *before* we look for an escape route."

"Did I say that out loud?"

She gave him two silent eye blinks. "Sure you did."

King thought she looked the way she had when he asked her what she was doing at the castle . . . before she came up with the vintage clothing story . . . that turned out to be true.

"Don't you remember saying it out loud? How could I have answered you, if you didn't?"

"Good point. Really? I said that out loud?"

"Um-hmm."

"You can't tell what I'm thinking? Never mind. Of course you can't. Let's swim. Warm water sex sure beats freezing to death and getting calcium slimed."

"You're one horny package of testosterone, Hurricane Boy."

"Look who's talking, Orgasmatron. Like you *don't* have a major case of bungee-jumping hormones."

"Are you suggesting that we interconnect our hyperactive hormones to warm up and indulge our come-hither pheromones at the same time?"

"Pheromones! That's what this is." King sighed in relief, so much relief, he knew she'd caught on.

"Sex for sport," she said, "and I'm on your team, right?"

Again with the mind reading? But nah; he hadn't thought about that since he tried to throw her out the first day . . . after which she happened to mention being a cheerleading team player looking for the big *O*. Weird. "You know, don't you, that even if we don't get out of here on our own, someone will eventually find us, right?"

"Because Gussie's wailing will drive them crazy if they don't?"

"Precisely. And she's worse now that she knows you. I never heard her wail as loud as she does when you leave the castle."

"I'm sure they'll find us eventually. But I'm freezing now."

"Let's warm up in the water, shall we? Wait," he said as she was about to ditch his hoodie. "Let's take it slow, undress each other."

"In different circumstances, I could learn to appreciate your unwavering sexual focus, but I'm freezing here. I don't know, Paxton, for somebody with a steel rod shoved up his—"

"Will you quit that? The rod's gone, already. You extracted it the day you told me it was there. Haven't you figured that out yet? Great guns! I never thought of you as a slow learner."

"I'm not the only slow learner here. It took you two blooming passes last night to find the spot I most wanted you to touch."

"That's called foreplay, sunshine. Get used to it. I'm the ranking commander when it comes to taking it slow."

"Jelly legs," she warned, falling against him.

"Jelly legs?" He encircled her with both arms, pulled her close, and she rested her cheek against his chest.

"Yep," she said looking up. "It's a sexual response of the female skeletal system. When a man does or says something that shoots straight to our . . . our—"

"Hormones?"

"Yeah, those. The bones in our legs turn to jelly."

King didn't want to let go of her to take her clothes off—how twisted was he? If that wasn't insane, he didn't know what was. Oh, yeah, now he remembered. His magnetic attraction to hot little miss sexy pants with attitude. But when he unzipped her hoodie and found the bold black message on her white tee, Orgasm Donor, he embraced insanity.

As a matter of fact, his willing recipient of her as-yet-to-be-donated orgasm sat up and begged. Who's insane now? Not me. "That shirt says you had an ulterior motive for dragging me out here."

"Yeah, and your dick's really upset about that." She cupped him.

"We're supposed to talk about how to handle Gussie," he said, gritting his teeth.

"We will . . . eventually . . . afterward."

"As long as I wasn't lured into a sexual trap for no good reason."

"Hah. If I had suggested a sexual trap, you would have raced me here."

"Okay, you got me. I'm a sucker for a sexy lady in need of a good—"

"Orgasm recipient?"

His eye crinkles cut deep. "First," he said, sliding her shorts down her legs and kissing her lemon lace panties, a sight to feed any man's lurid imagination, "let's get these clothes off you."

"Hey, I'm calling for some equal opportunity freezing here. I go bare-assed, you go bare-assed!" She unzipped his slacks and removed them along with his control, sliding them down his legs, her cheek grazing his boner, her peppermint hair tickling his thighs, making him ready to . . . "No fair, you're instigating preforeplay foreplay, and I'm the commander, here. Stop taking the lead."

Ignoring him, Harmony parted her lips and put the slightest pressure on his boner with her nibbling mouth, nothing between his blow pop and her lips but a pair of black silk briefs.

She looked up. "You *really* want me to stop?"

"Hell no! Lose the briefs."

"In a minute." She slid her hands up the backs of his

thighs, beneath his briefs to cup a bun in each hand, and even as she gently stroked his bandaged butt cheek, his big boy danced while she watched in fascination, up close and personal. Then she palmed her way around toward his happy place, and he about came when she cupped his balls in one hand and grasped his dick with the other.

"Does your man brain wanna come out and play?"

Like he wanted to take his next breath. He'd admit it; his man brain was doing his thinking for him.

She removed her hands from beneath his briefs, and he groaned; then she pulled them down and caught them on his dick.

"Long, thick, and ready to rumble," Harmony said, assessing him from all angles and seeming to like what she saw. "I can finally say it with all honesty. You da King! Hail to da King!"

His dick caught the chill in the air, almost embarrassing him by trying to go into hibernation. "Great guns, it's cold." He pulled off his shoes and socks and dipped a foot in the water. "Our prayers have been answered. It's a hot spring! I'm going in first to make sure there's nothing hiding beneath the surface."

"Yikes. Like snakes?"

"Like a calcified bottom with hard pointy tops that hurt. If there were snakes, they'd be boiled."

"Oh good." She took off her cork-heeled shoes and stood shivering at the edge: a blonde goddess in lemon lace, and all his . . . to play with   for a while . . . He needed to remember that she was only his to slake his lust with and to help slake hers. How did he get so lucky? He devoured the sight of her while he lowered himself into the water to scout around.

"It's safe," he said, surfacing a few minutes later. "Come on in, but slide in slow and easy. That's my girl, and tread water, because there are stalagmites down there."

"How can that be?"

"They formed before the hot spring trickled its way in here."

She floated beside him, sighing in appreciation. "This is heaven."

He curled an arm around her, so they skimmed the surface together, his boner returning to a formidable size as she teased it with her knees, on and off, almost by accident.

"If you think this is heaven," he whispered in her ear. "*Join* me for the real thing."

Chapter Twenty-two

HARMONY shivered in anticipation as King guided them to a corner of the hot spring, hooked his elbows on the calcified edge of nature's spa, and drew her between his legs. Her anchor. Her target. No, she must be the target, because King wielded the dart. Big, thick and long, his dart.

She wound her arms around his neck, her legs around his hips, and before she could put him where she wanted him, he stole her focus by kissing her. Oh, yeah. Foreplay. She forgot. This was new to her, this spicy male musk permeating her senses; hot, talented lips grazing her ear, melting her, slow nibbling at her nape, fine-tuning her sensual receptors and causing a slow rise in her heartbeat.

He tasted of salt and sweat. Man and sex. More like romance than lust, but more than romance. She could fall for this man. This was more than sex for sport, this prelude to enduring pleasure, except that King's version became a pleasure all its own. Ultimate foreplay.

He held her hips away from his, controlled her movement in the hot, licking spring, so only the tip of his shaft touched her, stroked her, wherever, however he wanted, depending on how he moved her. She flowered and opened to await his pleasure. She ran as hot as the spring, and yet he continued skimming her surfaces until her every nerve ending stood at attention, and the slightest abrasion, like his whiskers at the crown of her breasts, made her want him more. How much higher could she rise before she climaxed without him?

He looked up from his attention to her saluting nipple. "Do you have any idea how beautiful and luscious you are? Can you know what you do to me? I can't believe I tried to turn you away." He lifted her hand. "I don't care where you got the ring," he said, stroking it. "It made me see you in a different light." He laved her nipple, scattering shock waves, like mini orgasms, that she could hardly bear, yet rode with wonder. "Last night was probably the best sex I've ever had, and I didn't even have you," he admitted.

She kissed him then, because she didn't want him to see her tears. The best sex. Less than lust. Something mystical, no doubt, but not romantic. Certainly not love. They'd only known each other for a few days, after all.

He kissed her inadvertent tears, whispered his concern, pulled her toward and away from him letting his shaft slip the slightest bit in, then out as fast. A new experience, always to remember. Never to have with another. It wasn't possible.

Pay attention to the signs. Words to live by. But she'd missed the biggest sign of all: sex for sport—a warning she'd ignored. And yet that's all she'd ever wanted . . . until King.

She took him in, and he stopped controlling her. At his entry, her sharp burst of pleasure took her by surprise. His thickness and length stretched her, amazing, wondrous. He touched new pleasure points, deeper points, yet he raised her up. Rapture, and he'd barely entered her.

They moaned into each other's mouths.

Yes, he was the king or commander. Whatever. She'd never had a lover like him. Not that she'd had many, but last night had been better than all four.

Their presence in this Goddess cathedral was more than serendipity. It was synchronicity, the earth and all its elements in alignment so she could be here with King, lost to the world, but more alive than ever. Here, she found her true self. Mating with King. She could do that. She didn't need him to return any sentiment. Knowing how she felt, however premature, was enough.

The hot water added to their buoyant play, as they rode in harmony, her climax close, so close . . . yet he kept pushing it away, making her reach. He rode her hard. Someone screamed. Her. Him? Both of them. Over the edge in a rush down the far side of a rainbow they went, then over the falls into the sea, until they bobbed and drifted.

Heat pooled between her legs. A loss. He'd left her. Empty. She whimpered, and he consoled her. Nothing would be as beautiful as the experience they'd left behind. But when she opened her eyes, she saw beauty in his whiskey gaze. Concern. Caring. Honest and true. No walls. Vulnerable. Open to being cared for.

His vulnerability wouldn't last, but she'd cherish the moment. She kissed him and drew the nectar of the Goddess from his lips, abundance, joy. Entwining her shaky limbs with his, she drifted toward sleep, her cheek against his chest, his chin on her head, him cradling her as she floated free, warmed by the water that surrounded them like babes in the womb.

"Harmony, darling, wake up." Prince Charmy kissed her awake.

She opened her eyes. "Oh, it's you."

"Who did you expect?"

"Prince Charmy. He called me his darling in my dream. Couldn't have been you." She read King's confusion. "It's a fairy-tale dream I've carried around forever. My sisters make fun of me."

"What? I'm not good enough to be your prince?"

"Good? You're spectacular. But I never thought of Charmy in the sexual sense."

"Well, there'll be no happily ever after for you without sex, Orgasmatron. Time to upgrade the fairy tale."

"True enough. Look at us making love in nature's sacred place. I'm living a fairy tale, after all."

"Not for much longer. The air's getting cooler, if that's possible. Time to swim out and see if there's an escape route to be had before the sun goes down, or we're gonna have a long, cold night."

"You're aces at warm-ups," she said. "We'll make our own heat."

His laugh lines triple crinkled this time. She pushed off his chest and swam away. "King Paxton. I think you *do* know how to smile."

"Great guns, sunshine, don't tell anyone, especially not Aiden or Morgan, or my hard-ass rep will never recover."

King's walls remained down, Harmony realized, as they swam the serpentine spring toward a wide, round opening in a cliff, like a window to the sea. They held to its granite edge to look down on a suicide ledge of thorny rock, warm water sluicing past them over their hands, roaring down the side of the cliff into the sea a hundred feet below.

"Is that a dolphin?" she asked. "Never mind. It can't be."

"Yes it can. I saw dolphins around the island when I was a kid. Not long ago, a Newburyport whale watch tour had more than a hundred Atlantic dolphins playing around their boat."

Harmony pulled herself up on the edge of the opening to see if she could find more.

"Hey," King said, "you have a mermaid tattoo at the base of your spine."

Harmony slid back into the water. "Really? Who knew?"

"I've never seen a mermaid on a woman. Men yes, all the time. That's natural, but not on women. What gives?"

"Mia is a symbol of the Goddess and of female sexuality. The mermaid is a water spirit capable of utilizing the energy of the sea."

"You named her, like you named your dolphin vibrators. Why does that turn me on?"

"Everything turns you on."

"Everything about *you*," he said, but she read his regret for the disclosure. "Pretend I'm a sea captain," he said to distract her, "and take me down."

"To the sea in ships? That's a myth. Mermaids don't lure men to their deaths. Men go willingly, too stupid to realize that if they follow a mermaid into the ocean, they can't breathe. Mermaids have saved many a man from his death."

"I didn't mean to upset you."

Harmony shrugged. "No man has ever seen Mia. I thought of her as . . . a rite of passage, except, well, I planned to share her with someone special."

"I'm special."

"But you're not the *one*."

"The one? Oh, 'the *one*.'" King put some water distance between them. "No. No, I'm not. That's a beautiful waterfall," he said, scared spitless. "I've seen it from my boat."

"What kind of boat?" she asked, changing the subject so he wouldn't have a coronary.

"You never ask the expected question. My boat's a beauty, a ninety-foot wooden schooner called *The Sea Horse*."

"You're kidding? I love sailing, and I love sea horses. I have a sea horse tattoo."

He swam closer. "Seriously? Where?"

"That's for you to find out."

He put his arm around her shoulder. "Do you want to know if we can get out of here or not?"

She shrugged. "I know we can't."

"How do you know?"

"Your body language. You're being protective. We're sunk, you'll pardon the pun, and Mia had nothing to do with it."

"Mia is not under suspicion, but we are up the hot springs without a paddle."

"At least it's not a swamp of eternal stink, and we won't go hungry. We have bananas."

"If they're not mush, they're black by now. I dropped them on the way down."

"I know. They arrived before you did, and I rescued them. Frozen bananas are awesome, especially with chocolate sauce . . . like sex. *Hot* fudge sounds especially good right now." She shivered.

"Here, let's get away from the cool sea breeze and swim underwater to get warm on our way to lunch."

Beneath the green blue surface, they kissed and teased, frolicked and chased, and Harmony felt like a mermaid, cavorting with 'the *one*' fate intended for her. Wow, she *was* a sucker for a fairy tale.

Pulling her attention from King and futile fairy tales, she looked down to see the white caps of the stalagmites below them. So the spring was a relatively new addition to the cavern. She surfaced, sluicing water from her face and hair from her eyes. "What about the source of the spring?" she asked as King surfaced. "Maybe we could find our way out that way."

"The source has to be somewhere beneath the cavern floor beyond the spot where we made love," he said.

The roar of the falls was nothing to the sound of her heart roaring in her ears. He said they'd made love. He misspoke, of course, but, wow, he didn't catch himself. The poor man needed rescuing in more than the usual way.

"I'll bet I can't find a banana as big as your pecker," she said, diving beneath the surface to race him back to the cavern.

Chapter Twenty-three

HOW stupid was he? If he was ever going to stroke out, King thought, this would be the time. When had he *ever* thought of sex as making love? He didn't even consider the phrase viable.

Good thing the hellcat was pragmatic and comfortable with her sexuality. He might not have gotten away with that slip with another woman. He liked Harmony. Usually, if he liked a woman, he couldn't have sex with her, or if they had sex, friendship was out of the question. Harmony was different. "You ever have a man friend?" he asked, resurfacing to find her waiting.

"No, I grew up in a convent. What the hell kind of question is that? Of course I've had men friends. You thought I was a virgin?"

"See, there you go mixing *sex partner* with *friend*. That's why men and women can't be friends. Women don't have it in them."

"Whoa. Wait a minute. Are you asking me to be your

friend? Because you didn't blooming say it that way. You asked—"

"I get my mistake," he said. "Yeah, I think we could be friends."

"Friends . . . who . . . have sex together?"

"I love the idea! Perfect, isn't it? No commitments. No dating pressure. No, 'why didn't you call?' We could play it by ear, do lunch, catch a quickie, roust a ghost, fight a jack-in-the-box."

"Yeah," she said with a raised brow. "I do those things with all my *friends.*"

"So . . . our friendship would be unique. I can live with that. You?" He pulled himself from the water and sprinted to the bananas.

"King Paxton, don't you move!"

He froze.

She scoffed. "What do you have on your back?"

He lowered his head. "Busted."

"You bet, bozo. A mermaid tattoo. No wonder you went overboard about men getting them and not women. Care to explain?"

"My feet are freezing. Can I come back in the water first?"

"Only if you bring the bananas."

Raising them, he streaked back and jumped in, his arm raised to protect the bananas.

"Black," he said, surfacing. "I told you."

"Edible," she said. "Mermaid?"

King sighed. "We were sailing *The Sea Horse* in the Pacific, anchored near an island, went exploring, got rip-roaring too-stupid-to-live drunk, and we all got tattoos."

"We being? You, Aiden, and Morgan?"

"Who else?"

"What kind of tattoos did they get?"

King laughed. "Mine is tame compared to theirs. Aiden's,

well, never mind. You'll never know, because I swore I'd never tell, or die."

"That bad?"

King shook his head, but he chuckled. "I got a mermaid because I liked her curves." He skimmed his hand up Harmony's hip and along the side of a breast as he said it. "Like yours."

"Speaking of which . . ." She broke off a huge banana, felt him up beneath the water, then she felt up the banana. "See, it just doesn't measure up."

"Well, you gave it a pretty hard workout."

"I mean the banana, dumb ass."

"Hey, is that a name to call a friend?"

She laughed. What a sound. Like tinkling glass stars. He took a lock of her hair, brought it to his nose, and sniffed. "Peppermint's gone."

She reared back. "I'll wash it again. You smelled the peppermint? You got a nose like a bloodhound, or what?"

"It's normal enough," he said. "Like what's that perfume you use? Makes a man really take notice."

"I make it myself. It's patchouli, frangipani, and honeysuckle oils."

"You should bottle it."

"I'm sure somebody already has," she said. "What are the three scents you remember most from your childhood?"

He didn't have to think long. "Chipped beef, shoe polish, sweat."

"In the summer?"

"Military camp. Same smells."

"Some childhood."

"You're right. It sucked. But I always got a couple of weeks here on the island. *That* was cool. What three scents do you remember from your childhood?"

"Patchouli oil, smudge sticks, fresh lavender. I was always trying spells to bring my mother back and turn us into a family."

"You were a baby witch."

Her laugh charmed the pants off him. No, those were already off. All the better to—

"Like you were a baby soldier. We're pathetic. No wonder we play well together. We never played as kids."

"If I knew about spells for families, I probably would have tried a few."

"Watch and learn." She took a banana and raised it in the air:

> *"In the cave of the Goddess*
> *Mid the glitter of jeweled dew*
> *Grant these poor souls a family*
> *Hearts and homes to return to*
> *Loved ones to cherish,*
> *Nurture, protect, and love*
> *So below as above*
> *All that's holy, hear my plea*
> *Harm it none; this is my will; so mote it be."*

"Did you just spell us a family?"

"Not that it ever worked, but yeah. Who knows, maybe one of these days, our absentee parents will land on our respective doorsteps. I assumed yours were absent, with military school and all. Where were they?"

"My mother was/is career army. I lived at home with my dad until he ran off with a hairdresser. Then I lived at school. You?"

"A *woman* hairdresser?" she asked.

He laughed.

"Hey, I like that sound." Harmony echoed his thoughts of her. "It's a rusty laugh, but I could get attached. My mother ran before they cut the cord. Flew the nest before Dad came to pick us up from the hospital."

"That's why you said you and your sisters raised each other?"

"Yep. Dad was an absentee father even when he was present, usually with a liquor bottle in his hand. Now he's flown the coop, too. Maybe he found my mother, and they're lost together."

"My father wanted a woman who hung around. The hairdresser hung, until he died, actually, but she didn't want me hanging with them. I know, because I asked."

Harmony placed her head on his chest and stroked his arm, and King thought her empathy felt almost as good as sex. "It's hard to ask for family support," she said. "I've done it, too. We found our older sister—from my father's first marriage—when we needed her most. She didn't know we existed, but she took us in. Her name's Vickie. She was our best break ever. The shop was hers. Now we're partners."

This was getting too touchy-feely for him. He needed to get them back to earth. "You want a banana for dessert?" he asked.

"No thanks. Maybe we should save a couple for breakfast." She made curls in his wet chest hair. "We can have each other for dessert."

King set the bananas by the pool and floated into the kiss. He liked her sexual willingness. Ah, who was he kidding? He liked a lot of things about her. He wanted to make her childhood better. Weird. He lifted her and impaled her as they kissed. She sighed and moved along his shaft. Slick, sweet, and hungry, a seductress, pleasure her only goal. Life didn't get any better than this.

A cough echoed in the cavern, and Harmony pulled from the kiss. She looked over his shoulder. "Hey, scraggly stud muffin. How come you keep finding us like this? You a Peeping Tom or something?"

"I'm a disappointed rescuer, is what I am. And I'm thinking this doesn't bode well for our upcoming date."

"It doesn't," King said, turning Aiden's way, using his body to hide Harmony's. "You want to turn around so the lady can dress?"

"Sure, but . . ." Aiden picked up the lemon lace panties and bra and inspected them.

"Give me the damned things," King snapped.

"How about I give them to the lady?" Aiden asked hypothetically, as he gathered the rest of Harmony's things and put them on the edge of the spring.

King helped her out of the water and watched her dress, well, he guarded her privacy while she dressed. Yeah, right. That's what he was doing, but he couldn't find her sea horse tattoo before she gave him his clothes.

Harmony slicked her wet hair back and went to Aiden. "How did you get down here?"

"The same way you did, I presume?" He indicated the ice slide.

"Funny, we didn't hear you coming."

"We shouted our heads off. Thought you cracked yours in the fall."

"I'll bet we were underwater," Harmony said.

"Swimming," Aiden said, "that's what you were doing?"

"Are they down there?" Morgan called.

"They are." Aiden tied a rope around Harmony's waist. "Here comes Harmony. Take care." He tugged on the rope, and she slid up the slippery slope.

Aiden faced him. "You're gonna hurt that girl bad when you dump her. I hate to see it happen, because she's a hell of a lot better than the usual."

"She and I are friends," King said, sounding foolish even to himself.

Aiden barked a laugh. "If you're only friends, then I'm damned well gonna take her out on that date, after all."

"It's up to her," King said, itching again to hit something or someone. He and Harmony must be friends. She made him laugh, the way she was laughing with Morgan above them right now. She asked things he hated talking about, but her, he answered. Who knew you could talk to a woman? They were more than sex partners. He had no hold on her, but as her friend, he'd warn her off Aiden. She wasn't looking for commitment, but Aiden was tired of roaming, even if *he* didn't know it yet.

King rode the rope up to the cave and put an arm around Harmony, as if he'd missed her. He thanked Morgan, and Aiden, when he joined them, but he didn't think Harmony's thank-you kisses were necessary. "Where are the bicycles?" he asked.

"On their way back to the castle. It's dark out, you know. Everybody's been out looking all day. Aiden and I came to work on the dining room and heard the wailing before we hit the dock."

Harmony adjusted her hoodie to cover her Orgasm Donor shirt. "What made you think to look here?" she asked.

"We didn't think of it right away," Aiden said, "but King tried to get in when we were kids. I was with him a couple of times, but his nanny was strict, and she kept him in tow."

King closed his eyes as Harmony rounded on him. "*You* had a nanny?"

"Don't go there."

"But I thought you went to a military summer camp."

"He did, but even his nanny was military," Aiden said, "with a regime that could kill a normal kid. King got sentenced to two weeks with her here every summer, but he loved it."

"Will you shut up?" King snapped. "You gossip worse than a woman."

"I beg your pardon," Harmony said. "I'm a woman, and I've kept a hell of a lot more secrets than you have."

"Don't bet on it, Hellcat."

"You bared your soul to me down there."

"Wrong. My soul's a lot darker than you'll ever know."

"So much for friendship." Harmony walked to the castle in a huff.

"I don't think you've ever kept a female friend so long," Aiden said, and King decked him.

In the castle kitchen, he found Harmony talking to a teenager who was chewing her hair, staring at the floor, and giving one-word answers.

"What's going on here?" King asked, and the teen jumped.

"Sorry, I didn't mean to startle you. Did your boat run aground?"

"I'm looking for somebody," the kid mumbled.

"Somebody here?"

She nodded.

King rolled his eyes. It had been a long day, his butt cheek ached, and his fuse was short, but Harmony put her hand on his arm, and he calmed. Damn, she was using that peace maneuver again, and he wished to hell he didn't like it so much.

He sighed and tried to look into the teen's face. "What's your name?"

"Reggie," she said.

"Reggie? That's no name for a girl—Regina?"

She raised her head just enough to meet his eyes. "Daddy?"

Light headed, King tried to make sense of the rag-bag teen when a little boy, tiny, dark as Regina, peeked around her torn skirt.

"Are you my grampa?"

Chapter Twenty-four

"TAKE them to the formal parlor so you can talk in private," Harmony said, becoming his voice of reason. "I'll ask Gilda to make you a snack."

"This way," King told the girl, who picked up the little boy he hadn't answered yet, because frankly, he didn't know the answer. He didn't know what his own daughter looked like. "What happened to your mother?"

"She kicked me out when I came home pregnant."

"Wait, I need to know your last name."

She stopped. "Paxton. Reggie—Regina Paxton. Are you my father?"

"Your mother's full name?"

"Belinda Brewer Paxton," the girl said, handing him her son's birth certificate with her name, Regina Paxton, as his mother.

King reeled from the knowledge, which seemed nothing compared to what this girl must have gone through. "Yes," he said. "I am your father."

"Why did you stay away?"

He took her arm as they skirted the fallen chandelier. "Before you were born, your mother got a court order to keep me away."

"Figures."

The girl—his daughter—sat on the sofa, and the boy climbed into her lap.

King sat opposite them. "What's the boy's name?"

"Jake. Jake Paxton."

"And his father is?"

"A senior in high school this coming fall."

"Jake is what, two? So you got pregnant around . . . ninth grade?"

The girl shrank into herself.

"I thought Belinda would do a better job." King got up to pace.

Harmony brought in quartered sandwiches and chocolate cookies.

Regina and Jake looked at him—for permission to eat, King supposed, and his heart about broke. "Eat, eat," he said. "They need milk." He turned to Harmony, who was pouring a glass. "Good. Thank you." He handed it to his daughter.

She gave her son a sip and put the rest aside. He guessed, by her skeletal size, she fed the boy and went without.

Harmony gave him a second glass before he asked. He stood before his daughter. "This one's for you."

"Thank you," she whispered and set it aside.

"Drink it. There's more where that came from. We won't run out."

"Harmony, please stay," King said when she turned to go.

She sat on the sofa beside Regina and took Jake on her lap.

"Oh, no," Regina said. "I think he needs changing." She

slipped a bag off her shoulder and took out a plastic diaper thingy, and right there, his baby girl changed her baby boy.

King swallowed the very big lump in his throat and wondered how he'd screwed up so badly. "Where have you been since your mother threw you out?"

"Looking for you."

As if he'd been struck, King wilted against the chair back. "I didn't know."

"For three years?" Harmony asked.

"She crossed the country," King said. "Belinda lives in Malibu." A pregnant teen crossing the country looking for her useless father, who could have picked her up in his blasted helicopter in a few hours. "Did you try to call me?"

"Every big city I hit, I'd look you up," Regina said, "but I didn't know where you were, and the castle isn't listed. One of Mom's former friends took me in until Jake was nearly a year old. She took good care of us, even got a midwife to deliver Jake. She was like a mother to me. A nice lady. But her son came home to live, and well, he wasn't a nice man, so we left."

"Smart girl," King said, an undeserved paternal pride swelling his chest.

"I concentrated on taking care of Jake. Sometimes people took us in. Some good people. Some not. Most of the time, I lied about my age and stayed in shelters. I look older than I am, and I'm very responsible, so nobody questioned me. 'Who wants more kids in the system anyway?' I heard somebody say that, once. I think she was talking about me."

"Maybe the system would have found me for you," King said.

"Not before it took Jake away from me." Her son moved back to her lap, proving how wrong that would have been. King hated himself for abandoning his daughter to the mercies of a system, overworked on its best days. "How did you manage?"

"Sometimes I'd wait tables, if I found an owner who didn't mind Jake in the back room. He was a good baby." She combed his hair with her fingers. "Always quiet. I think he knew he had to be, didn't you, pup?"

"I was good so Mama could work," the boy said.

Regina tapped him on the nose with a finger. "I put every dime into feeding him, keeping him warm and safe. I made good choices and bad, but we made it. I knew about your island because Mom had a thing about the castle. She was really mad she couldn't take it away from you, by the way. So I headed for the only place you ever called home: Paxton Castle."

"Your mother threw you out on the street and didn't call me?"

"Evidently."

"My company phone number is on every check I send her. You should have asked her for it."

"I asked. She said she didn't have it."

The bitch, King thought.

Jake got off the sofa and came to stand in front of him, a familiar hungry-for-love look in his eyes. King knew it well. He took the boy on his lap. "You got a question, buddy?"

"*Are* you my grampa?"

"I am."

Jake looked at Regina. "I don't have to be afraid of my grampa, right?"

"No, pup. No strangers on the island, just family and friends we haven't met yet."

Jake nodded. "Good."

"How old are you?" King asked him.

"Two." Jake held up two fingers. "But I'm gonna be free soon. I saw a tractor in your garden. Bunnies live in gardens. My favorite color is blue. I can write my name. Wanna see?"

"No baby, we don't have any paper right now," Regina said. "Later maybe." Her expression questioned his plans for them.

"Oh, you're *staying*," King said, emotion forcing him to clear his throat. "We have to get the law on our side, but I'll take up that fight with gusto and with every resource at my disposal, a considerable arsenal, I might add."

Ignoring the misty sheen in Harmony's eyes, King ruffled his grandson's hair, and when the boy's little head rested on his chest, something in King broke, and he had to swallow hard. "How come this one's so smart? I didn't think kids this small talked like him." King bounced his . . . grandson—wow, did that put life into perspective. "Have you been home-schooling him on the road, Regina?"

"Reggie. He's eager to learn. At my last job, they called him Baby Einstein."

"How old are you, Reggie?" Harmony asked.

"Seventeen. Almost eighteen."

Harmony turned his way in shock, and King shrugged. "Yep, it runs in the family. I was a junior in high school when Regina was born."

"Reggie," she said.

"*That's* when I changed high schools," he told Harmony. He didn't want Regina to know that her imminent arrival had cost him a military school graduation.

His daughter, finally, with him after all these years. He wished he'd hugged her right away. Now he'd missed his chance, and he didn't know how to get it back. Regret threatened to choke him.

Harmony took Regina's hand, tugged her off the sofa, and brought her to him, so King got up with Jake and faced her.

Harmony stole Jake with a chocolate cookie, then she shoved Regina his way. King's arms went around that girl so fast and hard, he was afraid he'd break her, but she didn't seem to mind, because she held him in a bone crusher. At first she cried silently, then she all-out sobbed in his arms; his little girl, who'd lived though hell while he became a rich playboy with a sailboat and helicopter for toys. He was such a shit.

Through a mist, he watched Harmony carry Jake—his little head on her shoulder—from the formal parlor.

King picked up his daughter and carried her back to the sofa, where he sat with her on his lap, her face in his neck, and he let her cry her heart out. His own tears wet his face, no stopping them. He blamed Harmony for that. But maybe, for Regina's sake, it was a good thing Harmony had taken a can opener to his ramparts.

He was a first-class jerk. Back when he'd screwed up, he'd been glad Belinda wanted a divorce. Glad to be rid of her. And his daughter? Well, he'd managed to put her out of his mind most of the time, except when he signed the monthly child support checks. Son of a bitch. He'd paid child support for three years while Regina supported herself. Belinda was a shit, too. "You sure didn't luck out in the parent department," King said.

"I always imagined sitting on your lap," Regina said. "I dreamed about it for years, but maybe I'm too old now?"

"Your choice, but we could pretend this is the day you were born, and it's the first time I've ever seen you—because it is—and I could hold you for a bit, just for today."

She stayed where she was. "You never saw me?"

"I went to the hospital the day you were born, but your mother had me arrested before I saw you. Disobeying a no-contact order can do that to a guy. I came back to Salem when I got out of jail."

"How long were you and mom married?"

"Long enough to give you my name and to give her the right to a great deal of my money. About two weeks."

"Wow, you got off easy."

King chuckled. "No kidding."

Chapter Twenty-five

KING figured that he and Regina sat on that sofa for a couple of hours at least—her beside him, after his leg cramped—his arm around her, catching up on the years he'd missed: the horror of being potty trained by a maniac, her first day of nursery school—the only kid without a mother in tow. The pigtail years, her first visit from the tooth fairy, the year she stopped believing in Santa Claus, her first crush, her last . . . and the brutal end of her childhood.

King sighed. "Regina, I'm gonna tell you something."

"Reggie," she said.

"Right. This is the thing. You mistook sex for love, and for a love-starved teen, that's *really* easy to do. I know, because I made the same mistake. But as of this minute, we're going to put our mistakes, all of them, behind us, okay? But we're not going to forget that a lot of good came from them. You, for one, and Jake for another."

"You're like the best dad ever."

"I'm like the worst dad ever, but I'll change, I promise. I need you to forgive me, Regina."

"Reggie. And there's nothing to forgive."

"Are you kidding me? At the least, I should have sicced my lawyers on the case, once I hired lawyers. At the most, when my company took off, I should have stormed Malibu to prove I could be a good father. I deserved visitation rights."

"Well, when you put it that way . . . I forgive you."

King stroked her hair the way she'd stroked Jake's, loving her little-girl head on his shoulder. "I'll see my lawyer tomorrow," he said. "Make us a legal family and tie us up in a big *blue* bow." *No spells or rituals required,* he thought.

She smiled. "Speaking of blue, I need to make sure Jake's all right." She got up, and King did, too, but as they left the formal parlor, he put an arm around her shoulder. "Harmony's taking good care of him, I'm sure."

"Is she your . . . significant other?"

"No, she works here. Kind of a girl Friday, pain in the neck type."

"But you're friends?"

"Yes, we are."

"Just friends?"

"I haven't figured that out yet. Guess I'm not as mature as you." He winked.

Regina laughed, a great sound. He'd make it happen often. By God, he would.

They found Harmony and Jake asleep on Harmony's bed, both with a fresh-washed look and wearing literal-statement tees. God knew what notions the hellcat had already put in the boy's head. He only hoped she hadn't read him his shirt. Harmony slept facing Jake, three kittens between them.

"Do you have luggage?" he asked Regina.

She shook her head. "The clothes on our backs and a diaper bag."

"No problem." King rummaged through Harmony's

dresser for a pair of shorts and a tee. "Candy Fixes Everything," he read before handing her the shirt. "I think that's Harmony's mantra. Bathroom's that way. The tub has jets, and Harmony came with a whole suitcase of scented bath stuff; I kid you not. Use whatever you find. There's a box of new toothbrushes in the closet."

"I've gone to heaven."

"Hardly. We sleep dorm-style, but I'll fix that. For tonight, climb in with Harmony and Jake. It's an extraordinarily comfortable king-sized bed. If you need anything, I've got the next cot over. Do you think you'll be all right in a strange place?"

"Dad, you don't know from strange, and this won't be the first time I share a bed with a woman I don't know, but it'll be the nicest bed and the nicest woman." She patted his arm as if to console *him*.

"This place," she said. "It's a castle. Paxton Castle." She grinned. "My imaginary home at the end of the rainbow . . . come true. I feel as if I've clicked my ruby heels and made it back from Oz."

While Regina was in the bathroom, King sat on a chair and watched Harmony and Jake sleep. He had new priorities: a family. Hadn't the witch spelled them a family this afternoon? Nonsense. Regina had been traveling for a year.

Wow, he had a daughter and a grandson. A bright grandson . . . who would not be going off to some boarding school for gifted children. They'd find a school near home. Well, Regina would. He was only the grandfather. Her call, but she didn't seem to have Belinda's overpriced Hollywood ideas, thank God, so they should get along fine.

Regina came out of the bathroom looking like a little girl, kissed him on the cheek, a moment he'd cherish, and she climbed into bed. Jake turned into her arms. "Mama," he sighed. No sooner had Regina fallen asleep than Harmony climbed out of bed, took his hand, and led him to the musty sitting room next door.

On a Victorian sofa that had seen better days, she curled into him. "Tell me what happened, Grampa."

"I'm kinda tired, Hellcat."

"I'm kinda freaked, Frosty."

King sighed, bowing to the inevitable. His walls were cracked anyway. "To start with, you have to understand that at military school, I was taught control and discipline, and I ate it up."

"Because control was safer than getting kicked in the emotions?"

He looked down at her and put his chin on her head. "Smart-mouth witch. You're too wise for you lemon bikinis."

"Focus, Paxton."

"Okay. Discipline and control: I got straight A's for that, if for nothing else. But my control slipped once. Junior year. I got a gold-digging military-school groupie pregnant—a spoiled princess, it turned out, who wanted her own castle. The consequences, however, were permanent. I got expelled and became a lousy husband. Two weeks later, we split. In the divorce, I lost my unborn child and a lifetime of visitation rights, not to mention half my trust fund, and enough monthly support for an army."

"So you won't slip again," Harmony said.

"No, I won't. Not in this lifetime. I don't make the same mistake twice. I'm the kind who gets married once in a blue moon, so it'll never happen again. I won't let my emotions rule me . . . but my sexual appetite, that's another story. You understand where I'm coming from, right?"

"In every respect, and who can blame you?"

"I blame myself for Regina's sorry life, and, in some obscure way, for letting you down. Still friends?"

She cuffed him. "Sure."

He caught her gaze. "Can we go to bed now?"

"With a brilliant and impressionable two-year-old in the house? Not together. Not anymore."

King felt both a sense of pride and loss. He released his breath. "Probably best."

Harmony toyed with his earlobe. "Did you say there was a parlor car in the train shed?"

King sighed. "Let's get some sleep."

She patted his chest. "Tomorrow, the parlor car."

"We forgot the bananas," he said.

She made swirls in the fabric of his shirt. "Think we should go back for them? That was some hot tub."

"I was thinking of a private elevator to get down there. Nobody would know it's there but us."

She fanned herself. "I'm getting hot just thinking about it."

"That's my sexpot."

"Yours? Am I?"

"Until the castle is restored. You keep the wind quiet, remember? I'm worried the wind'll frighten Jake. I keep imagining him in the toy room."

Harmony shuddered. "You finally believe she's dangerous?"

"I have marginal proof. A bayonet wound in my ass that's throbbing without the padded bandage I lost in the hot spring, and blue toes from a bruising chandelier. Yeah, she could be dangerous."

"We didn't get a chance to finish our discussion," Harmony said. "We were rescued too soon. But have no fear, I'm hatching a plan to . . ." She looked around as if the walls, or ghosts, had ears. "My plan is to . . . make the wind happy," she whispered.

"Sounds as witchy as you are."

"You got that right."

"You're trying to scare me, again."

"You think that's scary? Consider this: We shared something of ourselves with each other today—besides sex—and we learned that neither of us felt wanted as children. Reggie spent the last three years feeling unwanted."

"*I* damned well want her."

"That's beside the point, and damned if you being a good dad isn't a turn-on, but I'm trying to paint you a picture here. As the unexpected child of a . . . child, Jake must have started life unwanted, if only for a few panicky days or months. You see where I'm going with this?"

"Uh, no, sorry. I was, er, reading your breasts again, and I got distracted. Playtime Is Never Over. Is that a hint?"

"I didn't want to scar your daughter and grandson."

"Thanks. What does Jake's shirt say?"

"I Brake for Unicorns. I got it in honor of my sister Vickie. Long story, very romantic, but the shirt's a commentary on how she found her Scot. Can we get back to the subject at hand?"

"Which is?" King kissed her head. "You smell of peppermint again."

"So does your grandson. We took a shower together."

"Lucky son of a . . . Paxton."

"Focus, King. I know you short-circuited today, but try, please. The connection is being *unwanted*—you, me, Reggie, Jake—we all have that in common, and for some karmic reason, we're together in an *unwanted* castle."

"I never said I didn't want the castle. I just don't want the headaches that come with it, the wind included."

"So you *do* want the castle?"

"In a way. My ex wants it, too, but that doesn't mean she's getting it. You know, my ex reminds me of Gussie in a lot of ways: controlling, self-centered, mean-spirited. The problem, as I see it, is that Regina considers the castle her home, at the end of the blooming rainbow, her dream come true."

"Another reason you shouldn't sell. You have a family, King. Exactly what you wanted. Start having meals in the kitchen. Redo a family wing. Jake needs structure. Routine. It wouldn't hurt your daughter any, either."

"Now wait a minute."

"Fatherhood's a tough job, *if* you do it right. Are you ready to tell Reggie that her home's up for grabs, that after a year of trekking across the country with a baby in tow, she *isn't* home?"

"You really piss me off, Cartwright."

"I think we've established that. But I turn you on, too." Harmony ran her sensuous fingers through his hair as she nudged his head down to hers, until their mouths nearly touched, anticipation running to all his ready parts.

"Playtime is never over," she whispered.

"Grampa, I can't sleep."

Chapter Twenty-six

HARMONY got off King's lap and put Jake there. "His little feet are cold," she said. "I'll get some socks."

When she got back, she put her socks on the boy and cuffed them at his knees, then she covered him with a blanket. "Your grampa will take good care of you." She kissed both heads. "Night night, you two."

Harmony leaned on the wall by the sitting room door to eavesdrop on Brass Ass Paxton, the most unlikely grandfather in the world.

"Sing me a song, Grampa," Jake said with a sleepy voice, and King stumbled his way into an amazing rendition of "Puff, the Magic Dragon."

A raging case of the warm fuzzies overcame her as she made her way to bed, and she realized that several new motives had been added to her psychic mandate. She *definitely* needed to send Gussie on her peaceful way. Now more than ever, she needed to encourage King to keep the castle, which would help him keep his family. Never mind that she wanted to belong to that family.

But how was she supposed to do all that? What else did she have to accomplish here? There was more, she knew, and where did the ring fit in? Unless the ring had already fulfilled its purpose by getting her in the door. King said it made him see her in a new light. Harmony got into bed, and Regina sat up and called Jake.

"He's okay, Reggie. Your father's singing him to sleep in the next room. They need some one-on-one time. They're enjoying it." Harmony figured that only selflessness would make a girl as responsible Reggie relax, and sure enough, she went back to sleep.

Overwhelmed by her known and unknown goals, Harmony guessed it was time to call for help. Telepathically, she called her sisters.

"Now, sisters mine, it's time to make our
magick shine.
Come into the search, I'm in the lurch.
The power of three is all that I see.
Making a home, never to roam,
A place of peace, shelter, and love.
Keeping it, saving it, setting it free.
Come to my aid, oh power of three.
Harm it none; this is my will; so mote it be."

Harmony woke to a cheerful, "Good morning, Tiger," but King wasn't talking to her. He was trying to keep his grandson from stepping on her face in his rush to get to his grandfather.

"Get up, Sunshine," he said looking down at her. "Breakfast in the kitchen in half an hour. Regina's already showered and helping Gilda cook."

"Reggie," Harmony said. "She wants you to call her Reggie."

"Right. I gave her another of your shirts and shorts. She fell in love with Will Work for Shoes."

"Hey, your daughter's got good taste. That's one of my faves."

King rolled his eyes. "Do you have one for Sleepy here? Something that won't haunt him in his teenage years?"

Harmony went to her drawer and pulled out her Boys R Us shirt. "How's this?" They pulled it over Jake's head as the boy stood on her bed. "Perfect, hey? I have red socks to go with it. Give me those cute toes," she coaxed as she put her socks on him. She nudged King. "When are you gonna get them some clothes?"

King caught Jake in his arms. "I got their sizes from Regina last night. Aiden and Morgan hadn't left. They're shopping on the way here."

"Do you have any idea how much a kid this size needs?"

"I *need* Mama," Jake said.

"No putting one over on you, my boy. Let's go find Mama, then."

"Hey," Harmony called. "I missed my morning snuggle."

King stopped. "I thought about that when I woke up."

"Hard to ignore, was it?"

"After yesterday? Do you doubt it?"

When Harmony sat down to breakfast, she had a feeling of déjà vu, as if she'd done it a hundred times, but that was wishful—not psychic—thinking.

Reggie hooted when she saw Harmony's shirt. "Will Work for Vintage Clothes! They're the best. I love vintage."

"Then you're in the right place." Harmony turned to King. "Can she help me search?"

"Sure, but you have to let her keep whatever she wants."

"That's fair, though I'm thinking she'll want vintage 1900s not 1800s."

Reggie looked from one to the other. "What are you talking about?"

Harmony accepted a plate of ham and eggs from Gilda. "I'm the buyer for my family's vintage clothing shop, here harvesting vintage clothes. Your dad says you get first choice. I've found some ancient stuff."

"Yuck. No, I want old stuff from when you were young, Dad."

"Ouch!" he said, throwing his napkin in his plate.

Tears filled Reggie's eyes. "I didn't mean to make you mad."

"Cupcake," he said squeezing her shoulder. "I was kidding. If you did upset me, I'd still love you. You'd still have a home with me."

Reggie looked up at him. "Really?"

"That wasn't how it worked in your world, was it Regina?" he asked.

"Okay, Dad, you love me no matter what, so here's the litmus test. My name is Reggie. I hate the name Regina. Please call me Reggie."

"Done." He kissed her, bent to kiss Harmony, realized his mistake, and swept awkwardly by her to kiss Jake. "I'm seeing my lawyer. Be back later."

"Is he the most reasonable man on earth or what?"

"What!" Gilda and Harmony said together.

Harmony laughed. "He's the most *unreasonable*."

Gilda laughed. "You got that right."

"Come on, Reggie." Harmony washed Jake's face. "Let's go find some seventies vintage."

Harmony took Reggie to a newer wing. "I think the closet in this room might have what you're looking for. It was decorated around the time your father was born here."

"Daddy was born here? Cool. Now I love it even more."

Harmony could practically feel the winds of change. "He'll be real happy to hear that."

Twin beds wore flowered orange, yellow, and lime coverlets. A white walk-in closet took up one wall, clothes racks sharing space with drawers and shelves. They found everything their retro hearts could desire. Punk and flower child outfits, micros, minis, and maxis, bell bottoms, caftans, jumpsuits, and pantsuits, some in psychedelic colors.

Open shelves above the clothes held shoes of every style, height, and color. Seeing them, Reggie did a retro disco happy dance that made Harmony and Jake laugh. She grabbed the ladder.

"Wait!" Harmony said. "Let's make sure it's safe first."

Reggie backed away as if she'd been slapped.

"Regg. I know you became a woman in the ninth grade, but you missed some life lessons. I didn't want you to get hurt. You didn't do anything wrong. If you did, your dad might dislike what you did, but he'd never dislike you."

"Thanks," Reggie said, lunging in for a hug but pulling back.

"Oh come here," Harmony said. "I want the hug." It was a strong hug. Warm. Friendly. "I'll check the ladder, then you can go up."

Harmony moved the ladder along its rail, and hung from every rung. "Okay, go for it."

Reggie climbed to the top and started pulling out shoes.

Harmony went to play with Jake on the floor. When a chill hit the room, she threw a blanket around Jake. When she turned to Reggie, the ladder was trembling.

It started tipping away from the wall, and Reggie dropped a pair of shoes so she could hold on. "Push it forward with your body," Harmony shouted.

If the ladder kept falling away from the wall, Reggie was gonna hit the floor and break her back.

Chapter Twenty-seven

HARMONY got behind a twin bed and pushed it forward with every bit of strength she had in her. Reggie landed on it and bounced, as did the ladder . . . in Jake's direction.

Harmony and Reggie screamed and lunged for him, but the ladder veered away from Jake, as if something had deflected it and sent it in another direction.

Harmony snatched Jake up and turned her back on the ladder to protect him. It crashed into a full-length mirror.

Still shaking, Reggie cried as she took her son. "A broken mirror," she said. "Seven years' bad luck."

"I didn't break it, Mama."

"We know, Scrumpling." Harmony wiped her own tears. "And no bad luck. That's an old wives' tale. We needed good luck, and we got it." They sat on the bed together to catch their breaths.

Gussie, Gussie, Gussie, Harmony thought. *You hate the daughter as much as the father, but you protect the grandson. Why?*

"Destiny and Storm," she called telepathically. *"Now. It's time now! Where the hell are you?"*

"Hot and smokin' witch patrol reporting for duty," Storm said, as they walked in.

"Thank God," Harmony said. "This is getting scary."

"Very scary," Reggie said.

"Reggie, these are my sisters. We're triplets."

"No freaking kidding."

"Storm and Destiny, meet Reggie, King Paxton's daughter, and this is her son, Jake."

Caramello flew into Destiny's arms, and Warlock hopped on Storm's shoulder and pawed at her hair until he tossed her wig to the floor.

Jake doubled over giggling.

Storm huffed, and with a flick of a hand, poofed her purple spiked hair. She picked up her cat and looked him in the eye. "Warlock, I know you like Mummy the way she is, but we have a job to do, and I have to look like Harmony, so *lay off the wig!*"

Jake's giggles became contagious.

"Jake," Storm said, "did you cry on the boat on your way here?"

"Yes," Reggie said. "He did. He'd never been in a boat before. How did you know?"

"I get a sense when kids are in distress. It's a psychic thing." She smoothed the boy's hair. "I'm glad you're okay now."

Tigerstar jumped on the bed, and she rubbed the top of her head on Jake's arm, then Regina's hip. Jake petted her, and Star purred and climbed on his lap to curl up. "She likes me!"

"She sure does," Harmony said, while Storm put her wig back on.

Reggie examined their faces. "Don't think I'm gonna remember which of you is which. The only way I can tell you're Harmony is because you're wearing different clothes."

"Which I need to fix." Harmony took off her shirt and replaced it with the orange and black one her sisters brought. "Hold on to Jake, Reggie, not for his protection, but for yours. We have to we see what we can do about the g-h-o-s-t."

Reggie laughed.

"No joke. Didn't you feel as if something *pulled* that ladder back?"

"Well yes, but—"

Harmony slipped into a pair of black shorts and shoes like her sisters. "Did you *not* see the ladder veer *away* from your son?"

"Very weird, I agree, but—"

"I believe you're safe as long as you've got Jake in your arms. When you get to the dorm, take an amethyst crystal from my top drawer and put it in your pocket. That'll help deflect her negativity."

"What you're saying isn't possible."

"It's as possible as a teen dragging a one-year-old across the country to find a father she's never met. A lot of people wouldn't believe your story, either."

Reggie tilted her head. "You're right. I defied the odds."

"And raised Baby Einstein while you were at it. So listen, weirder things have happened. It gets cold when the g-h-o-s-t shows. Do you remember getting cold?"

"Yes. I *was* freezing all of a sudden."

"Bingo. She's your ancestor, by the way."

"Wonderful, but on my mother's side, right?"

"No. Her problem is with you and your father. "We need the power of three as one to handle this, and that'll take all our concentration. We'll get our best shot without distractions; they break our power of concentration. If we're weak, the g-h-o-s-t is strong. Trust me on this. Don't tell anybody you saw triple. We have some serious psychic w-i-t-c-h peacemaking to do, so if anybody sees us, any one of us, we're all me, no questions asked. The less explaining, the more energy we conserve."

"Who's the w-i-t-c-h?" Reggie asked. "You or the g-h-o-s-t?"

"All of us," the three of them said.

Reggie shook her head. "Does my father know?"

"He doesn't know what my sisters look like or that they're here. Keep our secret for a few hours, and give us a chance to work our m-a-g-i-c-k. We'll come out of the broom closet before the day's over."

"I can spell, you know," Jake declared, arms crossed. "J-a-k-e." He nodded, annoyed that he couldn't understand them.

"Jake, you smart boy, will you take your mama back to the bedroom so she can rest?"

"Can I take the kittens?"

"They need to stay with us. Caramello belongs to Destiny. Warlock is Storm's. And Gingertigger is mine."

"Can Tigerstar come with us, then?"

"You know, I think she might like to do that." It looked as if Vickie's Tigerstar, a powerful familiar and wise to Gussie's presence, was lending her protective instincts to Reggie and Jake, a big relief.

Harmony walked them up the hall. "Be gentle when you tell your father about this."

Reggie hugged her. "You care about my dad, don't you?"

"What are you, psychic? Don't tell him; you'll scare him away."

Reggie laughed. "I won't tell a soul." She picked up her son.

Harmony's sisters met her halfway back. "The technocrat with the steel rod up his butt has a daughter?" Destiny asked.

"Never mind the daughter," Storm said. "Harmony's got the hots for the father. I told you she'd been getting laid." Storm caught her sleeve. "Is the brass ass good in the sack?"

Destiny cuffed her. "Geez, Storm."

Harmony made a fainting motion with the back of her hand against her brow, and they all three hooted. "Listen," Harmony said, "there are a couple of guys I want you to check out while you're pretending to be me. I need to know if my take on them is right or if I'm blocked."

"If you're blocked, it's because some guy's docked in your man radar," Storm explained with a wink.

Harmony rolled her eyes. "Check out Aiden McCloud. He's cute in a shaggy-dog sort of way, a guy who's at his best with a Harley or a woman under him, and whichever it is, all engines will be revved and purring."

"Okay, McCloud's mine to size," Storm said.

"The other one's Morgan Jarvis. He's an architect, and—you'll love this—a paranormal debunker. Give me your take on him before I say any more. Like us, Des, this one doesn't seem to know who he wants to be when he grows up. You'll know him when you see him."

Destiny frowned. "I resent that. I know who I am. I'm the manager of the Immortal Classic."

"That's what you do, not who you are," Harmony said. "You're only going through the motions."

Destiny folded her arms but didn't argue. The triplet thing had its uses. She was right, and Destiny knew it. Harmony sensed Paxton coming as her sisters ducked into the closet. How foolish, and yet their scheme would backfire if they became a sideshow. Better for their midsummer ritual preparations if they concentrated on their task. Every nosy question would suck their energy and diminish their collective power.

"What the hell happened in here?" King asked. "Are Reggie and Jake okay? Are you? I thought they were with you."

"Good paternal instincts, Paxton." She took his arm to lead him from the room. "We had a visit from Gussie. I have good news and bad."

He didn't take either well, she thought a few minutes later as he ran up the stairs to the dorm.

Aware the coast was now clear, her sisters joined her.

"We have to concentrate," Harmony said, "and work our way through this place, room by room. The negative entity is strong, so we have to be stronger. Do you have everything we need to bless and cleanse each room?"

Destiny ticked off their supplies on her fingers. "Salt, smudge stick, black candles, water, and a broom."

"Here, I found a source for amethyst crystals here on the island and brought one for each of us." She led them through the formal parlor, their kittens following. "This'll take a few days, but the more rooms we cleanse and protect, the easier it'll be to do the ritual."

"We're doing it, then?"

"I don't see that we have a choice." Harmony led them behind the small tapestry. "In a way, I'm glad Gussie expended a good amount of energy this afternoon, because our task here should be easier. Don't worry, none of the rooms will be as difficult as this one."

She placed her hand on the doorknob. "Brace yourselves. We're about to enter . . . the toy room."

Chapter Twenty-eight

IN the octagon creep show toy room, the kamikaze kittens went berserk.

Caramello hissed, hopped into the doll carriage, and bounced out, as if she'd been thrown.

The scent of candy apples wafted in as Warlock circled the wooden soldiers like a Halloween cat, black back arched and ready for battle. He charged and hit a soldier in the chest. It toppled like a bowling pin and took out the entire regiment in an artistic butterfly-wing domino effect.

The room rained bayonets. The girls screamed and the cats howled, but no splinters were reported.

Gingertigger launched herself to the top of the jack-in-the-box, but the music started, and the lid popped open, so Harmony's mewling kitten slid gracefully to the floor.

While Harmony used a broom to sweep away evil, Destiny distributed and lit black candles, and Storm sprinkled salt and herbs around the perimeters of the room. While they prepared their cleansing ritual, the cats hissed, charged, and assaulted every toy. Caramello rode the rocking horse, Warlock the tricycle.

Sometimes the toys went flying. Sometimes, the cats flew.

After Harmony performed the water blessing, she lit a smudge stick and held it as they circled the room, the three of them chanting.

> *"Mother Goddess, hear our prayer.*
> *With earth, fire, water, and air,*
> *Amethyst crystals bright and rare,*
> *Candles black and incense flare,*
> *The power of three as one declare*
> *All negative energy to beware.*
> *Finite peace this place ensnare.*
> *And it harm none; this will we bear.*
> *So mote it be, hear our prayer."*

By the third circle, the cats' hissing and bouncing slowed, and eventually they calmed and curled up together to sleep.

"We've done our job," Harmony said, "if there's nothing here to keep the psycho cats hopping."

"That was more exhausting than sex," Storm said.

"We've hardly started, though this is one of the darkest rooms. Next stop, the formal parlor."

In the parlor, her sisters sensed Gussie's lingering spirit, as Harmony had done, but they also sensed Paxton's return, so they slipped behind the small tapestry.

"Hellcat," Paxton said. "Thank God you're all right. Reggie said you saved their lives."

"She's exaggerating. I pushed a bed over to break her fall."

"Which was brilliant. Reggie thinks Gussie hates her and likes Jake."

"She's right. I sensed that Reggie would have broken her back if she hit that floor."

"What do you mean, you sensed?"

Damn, damn, damn. "I get a sense about things, like when you're coming around the corner, things like that."

"I sense that about you, too," he said. "It's called—"

"Passion?" she suggested to turn his thoughts.

"Too partner-focused, plus it requires a short-term commitment."

Harmony shook her head. "Big news. Lust then?"

"Too intimate. Scary intimate."

"Sex, then?"

"Okay. Where?"

"You're a horn dog letch."

"Stop it, you're turning me on." He focused on her shirt. "I'm a Witch with PMS. Any Questions? Part of me wants to run," he said, "but the part that's missed you—"

"Gotta go ghost-hunt." She waved him off. "Bye."

"You're killing me here."

"Better I should than the wailer."

King slipped his hands in his pockets. "Right. Bye."

Harmony got the telepathic message that her sisters had found a second door behind the tapestry and were exploring and circling back, so she went to the tunnel where she could concentrate on neutralizing Gussie and nobody could waylay or distract her.

By the time she returned to the parlor, she had to stop outside the door, because Storm had walked in on Aiden boxing the chandelier.

"Gonna pawn it for a jock strap?" Storm asked, and Harmony wilted against the wall.

"A witch with PMS?" Aiden said. "I have an awesome cure for PMS. Are you still up for that date?"

Harmony felt Storm's radar go up. "I'm up for a ride on your . . . Harley." She raised her arms and fluffed her wig to show off her breasts.

Harmony was gonna commit triplicide. Aiden thought *she* was coming on to him, slam it.

"What about you and King?"

Storm stilled and lowered her arms. *Now*, she remembered who she was supposed to be. "King and me?" Storm backed away. "King's got No Commitment engraved on his pecker."

Aiden raised a brow. "I'm not much better . . . at *commitments*, that is. Are you looking for companionship and a good . . . Harley ride, or a husband?"

"Oh, always a good . . . ride."

Harmony coughed.

"But I don't sleep around," Storm said, too fast to be sane.

"Since you're sharing King's 'Harley' these days," Aiden said. "I guess we'll have dinner but nothing more?"

"I . . . guess. Do you hear a baby crying?" Storm asked him.

Aiden frowned. "No."

Storm backed away from him to the opposite end of the large room and started back toward him. "Hey, the crying baby is loudest when I'm near you. Do you have children?"

Aiden barked a laugh. "Are you out of your mind?"

"Get rid of him," Harmony telepathically ordered, but Storm had turned and zeroed in on the full tapestried wall exuding Gussie's energy. "Can you get someone to take down that large tapestry and bring in a couple of spotlights to shine on the wall behind it? I need to take a better look."

Aiden taped the chandelier box closed. "There's nothing there."

"I think you're wrong. You restore antiques, right? Have a look. A hundred years of crud needs to come off, so we— so *I* can see what's beneath it."

"Really?" Aiden pulled the tapestry aside. "What do you think is back here? A crying baby?"

"No, but it's more than a wall."

"And you're more than a vintage clothing buyer." He winked. "I'll take care of it."

Harmony made sure Aiden was gone before she went in and cuffed her sister.

"Sorry," Storm said, rubbing her arm. "I was really attracted."

"Brutally so, and when the hell are you not?"

"This guy's a whole different brand of stud, in a weird, good, badass way. Being near him gave me snapshots of . . . I don't know; I couldn't identify the pictures, but I swear to the Oak King that I heard a baby crying."

"You'll forgive us if we don't hop to it every time you hear a baby cry," Harmony said. "Unless you think Aiden is maybe married?"

"No," Storm said. "That's not it. But I *was* right about Jake crying in the boat on the way here."

"Okay, I'll give you that one, but stop trying to hop on Aiden's 'Harley.' He thinks you're *me*."

Destiny joined them. "Way to pretend to be your lovesick sister, kid."

Harmony frowned. "I'm not lovesick."

Storm took exception as well. "I would have jump started the stud, if I was me."

"Big surprise." Harmony crossed her arms. "Let's do what we came to do, shall we? Concentrate on that wall."

Destiny touched her arm. "I just met Paxton in the hall. Yummers."

"Oh, oh. What happened?"

"He said I wasn't myself."

"I saw him, too," Storm said. "He looked puzzled."

"Did he try to cop a feel either time?"

"No, damn it," they said together.

"Oh joy. He suspects something. We're running out of time. He's on to us. Concentrate on the wall." Holding hands, they walked toward it, three by three, each focusing on the single place in the castle where a lively blaze of Gussie's spirit lingered.

While they did, their kittens played a hissing, head-butting, tumbling game with the tapestry and the wall itself.

She and her sisters formed a circle, but Harmony chanted alone.

> *"I received your past*
> *To bear in the present.*
> *Now open the door,*
> *That leads to the future.*
> *And it harm none; this is my will.*
> *So mote it be."*

She repeated the chant twice more before Storm broke the circle so they faced the wall, though they continued holding hands. "There's a painting," Storm said, "behind the tapestry, beneath the layers of premeditated grime."

Destiny nodded. "It's a story we need to know."

"Gussie's the painter. She was happy when she started," Harmony said, "and broken when she finished. You're right, Storm. She tried to cover it up."

"She *wants* us to see it, now," Destiny said. "And when we do, we'll understand."

Storm closed her eyes. "I'm sensing forgiveness, but I don't think it's from Gussie. Is there more than one ghost here?"

"Well, there's more than one of *something*," Aiden said, "or I'm hallucinating."

"Don't bet on it," King said.

The girls froze.

Chapter Twenty-nine

KING could hardly believe his eyes, yet he'd known *something* was up. The three of them looked identical . . . but not. There was a sameness yet a uniqueness about each, even from the back. Three dressed alike, in black statement shirts with orange lettering. PMS, indeed. A good ruse that would explain the little differences, should someone come upon the wrong . . . triplet? . . . unexpectedly. He'd nearly mistaken one, or two, of them for Harmony. Nearly. But not quite.

"I think we're having the same hallucination," Morgan said. "You three *act* like you know what you're doing, I'll give you that. I can't wait to see what's on that wall, if anything."

"I can't wait to see you side by side," Aiden said. And when they turned, he raised a victory fist in the air, and shouted, "Yes! I *wasn't* talking to Harmony most recently, was I? Which sassy witch was that?"

King saw the one in the middle wink.

"I admit," Morgan said, "that I thought Harmony was

one of the most beautiful women I'd ever met, and now I'm seeing triple, but I can't tell which one's Harmony. Bet you can't either, King."

"Oh, but I can."

Like Morgan, Aiden went for his wallet. "We're taking that bet."

King strolled over to Harmony, the one whose chin rose a notch higher, whose nipples pebbled when he got close, whose eyes revealed disbelief, whose lips parted in invitation. He looked her in the eye, hooked an arm around her waist, and kissed her senseless. Half a second into the kiss, she returned his enthusiasm, her fingers tangling in his hair. Definitely his. Well, not precisely *his*.

Morgan swore, and Aiden whistled.

King knew he should break the kiss, but he couldn't seem to get enough.

"Go, Daddy!" Reggie cheered.

And he'd had enough. King stepped away from Harmony while his daughter applauded. King's ears got hot, so he was sure they were beet red. One of Harmony's sisters gravitated to Aiden like a homing device.

"How long have you two been here?" King asked the newcomers.

"Hours," Destiny said. "We saw you trying to make out with our sister."

The discordant sound of music turned them to the piano. The kittens were dancing on and off the keys.

Morgan pulled aside the tapestry and palmed the wall. "You really think there's a mural behind the grime?"

"We do," Harmony said. "Aiden, Morgan, King, this is my sister Destiny, and the irreverent hussy is Storm. We're triplets."

"And you all think you're psychic," Morgan said.

"Takes one to know one," the three of them said together.

"You're psychic, besides being a witch?" King asked Harmony. "How does Morgan know?"

Harmony raised her brows. "How *does* Morgan know?"

Morgan stepped back. "From the way you were reading a painting that doesn't exist."

"Oh." Harmony sat on a sofa. "He's the debunker, Des."

"So *he* says."

Harmony looked from Morgan to Destiny and shrugged. "Whatever."

Jake held up three fingers. "Free."

"That means three," Reggie explained.

"Three of us, yes, and I already know that you can't say Harmony." She kissed Jake's hand. "But can you say Honey, instead?"

"I can say Honey."

It's settled then. "You can call me Honey."

"Free Honeys?"

"No, I'm Honey, that's Dessie, and that's Storm."

Jake nodded. "Honey, Dessie, and Strom."

"Figures," Storm said, picking him up. "You get the easy name wrong." She held him close and kissed his brow. "Say Storrrrrm."

"Strommm."

Storm held Jake tight for a minute, which didn't seem at all in character, King thought.

Two workers were taking down the tapestry. "Can we get those spotlights up?" Harmony asked. "Aiden, how long will it take you to clean the wall?"

"A couple of hours, maybe more. Depends on how dirty it is and what medium was used . . . in the event anyone painted anything."

"Gilda has supper ready," King said. "Let's eat first."

Harmony touched his hand. "We need a few minutes to change."

King watched them go. "How can you *not* tell them apart?" he asked his friends.

"I know what you mean," Aiden said, watching as well. "I know which one is Storm. She walks and flirts with sassitude."

"Which witch is the witch that starts with a *B*?" Morgan asked.

"Don't mix up the *B* witch and the *W* witch around them," King said. "You might find yourself growing a tail."

At supper, the triplet whose tight butterscotch V-neck tee said Destiny arrived first, wearing jeans and cowboy boots.

"What? No Spurs?" Morgan asked, before he ducked the pickle the cowgirl threw.

King was afraid the Storm triplet would scare Jake. She'd traded her blonde bombshell look for purple hair and lips, and a spiked dog collar. Her black spiderweb skirt made her look like a female vampire, and her boots probably came with a whip. But Aiden was beaming.

"Rev your engine?" Storm asked.

Aiden's eyes glazed over. "Vroom."

Last to the table, the hellcat arrived in peach spikes and matching tee with a gauzy rust orange skirt flowing around her legs, a tiger lily above her breasts and at each ear.

"Our father did this to us," Destiny said, opening her napkin. "He made us wear name shirts, at home, till we left for college."

"Irresponsible and clueless," Storm said. "We were trading shirts at Jake's age."

Harmony nodded. "It's Dad's fault we're hooked on literal statement shirts. I mean, we don't like these, but they have their uses."

"I've started *hoping* for messages," King admitted, "so call me a convert."

"Harmony," Storm chided. "Did you wear the *O* donor shirt?"

"She did." Aiden's appreciation annoyed King.

Aiden winked at Storm. "I gotta go start that wall." But he didn't move, probably because she didn't.

"What's with the gigundous boxes in the great hall?" Harmony asked, offering King the potatoes.

"Clothes, toddler furniture, supplies, mattresses. We're converting the dorm wing into bedrooms. The adults will use the furniture we've got."

"But it has negative energy." Harmony sighed and looked at her sisters. "We have some neutralizing to do. My sisters are staying for a few days. We have enough cots."

"We're filling up the dorm by the minute," Reggie said.

Harmony looked up, her fork halfway to her mouth. "Why? Who else is staying?"

"Aiden and I," Morgan said. "King asked us to stick around, roll up our sleeves, and move furniture."

"Yummy," Storm said. "A coed sleepover."

Reggie cleared her throat. "Yoo-hoo. Two-year-old in the dorm."

"Bummer," Storm said.

Aiden gave Storm a wink. "Keep me company while I clean the wall?"

"I'm outta here." Storm followed Aiden from the kitchen.

"I'm gonna get Jake ready for bed," Reggie said, "so by the time anybody comes up, he'll be asleep."

"We'll try to be quiet," King hefted Jake in his arms for a good night hug. "Night, sport. I'm sorry, Regg, I should have finished your room today."

"We've never had a room of our own. Jake won't wake up, he—no we—grew up in shelters, people coming and going all night, sometimes drunk. I sleep with one eye open, but nothing wakes him. Night," she said as she left.

King sat and felt the weight of her suffering. His fault. All his fault.

"I'm gonna watch Aiden do the wall," Destiny said. "We'll need you in a little while, Sis."

King gazed at Harmony.

Morgan scraped his chair back. "Three's a crowd, so I'm . . . like you care."

"Be there in a minute," Harmony said.

King wanted to take her for a stroll through the parlor car, but he needed some questions answered. "Why are your sisters really staying?"

"To neutralize the negative energy in the rooms and furniture. Not much around here is positive."

"I'm *positive* I want you in a bed."

"For the record, I'm . . . open . . . to the possibility. But our wailing resident is seriously scary. The cats went berserk in the toy room today. I need my sisters for backup."

"What does that mean?"

"Together, we combine our magick and harness our psychic energy. Together, we become the power of three as one. Together, we're powerful witches."

Chapter Thirty

HARMONY didn't have time to calm King, no matter how much the power of three unnerved him. "I have to go," she said. "My sisters and I need to interpret the message in that mural . . . together. We sense the mural's there for a reason."

"Are all witches psychic?" King asked. "Or are you unusual in that you're psychics in addition to being witches?"

"The two often go together. Don't tell me; you don't believe in psychics any more than you believe in witches or ghosts, right?"

"I believe you brought something frightening to life in this place."

"You narrow-minded son of a . . . witch."

"You've got my mother down perfectly," King said.

"I was talking about Gussie. You can't seriously blame me for her?"

"I can blame you for bringing her out of hiding."

"Excuse me, *I* shut her up. She's probably less malevolent

now than she's been in years, because I'm here. And she's more constrained now that my sisters are here."

"Then explain what happened to Reggie. That never happened before."

"Reggie's never been here before. Morgan said accidents always happen around you. They also happen around your daughter. And Gussie's been wailing for a century around the Paxtons. You can't blame me for that."

"Yet, what a coincidence. You come here for vintage clothes and end up taking care of our ghost . . . You want to tell me what's really going on?"

"It's . . . complicated."

"I'm listening." King sat beside her, took her hand, and rubbed his thumb over the Celtic ring. "I usually say 'it's complicated' to a woman looking for a commitment. It's called evasion. So, you want to tell me why my ghost shuts up when you show up, plus you're wearing a ring my grandfather described as one Nicodemus brought home from one of his seafaring jaunts?"

More than anything, Harmony wanted to lay her head on King's shoulder and hear him say he *believed* in her. She was glad he'd picked her out of the clone line. "I'm sure there are thousands of rings like this in the world."

King kissed the back of her hand. "I'm waiting."

"Okay. I found the ring in the hem of a gown I bought at a yard sale. When I put it on, I saw this castle in my mind, so I came here, and that's the truth. I think the gown and ring belonged to someone who lived here."

"Maybe the other half of the ring was in the sleeve?"

"Stop baiting me and tell me what you know about the ring."

"I like baiting you. When you get mad, your shoulders go back so your breasts pop out and call my name."

"Always thinking with your man brain."

"So what if you pictured this place? Why did you come?"

"When I put the ring on, I saw the castle in discord, and I fainted. I know you're gonna think this is nuts, but I saw coming here as a psychic mandate from the universe, as if there was something here that only I could fix. Though everyone in Salem knew the place was haunted by a witch . . . except you . . . I came the following day."

King touched her brow with the back of his hand. "I don't like that you fainted. Are you okay?"

"The darkness sucked me in. I'm fine . . . Tell me about the ring."

He played with her ring. "Nicodemus brought Gussie gifts when he came home from the sea. When he brought the ring, she'd peeked, and expected it, but he didn't give it to her. She was never the same."

Harmony sighed. "Which is why she wants vindication."

"Vindication? That has all kinds of meanings, and how do you know that's what she wants?"

"She told me . . ." Harmony read King's blatant disbelief. "I was wondering what she wanted, and the word came to me, as if she said it, with her icy breath on my neck."

King sat straighter. "Is she the reason for the sudden freezes around here?"

Harmony nodded. "You get cold when she shows, because she's stealing your energy and body heat. You felt her long before I got here, didn't you? Admit it."

"Hell," he said, running a hand through his hair. "I felt her when I was a kid, but nothing bad happened. As a matter of fact, I had some close calls. I almost drowned once, and I'd swear someone colder than the sea brought me to the surface."

"Like she saved Jake today. When did your accidents start?"

"After college."

"When you were a man like Nicodemus. Gussie likes children but not men."

"Or young women," King observed.

"Because a young woman likely got the other half of the ring."

King sat back in his chair. "That actually makes sense."

"Thanks for the vote of confidence."

"I wonder whose half you have." He lifted her hand and placed it against his face.

"Don't try making up now." Harmony reclaimed her hand. "I have the half that belonged to Lisette, the girl he gave it to."

"Lisette? You know that because . . . you sensed it?"

"Wearing the gown, Lisette's name came to me, and I envisioned her sewing something in the hem. I checked and found the ring." Harmony thought about that for a minute. "Maybe Lisette sent me here. If Gussie was upset with her, those empty picture frames might have held pictures of Lisette. I need to tell my sisters. I'll be in the parlor."

Her sisters were watching Aiden clean the wall. "Is he using a toothbrush?" Harmony asked.

Destiny shook her head. "It's *smaller* than a toothbrush." She crossed her arms. "He *says* he's an artist."

"Will somebody, *please*, get this artist a scrub brush?" Storm called from beside him.

Destiny and Harmony looked at each other and grinned.

"I see something!" Storm said. "Harm, Des, come here."

"Aren't you standing in the artist's light?" Destiny asked her.

"No," Aiden said. "She's fine. You know, I think this *is* a mural."

"No kidding, Rembrandt." Storm tried to spike his hair, but Aiden didn't seem to mind.

Harmony touched the colors on the clean bottom corner. "What makes you think it's a mural and not a regular painting?"

"The paint strokes I've uncovered so far are pretty damned big. Might take up the whole wall, which means you may as well go to bed. "I'll be at this all night."

Storm finger-wiped a spot on his cheek. "I'll stay up and help."

"She stays," Destiny said, "and the wall won't be what gets done."

"Bitch!" Storm snapped, and Aiden chuckled.

Destiny shook her head. "I'm off to bed. Coming, Sis?"

Harmony turned to go, but King leaned against a door-jamb, arms crossed, an aura of male need about him. His long frame was invested with tension, his square chin high, the light in his whiskey eyes hot, hungry, and provocative. "I'll be up later," she said.

Storm hooted, and Destiny shook her head. "Sisters!"

As Harmony closed in on King, he unfolded like a lazy panther sighting prey. She cupped his cheek, and he placed his hand over hers and slid it to the back of his neck as he brought their lips together.

"Ahem! You're not alone," Storm called.

"Train shed?" Harmony whispered low and throaty. "Chugga chugga."

"We're being spontaneous, now, right?"

"King, if you announce spontaneity, it's boring."

"Hey, no woman has ever called me boring."

"You had sex with women in comas."

"You've cured me. Or ruined me."

She took him by the hand. A few minutes later, they were about to cut through the toy room. "Hold on, McBullseye."

"I know. My ass is throbbing."

"Just your ass? How disappointing."

"Don't give me any sass." He led the way to the train shed. "The toy room didn't seem bad tonight."

"Duh. Because we cleansed it today. It's full of positive energy now. Witches are good for something."

"I can think of several delightful things."

The brightly lit train shed housed an amazingly well-preserved steam engine, its wheels as tall as her. The engine and parlor car capped a hill, each car balanced on opposing downward slopes, its track curved like a horse-shoe that ran beneath giant doors at each end. "This is ingenious," Harmony said.

"You think the train's amazing, wait till *I* get going!" He climbed on the engine and rang the bell. "It was a dark and stormy night," he whispered as he pulled her up and into his arms.

"The storm does lend our clandestine meeting a certain panache, but I'm still mad at you. I did not set Gussie loose."

"I apologize. I'm spooked after what happened to Reggie."

"You're a good dad."

"Sure am, for a whole day and a half now."

"Let's leave the guilt and regrets behind. Show me the parlor car."

"Not before you take a tour of the engine."

"This is not the engine I'm interested in."

"How many people can say they got laid in a Boston & Lowell steam engine?"

"Well," Harmony said, raising his shirt, "when you put it that way . . ." She kissed the line of hair from his navel to his zipper.

"Come here, Hellcat." King pulled her face up to his. "Open your mouth and show me a witch's passion to match a devil's desire."

Chapter Thirty-one

HARMONY gave the devil a run for his arousal, her every nerve ending near the surface. He turned her to liquid with nothing but the tremor beneath his fingertips. They drank from each other's lips, hungry, greedy.

King traced the shape of her breasts beneath her shirt, above her bra, then he moved his hands for a slow, tantalizing ramble down her belly, and lower still, until he knelt and slid both hands up her legs beneath her skirt.

Harmony closed her eyes. "Yes, there," she whispered, and she shuddered at his touch.

He stood, insinuating his leg between hers, pulled her against his heavy arousal, and she rode it, nothing between them but his zipper, her skirt, and a roaring of heat.

He pulled off her shirt and unhooked her tangerine bra. Her chilled breasts pebbled and ached as he kissed his way to a taut peak, nudging her charm bag aside. He took a nipple into his mouth, and pleasure radiated through her like sun rays on a summer day. She anticipated milking his cock the way he milked her lips, and she welcomed his greed with a spiraling of pleasure.

King raised his head to study her, his sex-drugged expression going from surprise to caution. "Lust," he said. "This is lust, right?"

"Oh, yeah."

Against the engine controls, he undid her skirt so a pillow of orange silk pooled at her feet. The air chilled the dampness on her panties as he knelt and shocked her by kissing that very spot. Her panties were gone in a blink, and King unfolded her to his gaze, tasting, licking, then working her with his tongue until she begged him to stop and begged for more.

He held her so she wouldn't fall when she came, and did it again. The man had a tongue that deserved an attendance award. He suckled and licked her until she flew from her body and met the moon.

When she thought she might pass out, he slid up her bikinis, hooked her bra, got her down from the engine, and carried her to the parlor car.

She came out of her sexual haze when she saw that the dimly lit car had a bedroom with a four-poster dressed in bronze fringe and silk.

"Before you say a word. It's a new mattress with the works."

"You set me up? You seducer, you. You purchased that mattress with wicked intent."

"And aren't you deliriously happy about it?"

She rested her head against his chest and toyed with his breast pocket. "Why did I think I was seducing you?"

"On the outside, you were. On the inside . . ." He shrugged. "Wait till your skin touches those silk sheets."

"How long have you been playing me?"

"Playing? Or playing?"

Harmony gave up the fight. She'd been reading his

mind and playing to his fantasies, so she guessed they were even. "Never mind the sheets. Wait till my skin touches yours."

His eyes twinkled. "I'm more than willing to give a skin-to-skin experiment the old scientific try."

"Do you like the danger of getting caught?"

"No. I hated getting caught in the cavern. No, Sunshine. It's the bod. Yours. There isn't another that gets me so hot." He set her down on the bed.

She jumped up. "Excuse me, but there are two bods *exactly* like mine."

King's head came up, alert, assessing, his brow furrowed. "I must be talking about the heart inside. Go figure. Never thought I'd recognize one."

"Wha'd'ya know? The man's got taste."

He winked. "Let me taste some more."

"Not yet," she said, evading his grasp, spooked by his addiction to her three-of-a-kind body. "Let's make it last. Let me play you a song."

"Music isn't what I'm in the mood for."

Wearing only the tangerine bra and bikinis, she sat on the piano bench to play and sing "King of the Road." She felt pretty much in control until King sat behind her and trapped her between his legs.

"Keep singing," he whispered as his arms came around her, and he slipped a hand inside the front of her bikinis. "This is for you, Harmony. Nobody but you."

She tried to continue singing and playing, but her fingers moved slower on the keys as her climax neared, and the lyrics disconnected from her brain. "Midnight train . . . third boxcar fifty cents . . . king of the—" She turned into his arms as she came, and she kissed him with the power of her climax.

He let her rest while he stroked that shivery spot at the base of her spine. "Ready for bed?" he asked against her brow.

Need purled through her. No man had ever worked so tirelessly for her pleasure. She slid a hand into his slacks, his eyes changing from whiskey, to honey, to caramel stirred by desire. "I'm hungry," she said.

King groaned and laughed at the same time.

She savored the sound and went for his mouth, upper lip to lower, lower to upper, until he swept her from the piano bench, and anticipation, like a wash of healing crystals, twinkled and spiraled through her. He put her on the bed, his clothes gone in a blink. Hers went faster.

King rose over her, hard against soft, thick probing muscle against willing flesh, pulsing warm, a mating dance on silk, a new sensual high. Sex with King in a bed, at last. "The ceiling is clear," she said.

"Observation dome."

"Too bad we can't see the stars."

Chuckling, he began an erotic journey with his lips, beginning at her nape and working his way down, her senses swimming with mindless pleasure. She needed more from King than from any other man, and when she realized it, she tried to keep the need from overwhelming her. "Come inside me."

He nipped at a breast, teased it with his tongue, and suckled her, and she came again, shocking them both.

"Scream your pleasure, Hellcat. I wanna hear you sing some more."

He looked proud of his power as he teased her inner thigh, but she grabbed his shoulders and brought his to face hers. "If you don't pluck me this blooming minute—"

He surged and filled her, stretching, invading, satisfying. Oh, good Goddess, the satisfaction. She raised herself to meet him, sighed, moaned, and sang her pleasure— "Alleluia!"—and wrapped her legs around him to keep him there. "Hard," she said. "I want it hard."

She came several roaring times as he rode her, her

ecstasy blending into throaty, incoherent sounds of gratitude and appreciation.

"I can't get enough," he said. "This is crazy, but I can't . . . get . . . enough!"

Feeling victorious, she watched him struggle to stay the course, but he lost the fight, and she rode his shuddering climax with him, one last amazing time, the stars flying about them, piercing and icy-hot.

Sated, satisfied, and elated, she kissed him wherever she could reach, his chest, his man nips, and finally his lips. She made love to his mouth, saddened by her all-consuming need for a man who could never be hers.

Despite her sorrow, she smiled at his attempts to get her beneath the covers. Once there, he entwined them like two halves of a Celtic puzzle ring.

"You were wonderful," she said, floating in a sleepy haze, sated, and drifting . . . drifting . . .

As if a rug had been pulled out from under her, she opened her eyes. "Are we moving?"

"Not possible." He pulled her close.

"King, we're rolling."

"Nope," he said. "Teams of men have tried to move these cars. They won't budge." He closed his eyes.

"We're buckled to the engine, right, to balance them on the opposing slopes?"

"Not necessary."

"Gussie gets her energy from the sea, especially during storms like this."

King opened his eyes. "Are we moving?"

"Dumb ass!"

She shoved him aside to get up, but the car hit something solid and threw her back on the bed. They lurched as wood splintered around them.

"We're breaking through the door," King said, climbing on top of her.

"Get off!" She shoved at him. "This is no time to get frisky!"

"I'm *protecting* you!"

Protection. Good idea. Harmony wove a protective sphere of bright white light around them, just before the bedposts snapped. The lace canopy fell, trapping them like flies in a spiderweb. Then the parlor car buckled, and the observation dome met the floor, pinning them in place—like flies under glass. Glass that didn't break?

"Oomph." Harmony fought for breath. "King, you're putting too much weight on me."

"The dome's wearing my ass print. We're meat in a dome-and-mattress sandwich, Sunshine."

"I can't believe the glass didn't break," she said.

"Strong," he said in her ear, "forerunner to the glass used in airplane windshields."

"Great." Raindrops hit the dome as lightning lit the sky. "We're halfway out the shed door, but we seem to be stuck," she said.

"Can you see the damn stars now?" he snapped, but the moon shone in blessing and reassured her, until the shed door collapsed on top of them, like a coffin lid sealing them in darkness. She prayed:

> *"Neath the blessing moon,*
> *Goddess protect us, rain anoint us.*
> *Lightning shine our way.*
> *Charged air, fill our lungs.*
> *Earth, bind our wheels.*
> *Harm it none; hear my plea.*
> *The is my will. So mote it be."*

"It's okay," King said. "Don't be afraid. We're not gonna run off a cliff. This is a sandy beach, and we're bound to run out of track soon."

"Thank the Goddess."

"Is it high tide or low?" he asked.

"What?" Harmony felt stupid, dazed, and confused by the question.

"The track runs—ran—where the land met Marblehead. I'm sure the track that got flooded must be gone by now, but . . ."

Harmony tamped down her panic and called on her beliefs. "Ground yourself, King. Picture your feet in the sand, throwing roots deep into the earth. Don't let go of the vision. Your roots will keep you in place, and your nervous energy will flow into them and strengthen them."

"I'd eat a rubber chicken if it would stop this car."

"That's not belief," Harmony snapped, "and desperation won't help." Their slow downhill roll seemed to come to a quiet end with little more than a shuffle of debris inside the car, but something pushed them backwards, hard, and the car teetered precariously, tilting almost on its side. "If we flipped like a pancake," Harmony said, "we'd be able to get out from under the mattress."

"And the box spring and bed frame, *if* we don't break all our bones or drown."

"Positive!" she snapped. "Speak and think positive!"

"This is no time to get hysterical."

She grabbed him by the skin of his nonexistent collar and pulled his face to hers. "This may be our *last* chance to get hysterical."

"Ow! Ouch! Sunshine, you're digging your nails into my shoulder."

She let go, and calmed. The car stopped moving. Her heart pounded in her ears. King's heart pummeled her chest. "We're safe," she said, but the car began to rock almost immediately. It listed from side to side and lurched forward with a bounce.

"Oh joy!" King said, being positive in a mocking way. "It *is* high tide. The ocean's trying to suck us in."

Chapter Thirty-two

KING took steady breaths while the sea rocked them in that car like a maniac mother trying to shove pillows over their faces. Okay, he was losing it. He'd told Harmony not to be hysterical, but he was scared to death.

He calmed before he spoke. "Any other witchy ideas to get us out?"

"Sure, I'll use the cell phone in my skin pocket. Oh no, I can't. There's no signal on this freaking island." She shrieked fit to bust his eardrum. "Wait. I *can* call my sisters!"

"Don't go bonkers on me. I'd rather die with a sane woman."

"King, if we die," she said, frighteningly sane all of a sudden, "let's come back in our next life together, okay? We have unfinished business."

She *was* losing it. "Okay," he said. "It's a date." He kissed her brow. "I wouldn't want to be in this spot with anyone else."

"I feel the same way about you."

This was more emotion than he liked. "About calling your sisters," he said. "I don't think it'll work. The castle's made of granite."

"I already called them. We have a triplet-to-triplet telepathic communication system. They're on their way."

"Great guns, she'd *already* lost it." She didn't even realize that the sea was sucking them farther into its depths.

At the sound of voices, King looked up and hit his head on the dome.

Men shouted orders. Women screamed and wept.

"Told you. My panic woke Des before I called. Storm and Aiden heard the crash, but it took them a while to find the source. They went for the gardeners and were almost back when I connected with Des. My sisters are crying because they're relieved we're safe."

"I won't feel safe until we're out of here."

"Positive. Stay positive."

"As positive as dying and reincarnating together? Right. Sorry. I'm the strong one. We're safe."

Harmony huffed. "Strong and humble. But, King, we're about to get caught with our pants down, so that macho thing's about to drown without us. It's going down to the sea in ships . . . with your tight-ass rep."

"Ah," King said. "Something to live for."

The sea carried them on a huge, rocking surge, and the men's shouts became frantic.

"Are we floating?" Harmony asked.

"No," King said, watching water bubble into the car along the breaks in the floor. "We're sinking."

"King? You should know that sex was never as good as it was with you."

His panic receded. "You never do say the expected thing. It was the best sex I ever had, too, and I've never said those words before."

"High praise." She kissed him, and for his part, if he was

going down with the parlor car, he wanted to go kissing Harmony.

The car rattled like when it crashed through the door, but it also heaved, groaned, and moved. Really moved. *Not* toward the sea, but away from it. "Thank God," King said.

"We're okay," Harmony said. "They're using pulleys and winches—is winch a word?—from the construction site to pull us from the water."

"You got that from your sisters?"

"Des is trying to reassure me, keep me calm, but she's giggling, so be ready for some teasing."

He met her brow with his. "Great."

Harmony started laughing, low at first, then with unbridled humor, until she could hardly breathe, and damned if it wasn't contagious. A woman who could laugh at herself and make him laugh at himself . . . What kind of magick would she pull from her bag of tricks next?

While their rescuers pulled the parlor car wreck up the beach, the shed door slid off, and King felt as if his casket had been rescued from its vault. "Spotlights on the world," he said. "I hope there's a blanket over my ass."

"Do you feel a breeze?"

"Nope, my butt's still kissing the dome."

"Hey, the storm's over."

"In more ways than one. When we get out of this, can you do something about Gussie? I don't care how drastic. She's gotta go."

Harmony sighed. "That saves an argument. Glad I'm gonna live to appreciate it."

"See any of our rescuers?"

Harmony stretched to peek beyond the side of his head. "Pretend . . . you're a fish in an aquarium."

He groaned. "Who's peering in at us?"

"Everybody. The gardeners, Gilda and her husband. They're waving, and they appear to be able to see us quite clearly."

"How can you tell?"

"They're all grinning. Did you *ever* see Gilda's husband grin before?"

"Never." King groaned again.

"Storm has her *snout* pressed to the glass like a Peeping Tom porker."

"I heard that!"

"Then get us the hell out of here," Harmony snapped.

"Ouch!" King felt a lessening of pressure and a fresh breeze. "I take it the dome's coming off?"

"Inch by inch," Harmony said. "Why? Did it hurt?"

"Only when it ripped my butt bandage off."

Harmony snickered. "Thanks for climbing on top to protect me. Bet you never thought you'd get rescued sunny-side up."

King gazed into her eyes. "I think I have the shape of you imprinted on my ha . . . happy man brain." He'd nearly said *heart*. Must be a near-death thing. "Feels good to lift and turn my head," he said. "Hey, I can flex my ass cheeks again . . . in public, of course, kind of like living my worst nightmare."

"*We're* living the nightmare," his curvaceous mattress said, "but in my version, we die. Suck it up, McBulls-eye, and thank the stars you're here to be humiliated."

The dome fell to the sand beside them. More spotlights went on.

Their rescuers applauded.

"Way to go!" Storm yelled. "You nearly fucked yourselves to death."

Chapter Thirty-three

"AND you think I have a smart mouth," Harmony said. "But look at the bright side. At least there's no Live at Five news crew here."

"We need blankets," King called, and several landed on them as their rescuers' laughter receded.

"Are they gone?" Harmony asked.

"Yeah, they're going in through the train shed."

"Thank the Goddess." Together she and King removed the lace canopy and bedposts. "I gotta stretch in the worst way," Harmony said, getting up. "Oh, ouch, everything aches."

King arched and rubbed his ass. "I've really been taking a licking."

"But you keep on ticking."

King hooked her around the waist and brought her naked body against his. "Got any energy left?"

"Are you kidding me?"

He groaned. "Not *that* kind of energy. I want the mattress and box spring in the Dumpster. Less explaining when the crew fixes the shed door."

"They'll *see* the mattress in there."

"Won't matter. Tomorrow, we're throwing out a dozen mattresses." King shrugged. "So we started early."

"You actually think our rescuers will keep their mouths shut?"

"They'll razz the hell out of us, but I don't think any of them will tell the crew."

"Can I tell you how much I don't want to remove the evidence right now?"

He kissed her brow. "Better than drowning, right?"

They got back to the dorm an hour later, everyone but Aiden and Storm asleep. Tiptoeing around in the dark, they took turns in the bathroom and climbed into their respective beds.

"I figured you went to the tower," Morgan said into the darkness. "I kept waiting for you to fall through the ceiling."

"They don't go looking for kinky," Destiny said. "It just finds them."

Harmony gasped. "Des!"

"They're just jealous," King said.

"I'm really, really glad my son sleeps soundly," Reggie said.

"Oh God," King said. "My daughter heard that."

"Don't worry," Des said, "nobody told her what happened."

Reggie scoffed. "I can guess."

"Not in a million years!" Morgan chuckled, and that was the closest Harmony had come to liking him.

Reggie sighed theatrically. "I imagined my dad would be a pipe and slippers kind of guy, but what do I get? A new millennium stud puppy. I'm so glad Jake is a sound sleeper."

"Me, too, sweetheart. At dawn, we start giving everybody their own rooms."

"It's already dawn," Morgan said.

King cleared his throat. "At noon, we start giving every-body their own rooms."

Storm woke Harmony at nine. "The mural's done. Wait till you see."

Harmony turned to King's cot, but he was gone. She'd slept later than anyone. Great.

When she got to the parlor, she saw that the mural itself did, indeed, fill the entire wall. Storm was sprinkling salt and protective herbs in front of it.

Destiny stood back, examining it, while Gingertigger and Caramello paced the length of it like guard soldiers, stopping to hiss or charge the mural, only to bounce off and charge, pace, and hiss again.

Tigerstar stood in front of the Queen Anne chair with her back arched. Warlock used the same stance beside the piano.

Before long, Aiden, King, and her sisters gathered round in earnest, as if they'd waited for her. She and her sisters clasped hands. "It's bizarre," Harmony said. "Un-even."

Aiden nodded. "From its condition and the types of paint and tints used, I think it was painted over a period of ten or twelve years. The brushstrokes reveal time-lapse in-consistencies, including a growing unsteadiness that would indicate the painter's aging hand."

King walked to the far end. "I don't see a signature."

Harmony swept the mural with her gaze. "At first sight, I'd say the signature runs horizontally along the bottom. The way the mural is sectioned off vertically in different colors and shades reveals the painter's mood, right? The colors also mimic the mood of the dolphins at the bottom of each respective section.

"Bright colors equal laughing, playing dolphins in a bright sea. Dark colors equal dolphins beneath a gray sea. Oh, and look at the end. One lone, beached dolphin. Who died alone here? Gussie? Who collected dolphins? Gussie. The dolphins are her signature."

"Look at that last section above the beached dolphin," Storm said.

Harmony shivered. "A young woman, Lisette, stepping into the sea . . . wearing the gown I bought at the yard sale, proof I came to the right place."

Destiny nodded. "Let's concentrate on reading the mural from the beginning so we don't jump to any conclusions."

Reggie came in with Jake by the hand and sat on the sofa facing the wall. "Can we watch?" she asked.

"Of course," Harmony said.

Reggie put toys on the floor at her feet, and Jake sat down to play.

Harmony got the warm fuzzies again when she turned to King, who was watching Jake. "King, since you were born here, will you hold my hand? As a psychometric, I'll get as much knowledge from touching you, through your connection to the castle, as from the painting."

King squeezed her hand, which she found reassuring. "The first section, in pastel colors," she said, "portrays a child asleep on the beach, and below, two happy dolphins are swimming in a pastel sea."

"The child's not asleep," Destiny said. "She's half-drowned."

"She washed ashore in a storm." Storm elbowed Aiden. "Funny how well I can read storms."

"She washed ashore here," King said. "That's the island beach. I recognize the outcropping of rocks in the distance."

"Good. We've nailed the location. The girl, a little older, is playing in a nonthreatening toy room with a doll carriage. She's part of a happy family, I'm assuming, since the section is painted in bright colors."

Brahms's "Lullaby" began playing on the piano, the keys moving with no one playing. Harmony hadn't mentioned the phenomenon, nor that she suspected it meant they were getting close to the truth.

Warlock backed away from the piano, while Caramello and Gingertigger ran over to flank him, as if he might need reinforcements.

Tigerstar left the Queen Anne chair to curl up beside Jake, but the boy looked up. "The lady's crying," he said.

The music stopped, and Reggie took Jake on her lap. "What lady, baby? Tell Mama."

"The lady in the chair."

Whoa, Harmony thought.

King took Jake and brought him to the chair. "You're not afraid of her?"

Jake smiled at the chair. "She's nice, but sad and cold." He turned to his mother. "Can we get her a blanket, like we got at a shelter once?"

"Sure, baby," Reggie said.

King swallowed. "Tell Grampa what the lady looks like."

Jake smiled. "*You* know." He pointed to the Queen Anne chair. "See, she's got a purple dress with stars on her neck and ears, and a fish like those"—he pointed to the mural—"on her dress."

Harmony bit her lip. *Gussie.* Jake saw Gussie. Young children saw ghosts because they hadn't been trained yet not to. Harmony hadn't expected the confirmation. But if Gussie sat in the chair, who was playing . . . "Jake, do you see anyone sitting at the piano over there?"

He giggled when he looked. "Silly Honey. There's nobody there."

"Yep, silly me."

King brought him back to Reggie, and Harmony turned to her sisters. "I saw and heard the piano when I sensed the wall was significant. What do you think it means?"

"Lisette's here," Storm said. "In the present."

"You think she was playing the piano just now?"

"Absolutely."

"I think the music is some kind of sign," Destiny said. "It's telling us that what we're doing is significant. Let's get back to reading the mural to see what else we can learn."

"Right," Harmony said. "Okay. A mother and baby dolphin in a bright section are playing beside a ship in full sail, and a man on deck is waving to them."

Destiny scanned the painting. "That theme is repeated often. He's sailing away in almost every section."

"That would be Gussie's husband, Nicodemus," King said. "He captained his own ships and spent years at sea."

"Notice how the colors stay bright until the girl's grown up." Storm indicated the section she referred to. "The color dims where the captain is on shore, leaning on his cane, watching Lisette as a beautiful young woman. His expression is painted to look . . . ominous."

"Nicodemus gave half of the Celtic puzzle ring to Lisette," Harmony said. "So his interest in her would appear ominous to Gussie."

"Neither the colors nor the dolphins are happy there," King said. "What do you think, Aiden?"

"I think this could be a happy home again if somebody put some heart into it."

King raised a brow. "I was asking your opinion of the painting."

Aiden gave his friend a no loss/no gain shrug. "The brushstrokes are bolder there than anywhere in the painting. The painter was most likely upset or agitated when he or she painted that section."

"You know what else is repeated often?" Destiny said. "The round mirror with the dolphin finial. It can't have been in every room of the house, yet that's how it's portrayed."

Storm nodded and grinned. "It has to be her scrying mirror, which means the mural itself could be some kind of spell."

"Not possible," Destiny said.

"You're both right." Harmony touched a depiction of the mirror and closed her eyes. When she opened them, she smiled. "What your scrying mirror shows you, mine may not show me, right? Gussie is showing us that this is her vision."

The piano played the lullaby again.

"Another point for our side," Storm said. "And another piece of the puzzle solved."

"Great call, Harmony," Destiny said. "Must be why you're the oldest."

Harmony traced a sepia-toned close-up cameo of the ring's embracing couple. Near it, Nicodemus is sailing away beneath a hovering angel and a lightning bolt. She turned to King. "How did Nicodemus die?"

"At sea, in a thunderstorm, as you already suspect."

"One powerful witch," Storm said.

Chapter Thirty-four

HARMONY hoped with all her heart that reading the mural correctly would help bring peace to the castle.

"If Gussie loved Lisette and Nicodemus," Storm said, "their treachery probably hurt her deeply."

"*If* Lisette and Nicodemus *were* treacherous." Destiny got that familiar faraway look they knew so well. "Maybe Gussie only *thought* they were treacherous. She's known to have caused discord—still does. Someone who's naturally negative and devious expects others to be that way. Suppose her assumptions about Lisette and Nicodemus were wrong. She was obviously paranoid."

"Des is the Pollyanna in the family," Storm told King and Aiden.

"Suppose Lisette and Nicodemus had nothing more than a father/daughter relationship," Destiny said. "King, you and Reggie had a lot of catching up to do when she got here, right? Maybe Lisette and Nicodemus liked to catch up after his voyages, but Gussie didn't like them getting along. Sound familiar?"

"Keep talking," Harmony said.

"Okay, I will. Suppose Nicodemus and Lisette . . . escaped . . . Gussie's watchful eye to catch up and keep her from coming between them. We *know* a family who pretends they don't talk to each other so the instigator can't come between them. They go camping together, take care of each other's kids, and as long as the argument-causing matriarch doesn't know, they get along fine. If the matriarch knows, she causes a rift between them."

"You think Gussie suspected a romance where none existed?"

"I do, and my instincts are strong on this." Destiny went to stroke the figure of Lisette wearing the gown. "I think King and Reggie remind Gussie of Nicodemus and Lisette."

Storm shook her head. "That would make more sense if King had nearly died *alone* last night—"

"Daddy, you nearly died last night?"

"It's okay, kitten," King said, putting an arm around Reggie's shoulder. "I'm okay."

"Sorry," Storm said. "My point is that Harmony nearly died, too."

"Here's a wild thought," Destiny said. "King and Harmony were nearly sent to sea . . . where Nicodemus died, where Lisette started her journey to Salem. Gussie, I believe we've established, was mentally ill. If Gussie loved dolphins, she loved the sea, so sending people to the sea could have been her way of bringing them peace."

The piano played again, loud and with feeling.

Storm shook her head. "I don't know, Des. I think Gussie's screwing with your brain. I think she killed them."

"Do you see her killing anyone in this mural?" Destiny asked.

Storm smacked the mural. "I see angels hovering over the people who died."

"But Lisette *didn't* die," Destiny said. "She made it to Salem, or Harmony wouldn't have found her gown. Gussie only *assumed* she died."

Harmony's head went up, and she joined her sisters beside the last and darkest section of the mural. "The gown found *me*. Maybe Lisette led me to it, so I'd find the ring and come here."

"That's my point." Destiny turned to include everyone. "A beached dolphin is a dying dolphin. Losing Nicodemus and Lisette broke Gussie's heart."

Storm scoffed. "Or losing the ring broke her heart. Lisette sewed it into the gown's hem, don't forget."

"Because it was her last gift from her father," Harmony said. "He died before she stepped in the sea. Lisette was left alone with a mentally ill woman who believed Lisette betrayed her. She might have loved Gussie, but she knew she wasn't safe staying with her."

The lullaby played again, with emotion. Harmony thought they might have gotten it right. "I'll be. Lisette wanted Gussie to think she was dead. Lisette outsmarted Gussie."

Aiden's staging collapsed in a thunderous heap, sending wood shards, dirty water, and cleaning solution in every direction.

Reggie covered Jake with her body.

Storm and Destiny screamed, while King put himself between Harmony and flying debris. "Hey," Harmony said, "thanks, but I thought I was supposed to protect you."

"So why's your arm bleeding? You insulted Gussie, and you were closer to the staging than anyone, so I figured you needed protecting." King looked at her cut as Morgan came in. "Morgan, get the first aid kit. Is anybody else hurt?"

"I am," Reggie said, a hand to her bloody cheek.

King didn't seem to know which of them to tend first.

"Take care of Reggie," Harmony said.

Destiny took Jake. "You okay, buddy?"

The boy nodded, but he looked with concern at his mother. "Kiss Mama better?"

"In a minute, scrumpling."

Storm took the first aid kit from Morgan. "Gussie's *still* manipulating the people around her."

"True," Destiny said, putting Jake down beside his mother.

"Reggie, are you all right?" Harmony asked.

"Who wouldn't be with *two* Paxton men at her beck and call?"

"The splinter only caught her ear," King said, "but I thought it split her cheek." He sat on the sofa beside his daughter, looking pale. "Are *you* okay, Harmony?"

Morgan barked a mocking laugh. "Are you gonna faint, old boy, because of a few splinters? Hell, I've seen you walk away from death. You're losing your edge, Paxton, because of a couple of women."

King shot to his feet. "I don't know what's eating you, but apologize."

Morgan raised his hands. "Kidding." But his neck and ears turned ruddy. "I apologize. I didn't mean to be a shi—" He caught Jake's gaze. "Short-sighted, bigmouthed idiot."

"He means it." Destiny regarded him with surprise. "Morgan, even your aura's embarrassed."

Harmony turned to her sister. "You don't read auras."

Destiny pointed a thumb over her shoulder toward Morgan. "I can read his. It's dirty."

"I resent that," Morgan snapped.

Destiny raised a satisfied brow. "That's why I said it, but you are screwed up."

Morgan frowned, and Destiny ignored him. "I think Gussie caused strife so she could be the peacemaker and center of attention. It's a sickness."

"She and Nicodemus never had children, so when Lisette washed up on shore, the girl must have seemed like a gift," Harmony said. "A gift who betrayed her with her husband, or so she thought."

"King?" Storm asked. "How can you be the heir, if they never had children?"

"I descended from Nicodemus's black sheep brother."

"Figures," her sisters said.

"Thanks," King said, "but that doesn't change the fact that you're doing a lot of speculating."

"Speculating?" Storm hooked arms with her and Destiny, so they stood three against the world. "We're psychic. Get the picture?"

"Psychics make mistakes," Morgan said.

Destiny rounded on him. "Psychics don't exist in a debunker's world, so how would you know?"

"Forgot." Morgan snapped his fingers. "No such thing as psychics, witches, or ghosts. So leave me out of this."

Destiny raised her chin. "Never forget who you're pretending to be. Where have you been all morning?"

"I was pretending to get the new bedding set up. Jake, you have a great new room. And there are eleven other bedrooms with good mattresses. You just have to choose a room and some furniture now."

"Not before we protect and bless the rooms and neutralize the furniture," Storm said. "I wouldn't stay in any of them unprotected with that psychotic witch on the loose."

The lights went bright, then everything went black.

"Oh happy day," Storm said. "I pissed her off again."

They heard King's pager go off.

"I'm sure that's the foreman telling me the lights went out," he said, "but I'm not leaving anybody in the dark. Grab a hand, and I'll lead you to the site, and out the door, if necessary. Roll call, sound off."

When Jake heard everyone accounting for themselves, he yelled, "Jake Paxton and Mommy, too."

Curt, King's foreman, said he didn't know what caused the power surge, but a backhoe cut the main power line.

"Nobody's hurt, then?" King asked.

"Nah. The crew's outside till we get the power on and they can come back to work."

Harmony saw lights and did a double take. The empty elevator behind the main stairs came down lit like a Christmas tree. "Could the elevator be on a separate circuit?"

Curt whistled when he saw it. "You don't understand. We cut the main. Whatever's running that elevator is *not* connected to a power line."

"Make it stop," Jake said. "The lady wants to get out."

"Is it the lady in purple?" Harmony asked.

Jake nodded. "And she's even sadder."

The elevator rose again, and when it came back down, Jake sighed. "She's gone, but that's okay because she wanted to get out."

She wants to get out, Harmony thought. *She wants vindication.* Hadn't Destiny come darned closed to vindicating her this morning? Maybe the right spell . . .

King hugged Jake, as if he'd protect him from everything, if he could.

Harmony sighed. A sucker for a good father, she was falling hard. "Lotta karma going on around here," she said.

"Gussie may have wanted the ring at the beginning, but I'm not sure *she* knows what she wants, now," King said.

"Us either," Storm and Destiny agreed.

"But she does want Harmony here," Storm added.

"Think about what you just said. She wants harmony here. Maybe that doesn't mean she wants me. Maybe she wants peace."

"It seems to me," Reggie said, "that her husband gave her things but never himself. Maybe that's all she ever really wanted. I know how that feels."

King paled, and Reggie touched his arm. "I don't feel that way now, Daddy. Mom used to say you didn't want me, but your guilt money bought me things." She leaned into King, holding Jake, and Jake stroked his mother's hair.

"I didn't want things," Reggie whispered. "I wanted my dad."

"You know better now, right?" King pulled her closer.

"I do."

"Then this might be the right time to tell you that I applied for your custody, yours *and* Jake's, until you're eighteen and can assume custody, though I hope you'll stay with me when you do."

Reggie threw her arms around his neck, and Harmony fell even deeper.

"Don't count your chickens. Applying for custody is the easy part, compared to the real battle."

"Mom." Reggie groaned.

King nodded, looking as miserable as his daughter. "My lawyer's making inquiries as to whether she reported you missing. If she didn't, we have a case."

"And if she did?"

"I go to jail for having you here."

Chapter Thirty-five

"DON'T worry, kitten," King said over supper a short while after the power was restored. "I don't plan to go to jail, but let's not worry about that unless we have to. My lawyer thinks we have a case. I gave him the name of the woman you stayed with, so he can question her, by the way."

"Daddy, don't let Mom have me."

"She hasn't been worried enough to call me over the last three years, so that's not likely to happen."

"I don't want to go back."

"I won't let you go. My lawyer will fight for us. But we're straddling a legal tightrope. You need to know that. I want you, Regg, and I want Jake. Whatever happens, remember this: I'm here to protect you from *dead* East Coast witches and *living* West Coast ones."

"Hey," Harmony said. "You're implying that *witch* starts with a *b*. Cut that out. The two are not interchangeable."

"My apologies. You're right."

After supper, King took a walk around the castle. His family was in danger—his family, meaning: Harmony, Reggie, and Jake. Damn. His feelings for Reggie and Jake were normal. What he felt for Harmony was . . . indefinable. He was running scared without moving, when usually nothing scared him. Or nothing used to. Now three people, no two . . . no three . . . mattered more than his own life. Two, he could claim. One he would have to let go . . . eventually.

Right now, keeping them safe was all that mattered. He was thinking of getting them out of the castle.

The crew needed to go, too. He'd pay them to stay away for a week or so. Not their fault Gussie was running amok.

"King!" Harmony, her hair blowing in the wind, stood on a cliff above him. She made a motion for him to come. "Jake's in trouble," she shouted.

KING died a thousand deaths at the sight of Jake crawling along the beam suspended over the great hall by flexible pulleys. "Raise a net," he shouted to the crew. Thank God they kept safety netting on site.

Jake's knee slipped before they got the nets up, and King, and everyone else, gasped . . . but something, or someone, stopped him from falling, and he managed to regain his balance.

"Where's Reggie?" King asked.

"I don't . . . oh . . . she's up in the gallery." Harmony pointed, and King's heart sank again. His daughter hung from the gallery rail, trying to reach the end of the beam, while it rose up and away from her as Jake's weight tipped it downward at his end.

The crew had the nets beneath Jake now, but there was none beneath Reggie.

King ran, climbed the rail, caught his daughter around the waist, and hauled her to safety. Jake fell and screamed, and King got distracted, lost his balance, and did the same. He broke his ankle, he thought, flat on his back, his head going muzzy, people running his way when they should be taking care of Jake.

Reggie broke through the crowd with Jake in her arms, and King released his breath. "Thank God."

"Grampa! That was fun! Can we do it again?"

King blacked out.

"It's just a sprain," Curt said from a distance.

When King opened his eyes, he wasn't in the great hall but with Harmony in the dorm.

"Does it hurt terribly?" She sat beside him on his cot.

"Screw that. How's Jake?"

"Not a scratch on him, which is more than we can say for you."

"It doesn't hurt that bad. Ouch!"

"That's what I thought." She handed him a glass of water and a couple of aspirin.

He downed them in one sip.

Harmony stroked the hair from his brow, which he liked. "I don't think the fall made you black out, I think terror for your family did."

"Tell my crew that."

"What do you care what they think?" She cupped her hands over his throbbing ankle, and King felt an escalating warmth that eased the pain somewhat.

"I'm the boss. I'm supposed to be invincible."

"Any of their kids or grandkids hangs from the ceiling, they'll black out, too. They know that. Curt and a couple of others looked pretty green."

"I gotta get back down there. Help me up."

"Sure, but can you fly without a helicopter?" He let her hold him while he tried to put weight on his ankle, but no go, not without her support. Wonderful. That'd make him look like the boss.

"Wait a sec," she said. "I'll be right back."

She brought him an old, gold-tipped cane he'd seen over the years. "I got such a sense of the ring when I took this from the cane stand," she said. "I took everything out, and dumped the stand upside down, sure the other half of the ring was in there." She shrugged. "But it wasn't." She raised the cane. "Look familiar? I think it's the cane Nicodemus is using in the mural."

King swore. "I'll let you in on a secret. That mural makes me want to black out, too. I've got to get my family out of this place."

"How about we get Gussie out, instead?"

"I'm listening," he said, "but so is she, right?"

"My sisters and I have been talking about—" Harmony put her lips to his ear, and he cupped her head because he liked her this close. "A ritual," she whispered.

"Which means?"

"Either we go for a bike ride, or you trust me on this."

"When?"

"In a week and a half. We have to wait for the summer solstice to tap into the sun's strength and vitality."

He understood then that she meant a witchy ritual, and damned if he wasn't grateful she had an idea, any idea, witchy or twitchy, or moon magickal. He'd take anything right now. "Think we can hang on that long?"

"My sisters and I have been casting protection spells all over the house for the past couple of days, rather blatantly now that we've been outed, so you might have some explaining to do."

"How the hell do I explain that?"

"Tell them we're fighting fire with fire. They'll get it or they won't, but they're men. They won't ask for directions."

King barked a laugh. "Is that witch wisdom or feminine intuition? Help me up."

She tried, and he got dizzy. "What kind of pills did you give me?"

"Pain pills from Curt's first aid kit. He said you wouldn't feel a thing after you took them . . . oh, oh."

King shifted from his cot to her bed, fell into it, and pulled her down with him.

"Are you getting friendly or woozy?"

"Woozy friendly?" He traced the letters over her breasts. "Licensed to Thrill. Care to give me a demo?"

"Let me lock that door so I can take your mind off the pain."

"People are gonna come knocking."

"No, they're not. The crew's left for the day, and everyone has their own bedroom as of an hour ago."

"Oh, Sunshine, get over here, so I don't fall asleep before the main event."

"I can come fast."

Chapter Thirty-six

A few days later, a letter from his lawyer made King sit Reggie down while Gilda played with Jake outside. "Sweetheart, I have some bad news, but before you hear it, I think I have a solution. Are you ready?"

"No, but I'm glad Jake's having fun so he'll remember his home."

"Stop playing psychic; you're off the mark, but let's go sit in the sun and watch him play." King grabbed his cane and followed her out. She picked a piece of spearmint from the herb garden by the kitchen door, crushed it, and held it under his nose. Harmony's influence, he thought. "Fresh. Clean," he said. "Makes me want to chew some gum."

Reggie smiled. "I love this place."

That didn't make him feel much better. They sat on a marble bench while Jake chased butterflies around the dolphin fountain.

Reggie laid her head on his shoulder. "I'm braced."

King stroked her hair. "Your mother got wind of my

lawyers' inquiries and traced them back to me. She's filed a countersuit for your custody."

"I won't go."

"Not an issue, but . . . she didn't apply for Jake's custody. That's good. It'll work in our favor."

"To her, Jake doesn't exist. He wouldn't fit her social stratosphere."

"Into Malibu society, is she?"

"Big time. Last boy toy I remember was a soap star half her age."

"Knowing that might help. It means she won't want her world to know she's a grandmother. I'm going to California to settle the future, for good."

"Can't she have you arrested there?"

"I won't have contact with you while I'm there, so I won't be breaking any laws. But I might try to convince her that I can have her arrested for stealing three years' worth of child support."

"Whatever you do," Reggie said, "don't give her the castle. I'm not kidding. This is our home."

King guessed he wasn't the only one who suspected that gold-digging Belinda would give up her daughter for money. He hadn't quite realized how much Reggie loved the castle, nor that she already considered it home. Could his valiant girl stand another disappointment? And could *he*, in all honesty, be the one to disappoint her?

"Did she look for me, by the way?" Reggie asked. "Did Mom look for me?" she repeated.

"Yes, she hired a private investigator to find you, but he went out of business."

"That's lame. She's usually better at covering her tracks than that."

So much for his ploy to make her think her mother gave a rat's ass. "She's running scared, I think, so I'm off to play bad guy/bad guy."

Tears spilled over Reggie's big, dark eyes. "She doesn't

want my beautiful boy, Dad. I know she doesn't want me, but how could she not want him?"

"Come here. Give your old dad a hug."

"You? Old? Storm says you're a prime stud."

"Storm should keep her opinions to herself!"

Reggie laughed. "What fun would that be?"

Harmony and her sisters had become quite an influence on Reggie in the short time she'd been there. His daughter's shirt of the day said, You Cease to Amuse Me, despite her full closet of new and retro clothes. He kissed her brow as Jake came over. "Grampa, take this with you to Caniforna." The smiling urchin presented him with a mud pie.

"Baby Einstein, you never miss a trick." King ruffled his hair and squeezed Reggie's shoulder, as she wiped Jake's face with the corner of her shirt. "I have to find Harmony," King said, "to make sure she *and* her sisters can stay to keep you safe while I'm gone."

Half an hour later, he found Harmony in the billiard room, but his request caught her off guard. "When are you going?" She circled the room waving a smoky . . . something. "It's a smudge stick," she said, answering his unspoken question.

"I'd like to leave tomorrow morning, if I can."

"Of all the times." Harmony sent her sisters a look. "The thing is, we've been rushing the protection spells so we could go back to Salem for the weekend. Our sister Vickie's coming home from Scotland, and we have a welcome-home party planned."

King released his breath. "I hate the thought of leaving Reggie and Jake's futures hanging. Besides, in this case, a surprise strike is critical."

"Can we take Reggie and Jake home with us?"

"You'd do that?"

"We love them. Of course we would." Harmony looked at her sisters, and they enthusiastically agreed.

Relief and gratitude flooded him. "Reggie will love it.

And if things go bad, Belinda won't know where to find her."

"Things could get ugly, huh?"

"Belinda doesn't do nice. A mutual friend told me a few years back that she got her parents to sign their house over to her, then she moved them to senior housing and sold it."

Storm shivered, as if she knew Belinda.

"Storm, do you sense something?" Harmony asked.

"The woman gives mean-spirited new meaning. She's . . . small. Her world is narrow. She's selfish and malicious. Like a dog with a bone, she doesn't give it up unless she can bite someone for fun."

"I know all that," King said, "but hearing it makes me realize I should have fought for Reggie years ago."

Harmony picked a piece of lint off his shirt. "You were a kid. Forgive yourself." She slid her palm down his cheek and stepped away. "Your chicks will be safe with us. They'll have a blast. So will we. Go to California and kick some bad Malibu ass."

"If your sisters weren't here, I'd kiss you."

"Go ahead," Storm said. "Kinky."

King didn't feel much like smiling, but he gave the rebel a wink. He also gave his crew an unexpected vacation, with pay. He might not look much like the boss leaning on his cane, but they treated him with new respect after that.

At dawn the next morning, Harmony walked him to his helicopter and kissed him good-bye, nothing compared to the send off she'd given him the night before, which included a gift from his own wine cellar that she'd utilized brilliantly. "Châteauneuf-du-Pape will never taste as fine," he whispered against her lips.

She cupped his cheek. "Take care of you." Her smile failed to hide her concern. "Call my cell and let us know what's happening, okay? Reggie will be nervous, and so will I."

"I'll do that."

Late that afternoon, in Malibu, sitting across from Belinda's house, King didn't need a detective to tell him that his ex hadn't been able to afford a gardener or house painter for a while.

It took her a long time to answer her door, and when she did, she smiled, which scared him worse than the flaws in her once-flawless skin.

A bottle of Jack Daniel's sat open on the bar behind her.

"You're not gonna talk me out of getting Regina back," she said.

"She'd rather be called Reggie."

"You stole her."

"You threw her out, and she came to me, but I'm here to fix that. I brought her back to you. Write me a check for the three years of child support you stole, and she's yours."

"How about you don't have to pay for the next three years?"

King shook his head. "How about I don't have to pay for the next six months?"

"Even better," Belinda said.

"You don't know how old your daughter is. Child support ends when she turns eighteen in six months."

The look on Belinda's face told him she hadn't counted on that. She must have promised her lawyer a cut of the money tree she planned to shake, because the partied-out playgirl before him couldn't afford a custody battle.

"I can't afford—"

"To maintain your lifestyle. I can tell. Suppose I give you two choices," King said. "I bring Reggie and her son here from the hotel, and the world knows you're a grandmother, or you sign custody over to me. I've got the papers right here."

Belinda smiled her evil/nice cat smile, the kind the unsuspecting world would think was sweet. He knew. He'd fallen for it once. "Suppose I give you . . . *one* choice," she said. "A few days in jail should help you come up with a better offer."

Her doorbell rang. "Get a life," she said before she let the cops in.

They arrested him on the spot . . . for kidnapping.

Chapter Thirty-seven

HARMONY ran up the steps from the boat dock to see if King's helicopter sat on its landing pad. She was disappointed he wasn't there yet. It had taken days for his lawyer to spring him. Kidnapping charges were serious business. Evidently, Belinda the Bitch had friends in high places. Harmony had missed him so much that she wanted to welcome him home alone.

Reggie understood, so she and Jake were still with Destiny and Storm. They planned to tour Salem and take in some of the sights. They'd be back in a few days for the summer solstice, but for now King Paxton was all hers.

The goons who'd tried to keep her out the first day tipped their hats and unlocked the castle door for her. It was creepy inside, alone, without lights. Good thing she knew her way to the dorm. She and King shared it now, and the cots were gone.

He was due back any minute, so she took a quick shower, perfumed the right places, and slipped into a lime lace babydoll cami with matching bikinis.

He stepped into the room a minute later. He'd probably landed while she was in the shower.

"Jailbird!" she said in greeting, but he said nothing. His hungry gaze was transfixed by the blonde triangle of hair beneath her translucent bikinis. Harmony rolled to her stomach, crossed her legs in the air, and looked at him over her shoulder.

He dropped his bag and cane, and lunged. She screamed as he landed on top of her. She laughed as he planted kisses all over her. She hadn't expected such a bodacious welcome from her nonspontaneous . . . lover. Yeah, that's what he was . . . her lover. Why not admit it?

He pulled down one side of her cami, exposed a breast, and took it in his mouth. Then he kissed her triquetra, the tattoed symbol of three in a heart low on her right breast.

"God, I love this," she said. "You're spoiling me for any other man."

"Damned straight I am."

"Whoa, careful there, mister. That statement cuts a bit too close to the sharp edge of commitment. You don't want to go charging into a toy room without bulletproof shorts."

"I'm charging in *without* my shorts. How's that for spontaneous?" He pulled back and gazed, entranced, at her full and ready breast glistening from his mouth.

"Like what you see, flyboy?"

"Like it? I'm gonna devour it."

"I want you inside me." She lay down and raised her knees in a not-so-subtle invitation.

"You scare me, Hellcat. I'm not sure I'll ever get enough of you."

"There's enough for more." Something that happened in California had changed him, set him on a new course, though it was difficult to read him. At any rate, his movements were unhurried, profound, unselfish . . . overwhelming. He used his man brain to good purpose, setting his compass on her, not him. He didn't move with the intention of taking pleasure but of giving it. This was less sex and more a mating, less about the body than the . . . heart.

Couldn't be.

Emotions, maybe, but not the heart. Despite a thin veneer of self-protection, Harmony followed where King led. While he worked to pleasure her, she pleasured him.

New territory, this. Walls to scale and pull down, walls protected by iron-spiked fences that could tear the climber to ribbons, but she tried to scale them anyway. Forever became a possibility, at least for her orgasm. She'd never had one that lasted so long. Their cries mated in the quiet dusk, but they seemed to rise higher, and higher still, the two of them exploding and colliding like shattering stars spilling light across the galaxy.

Energized yet sated, breathless, they lay tangled, touching, kissing, nipping, wordlessly, as they drifted back to the world like feathers floating on a midsummer breeze.

King pulled wet tendrils of hair from her face. "Where the hell did you come from?"

"Why? Am I so different from your other women? Is it because I'm not lying here like a dead fish?"

"Stop making jokes." He kissed her exposed skin, adored his way up her legs, discovered and adored the Celtic rust and gold sea horse tattoo on her hip. "What does the sea horse stand for?" he asked. "Knowing you, it must have a meaning."

"I'll tell you after the solstice ritual," she said. "I don't want to raise your expectations."

"I love a mystery, but I have to be honest. I have the world's worst taste in women."

"Gee, thanks."

"Except for you, which is why you scare me. All exceptions do, because there's always an exception to the exception. Belinda is a prime example of the bitch factor in my usual choices."

"Why do you think that is?"

"Hell if I know."

"Maybe you like women who are mean-spirited and nasty?"

"Are you out of your mind?"

"If you choose a not emotionally available woman, your emotions remain intact, untouched, invulnerable."

"Screw you."

"Please do."

He slipped inside her again. Nothing slow, languid, or generous about his movements this time, he took her with savage intent. His plundering kisses and inciting caresses at her center led them to another death-defying but mutually satisfying climax. Moonbeams transported them like a magic carpet to a land of ecstasy.

Waves of aftershock rippled through her, and she drifted, only to wake up as King sat beside her, fresh from the shower.

He opened a tiny tin of candies. "Peppermint breast?" he offered.

She took one, examined it, popped it into her mouth, and crunched it.

"Damn," he said. "You bit right into it. I could *not* do that to a gummy penis."

He stood and she roared, because she'd just noticed that his white boxers announced Free Toy Inside, in fire engine red.

He looked so proud. "See, peppermint breasts and literal statement shorts . . . I can be spontaneous."

"One spontaneous moment does not a free spirit make," she said, but she went looking for the prize, anyway, and she got herself a handful. "Fantasmaglorious!" She pulled down his shorts. "All hail to the king! It's a keeper." And keep it, she did.

She kept it happy . . . for three days.

Harmony woke first on their last morning together. No more shared nights of sex, lust, love . . . whatever.

Sometimes she thought King was trying to show her how he felt without saying the words. At other times, she thought he got close to speaking the words, but not close enough.

She'd always hoped for a man who could make a commitment, but she'd found King Paxton instead, and she couldn't think of anybody she'd rather wake up beside. Fortunately or unfortunately, given their ghostly situation, their futures were on hold until she could complete the most important part of her psychic mandate and free the castle of Gussie.

Her sisters, with Reggie and Jake, would arrive tonight. Now would be her last chance to put her energy into making love to King before they were surrounded by the energy of others. Energies, however wonderful, and welcome, that would take their focus from each other.

Last chance, she thought looking over at the sleeping beast, admiring his raven hair of natural waves, remembering the depth of his whiskey eyes and the skill in his work-of-art bod, sculpted and wide-shouldered, thick-muscled and strong.

Virile. Voracious. Vulnerable—whether he wanted to believe it or not—and vocal in his pleasure.

Withering witch balls, she was spooky in love. Dipped and glazed. Waxed and scaled. No gilding the lily. Her love was pure, unadulterated, problematic, complicated, irrevocable, and polished to a magick mirror shine.

Chapter Thirty-eight

"HAPPY Midsummer's Eve!" Harmony said three hours later, flitting from King's sleepy reach. "I have so much to do, and it's nearly noon. My sisters will be back sometime this afternoon with Jake and Reggie, and—hey, look at you tenting the covers. You *are* voracious. A lesser man would have—"

"Died of pleasure by now?"

"I think you're ready for a midsummer gift." She handed him a small yellow and orange bright box with a red bow. I wrapped it in summer colors to honor the sun on its longest day."

"Then it's the sun's day, not mine," he said sitting up in bed, all sleep-mussed with his unruly hair falling on his brow and the covers falling to his deliciously tempting lap. "Why the gift?"

"It's a midsummer tradition you might want to pass on someday, but not to me."

King unwrapped the box, almost wary of its contents. Obviously, he hadn't received many gifts in his life, nor did he seem capable of showing gratitude, and when he opened the box and removed the ancient key, he looked puzzled. "I'm almost afraid to ask."

"It's a magick key that will open whatever is locked to you."

King gave her a cocky look. "Will it open a Victoria's Secret?" He threw off his covers and rose, primed . . . for anything. "If so, I'm ready."

"No kidding, McHorny." She flicked that sexy lock from his brow, but it stayed as stubborn as him. "The key is symbolic. You'll use it when you're ready."

"Or not. I don't do games. Maybe I should get that printed on a shirt so you'll understand." He went to the bathroom and shut the door.

"Get a life," she yelled after him.

She'd intended the key to unlock his walls and release his emotions, and she guessed it worked, because he was royally pissed. She dressed and went downstairs.

Morgan and Aiden were waiting in the kitchen.

"Storm invited us to the midsummer festivities," Aiden said, standing when she came in. "If that's okay?"

They were curious, Harmony knew, though Morgan would try to debunk the whole thing. "The more the merrier," she said, enlisting their help.

After a while, McHorny with attitude joined them.

Harmony looked around the great hall. "This is the best place to confront the situation, on home turf, as it were. To prepare for tomorrow's dawn ritual, I want to set up in the east corner of the room where I can petition the sunrise on the sun's special day." Hands on hips, she showed the three where to clear the construction debris.

She marked off an area by walking it. "Clear about twenty by twenty feet, here. Then go up to the library in the old wing, and get the Victorian tiger oak writing table. It has oak kings carved on the legs—you can't miss it. King, show Morgan and Aiden the way, but let them carry it.

While you're gone, I'll sweep away the negative debris, literally and figuratively, so you can put the table in the center of the clearing."

In the morning, she'd do a ritual cleansing, because today she needed more than a *ceremonial* broom to sweep.

A short while later, the men carried the table downstairs and centered it in her space. Aiden and Morgan groaned as they set it down. "That's got to be the heaviest table in the house," King said.

"I know. Isn't it great? I'm psyched. The Holly King and Oak King are symbols of protection. They battle for rule at midsummer and Yule. The oak is king of spring and summer and the holly of fall and winter, which makes this the best Celtic altar ever."

The men stole glances at each other.

"Are the big macho men afraid of an altar? Don't worry. We hardly ever sacrifice humans anymore." She cocked a brow at King. "Though I could make an exception."

Aiden elbowed him. "You gotta stop pissin' off the witch."

King firmed his jaw, and Harmony raised a brow. "The gardeners said I could borrow some of the balled burlap saplings, so can you get the oaks and hollies from the shed? Nine, if you please."

Morgan jingled the change in his pocket. "Can I ask why?"

"Sure. My sisters and I are hereditary Pictish witches—like our ancestor Lili from the nineteenth century—and our craft is based on the Celtic and Druidic traditions, hence woodland rituals near oaks. But since the focus of our ritual is inside, we're bringing the trees to us. In case you're interested, Mr. Debunker, I'll be using a hawthorn wand tomorrow for psychic protection."

"I assure you that you'll need no psychic protection from me."

"I should hope not, Morgan the Mystic." Harmony drew

a circle on the unfinished stone floor in blue carpenter's chalk. "I don't normally *draw* the circle, but you're men, so I'm forcing you to use a map for tree placement, whether you want to or not."

"I guess she told you," Aiden said to Morgan. And King gave Morgan an empathetic backslap. Storm and Destiny returned with Jake and Reggie, then, and Jake went to King and leaned in, curling his small arm around his grandfather's leg, as if King had been home base forever.

Reggie kissed King's cheek. "We missed you, Dad."

King thawed in place.

"Besides getting arrested, how goes the custody battle?" she asked. "I know you said we'd be fine on the phone, but dish."

"I have custody of the two of you until the hearing. Don't tell anyone, but after the kidnapping trick your mother pulled in California, my lawyer plans to tie everything in a legal knot for the next six months, until you're eighteen. If the bi—big child support stealer won't play fair, neither will I."

"Yes!" Reggie threw her arms around him. "This day is absolutely perfect. Now I'm really excited about the mid summer celebration. I can't wait to start. Harmony, what can I do to help?"

His daughter's excitement over the witchy celebration seemed to set a new steel rod in King's spine.

"You can help Storm pick herbs in the kitchen garden, later," Harmony said. "And Jake, can you play the drum at our bonfire tonight?"

He looked disappointed. "But Dessie made me a dragon costume."

"Well then, our dragon can play the drums. Wha'd'ya say?"

He raised an arm in victory. "Ye-esss!"

"Why a dragon?" Aiden asked.

"It's a leftover from Saint George and the dragon,"

Storm said. "By rights we should have a unicorn, and some horses, as well, but we're partial to dragons."

Aiden raised his glass her way. "Really glad to hear it."

King glanced at Aiden with surprise as Destiny came in with a big box. "Where do you want me to put our robes and ritual supplies?" she asked, raising the box—awkward, and clumsy, but not heavy.

Morgan came in with a sapling in each hand. "Where do you want the saplings?"

"On the blue chalk circle, remember?" Harmony said.

But when Morgan saw Destiny juggling the box, he set down the trees and took the box from her, as if she were a fragile pixie princess.

For his efforts, Destiny snubbed him.

"Where to?" he asked.

"A gentleman debunker," Harmony quipped. "Imagine that. Put it in the dorm."

King rubbed his hands together, getting into the spirit or falling in with Jake and Reggie's enthusiasm. Either way, *thank the Goddess*. "What's next?" he asked.

"Next, my sisters and I will take a cleansing and protective ritual bath in the ocean to prepare for our midnight bonfire and dawn ritual."

"Naked?" Jake asked.

Chapter Thirty-nine

AT his grandson's bald question, King swallowed his tongue and coughed up a fur ball, at least that's how he felt.

Morgan and Aiden grinned like baboons.

The triplets were going swimming . . . in the beautiful, beautiful buff. And *they* were nearly as pleased as King and his friends were. Well, at least he was cool with the idea—well, *hot* with it, actually—though he was only hot because Harmony was doing it.

Damned if he didn't want to get naked and swim with her. Not too smart after her symbolic key, and their night of glorious sex, during which he'd lost all control, which he hated more than, well, coughing up a fur ball.

Nevertheless, last night had been the best, and scariest, sex ever. It was out of body scary. I want *more* scary. I can't live *without* her scary. And who could blame him? Any man who had sex with the Orgasmatron would be turned on, and scared, except that he didn't want any other man having sex with her.

Harmony Cartwright had perfected the art of the multiple orgasm. She took charge and rode the big *O* into extended multiples, times infinity, one after another. He should be wearing slings and bandages, after last night. What a workout. Good thing he was already using a cane. He ached everywhere: in his back, his arms, and especially in his contented cock. Except it wasn't that contented anymore, with the naked swimming and all.

She'd ridden him hard all night, and he was ready to do her again. Go figure. More than ready, because, well, she'd inspired, manipulated, choreographed . . . *his* first multiple orgasm. Okay, only two in a row, but he'd nearly died of rapture. Damned if he hadn't wanted more . . . until that emotional commitment key thing, a gift he didn't have the guts to use.

Some pleasures in life weren't good for you, and he guessed Hellcat Harmony was one of them.

"Dad," Reggie said, pulling him back to his surroundings.

"You rang?"

"Jake and I are going upstairs to take our own ritual baths. Harmony gave me some of the eucalyptus, lemongrass, rosemary, and lavender oil she and her sisters are going to put on before their swim. After that, Jake and I are taking a nap . . . a *long* nap."

"I think that's a very good idea," King said as he watched them go.

When he turned back to the room, he saw Harmony watching him, as if she could peel away his layers to reveal his secrets. He wasn't fond of that probing, intrusive look of hers. But, great guns, was he fond of *her*.

"Let's go undress," she told her sisters, while she watched him. "We've got a bonfire and a ritual to prepare for."

King shook his head. "Shouldn't you conserve your energy for a ritual?"

Harmony tilted her head, as if she were about to impart a great secret. "Certain . . . sensual . . . exercises . . . *increase* our power."

"Then you must be pretty damned powerful." The echo of his words mocked him. Good thing Reggie and Jake had gone up.

Eighteen minutes later, the gorgeous, sexy, unselfconscious trio came downstairs wearing identical short black lace beach robes . . . and what—if anything—beneath them?

After the girls crossed the kitchen to go out the back door to the beach, Morgan and Aiden rushed to the kitchen window, and King limped sedately behind. "Did they make it to the beach yet?"

"Not yet," Morgan said, his face plastered to the glass.

King looked down his nose at their hormonal-teen-type snooping, and yet, he was going to join them. He turned to go back into the great hall. "We can get closer and see better from the old tower," he called from behind the stairs. "Beat you up there."

"No fair," Aiden called as the goofs went running up the stairs, "we don't remember the way."

King hit the Up button on the elevator.

When Aiden and Morgan got to the tower, trying to catch their breaths, he had already opened the shutters and casement. "Two grown men racing up the stairs to play Peeping Tom," he said.

Aiden chuckled. "The way I see it, we're three sexually healthy adult males, watching three sexually healthy adult females, who invited us to watch. There go the robes."

"Now that's what I call a sand-witch," King said. "Must be why my mouth is watering."

Morgan clapped a hand to his chest. "They're spreading oil on each other. I think I'm having a heart attack."

Aiden looked to the heavens as if in thanks. "Life doesn't get any better than this."

Morgan scoffed. "Sure it does. *We* get to spread the oil on them."

"Then they spread it on us," King said, fueling the fantasy.

Aiden lit up. "You think it's *edible* oil?"

Morgan barked a laugh.

"We're sick bastards," King said, transfixed by the sight. "Look at them, three stunning, voluptuous mermaids, symbols of feminine sexuality, stars of the sea, returning to the place of their birth."

"The mermaid," Aiden said, "is the siren whose irresistible call leads men to their doom."

Morgan shook his head. "Not really. The mermaid as siren is only an ancient myth, though her lure *is* powerful."

King gaped. "They teach you that at the seminary?"

"Aren't mermaids a link between passion and destruction?" Aiden asked.

"Then give me passion," King said.

Aiden nodded. "And give me destruction."

"Hey how did we get on a mermaid kick? Oh, yeah," Morgan said. "King started it."

"Pretty poetic for a straitlaced brass ass." Aiden slapped him on the back. "Are you converting, King?"

"To what? Witchcraft?"

"No," Aiden said. "Humanity. Are you growing a heart?"

King nodded toward the girls, up to their beautiful asses in water. "*She* wants me to."

"Fancy that," Aiden said. "Can't imagine why."

"Didn't you pay your penance yet, King?" Morgan asked. "About time you got a life, don't you think?"

"Son of a bitch. That's the third time I've heard that this week."

"I rest my case." Morgan leaned out the window. "Third time's the charm."

"Let's mosey on out there and sit on the beach," Aiden suggested.

"Who are you, Doc Holliday? Mosey?" King shook his head.

"Oh come on," Aiden said. "You know you want to go down there as much as I do."

"I don't know," Morgan admitted. "You know the witch everybody else thinks is the gentle and quiet Pollyanna?"

"The one you call a bitch," Aiden said.

"Yeah, her. She looks me in the eye, and I shut down."

"Sexually?" King asked.

Morgan blew out a breath. "I'd probably be better off. No, my brain shuts down and I stand there dumb as a rock. And my cock, well, that's like a rock, too."

Aiden looked confused. "How can she scare you, if you don't believe in the paranormal?"

"It's not the witch that scares me, but damned if I know what does. She's the most mysterious of the three, don't you think?"

"Maybe," King said. "But Harmony's the most open. Too open, I think. Scary open."

"'Cause you could fall in, huh?" Aiden kept an eye on the girls. "Storm, she's the rebel. I could really get into rebels."

Morgan elbowed him. "Cut the crap. You already have."

"I wish." Aiden paled. "Did you forget about the islands?"

Morgan shook his head. "That was more than a year ago. *You* turning celibate on us now?"

"He's right," King said. "You gotta let the beast out of his cage. You won't find a woman more open to adventure than Storm."

Aiden nodded. "I've been thinking along the same lines lately."

"Think harder," Morgan said.

Aiden winced. "Couldn't get any harder."

The girls' laughter caught their attention, the sound sluicing over King like cool air on a warm day, except that it raised his body temperature instead of cooling it.

Morgan did a double take and gave his full attention to the scene on the beach. "Guys, Harmony's waving us down. Let's go."

Chapter Forty

KING stood there alone, for some time after Aiden and Morgan left to go down to the beach and ogle the mermaids, and he wondered how long he could keep the construction on the castle going so as to keep Harmony around.

If construction stayed on target, he'd lose her.

If it took too long, he'd lose his buyer.

If he sold the place, he'd break his daughter's heart.

He closed the window and latched the shutters. If the mermaids *were* witches, *real* witches, and if they did get Gussie the hell out, Harmony would have no more reason to stay. Talk about a case of good news/bad news.

Ten minutes later, like perverts fresh out of peep school, King and his friends sat in the sand beside the girls' lace robes and watched like drooling goobers as the sexpots frolicked in the water.

"They do look like mermaids," Aiden said.

Morgan laughed. "Aiden, you got a little drool on your shirt."

"Come on in," Storm called.

Aiden cupped his hand around his mouth. "What?"

"Join us . . . in the water."

Aiden shot to his feet.

King threw a handful of sand at his horn-dog ass. "Hey, Rover, try not to sit up and beg."

Morgan grabbed Aiden's shirttail. "You're *not* gonna let them see how eager you are."

"The hell I'm not." Aiden slipped off his shirt, ran and dove in, pants and all.

Storm screamed when he came up beside her and pushed her under; then she shot out of the water and returned the compliment. They swam away from the pack, around an outcropping of rocks to the left, and into a world of their own.

"I always admired Aiden's up-for-anything-attitude," King said.

"I admire it so much, I'm going in, too." Morgan walked into the water, removing his shirt and tossing it toward shore, but it drifted out to sea.

King chuckled.

Morgan gravitated toward Destiny, despite his dumb-as-a-rock fear, and the two of them treaded water as they talked and left Harmony to her own devices.

King felt like a loser until she swam his way. Maybe she'd walk out of the receding sea like a nymph, lure him to the tower, and ravage him. A pretty scary thought when you figure where the toy room and parlor car got them.

Harmony stood in the water, her perfect body glistening from the sea, her sun-kissed hair riding her shoulders and partially covering one breast. One. The other, a testament to perfection, with its wide, dark aureoles, became the focus of his heated attention.

With his blood running south and his heart in his dry mouth, King stood and shed every stitch while she watched. He used his cane to walk into the water, and when he got deep enough to swim, he threw the cane to the sand with a better pitch than Morgan. He wouldn't need it later. Harmony would help him walk back to the beach.

As he swam toward her, she backed away, leading him like a siren toward the right and away from Destiny and Morgan.

When he got close enough to touch her, his mermaid dove into the water and disappeared.

Like a goddess, she rose to stand beside kissing rock, of all places, waiting for him until she disappeared behind it.

The space between kissing rock and the next outgrowth formed a small entry into an area that had always reminded him of a private lagoon. There he found Harmony floating toward the mouth of the magick water cave—or so he'd dubbed it as a kid—a seductive mermaid awaiting, no, *inviting* ravishment. Or was she waiting to lure him to some dark, underwater doom?

She tossed back her hair, revealing her glistening breasts, her nipples pebbled with dew and arousal. The salacious sea licked at the triangle of blonde curls between her legs, washing away the sand as if preparing her for his invasion, while she looked as if she felt every pleasurable sea stroke.

Harmony—the goddess of magick who'd invaded his life and invited him with sultry looks to invade her body.

When he reached her, King hovered over her, his legs floating while he held himself over her, skimming her with his body, her hair making slick waves in the wet sand beneath her head. His ready rod probed at her flowering center.

The sun warming his back, his heart beating like a drum, he slipped into her hot, slick core. She arched to pull him deeper, and he buried himself to the hilt.

He stopped to appreciate the amazing experience of her pulsing around him, milking him with her greedy muscles, a feminine magick he'd never experienced or never took the time to notice and savor until Harmony.

Every pulse of her womb shot darts of pleasure to every remote region of his body, even his heart. At the insight, King nearly pulled out, but he couldn't tear himself away. Couldn't bear the shock of separation.

Again she arched, their eyes meeting, her look pleading. And after he pulled back, almost, almost all the way, he buried himself again, deep and hard, and she smiled, closed her eyes, and sighed.

He tried to make peace with the degree of heightened sexual energy this woman provoked, his every nerve ending scraped raw, but she wrapped her legs around him and claimed him, and there was no more thinking for him. Then she clawed her fingernails down his back, branding him, enlarging his rod, expanding his capacity for pleasure and his awareness of the woman who inspired it.

Sex for sport no longer seemed enough.

The hellcat drew in her claws and cupped his balls, easy—praise be—but unmerciful in her frenzy to give and receive pleasure. When she stroked him deep at his root, she made him thicker and heavier, but he stubbornly clung to rising pleasure.

She bit his nipple, and he snapped.

Unable to stay the course, he rode her mercilessly, while she wanted harder, deeper, faster. She said she wanted pleasure to lift them from the sea and carry them so close to the sun they'd burn . . . and, by God, it did!

He buried his shout in their kiss and swallowed hers whole.

A series of tiny tremors, small waves of ecstasy, remnants of quiet rapture and unquiet satisfaction, stayed with him as King lay entwined with his mermaid, the water lapping lower along their torsos, causing a pleasant stir against his sensitive nerve endings. He rinsed her mound with seawater, and dusted the sand from his hands before he found her center, stroked her, and raised her up again, and when she took his comatose rod in her hand, and rinsed him of sand as well, he rose like Lazarus from the dead, and they did the dance again.

Nothing slow, just a mind-shattering bliss that came and went as fast as a jet through the sky. A minute later, she fell back to catch her breath. "That was some itch, Paxton, or was it an urge?"

"More than that," he admitted, against his better judgment.

"Ah, well, good sex then, if a bit sandy now and again."

"A notch better than sex, I think."

Harmony raised her head. "Not lust? It couldn't have been lust. That's rather intimate. Scary intimate," she added. "Your words."

"I might have a problem," he said.

She rolled to her side to face him and give him her full attention, eyes bright, her head in her hand. "Do tell."

"I think it might've been passion."

"Whoa. Wait a minute. Are you telling me that you feel a partner-focused short-term-commitment type passion . . . for me?"

"Well, I don't feel it for your sisters, and you *are* three peas from the same pod—"

"Technically no. We're not. See the first pod split, and I grew in one half. Then the other half split, but didn't separate, so Des and Storm grew in the other half."

"*That* would explain why I'm not attracted to them," King said. "They *are* different. Maybe it *was* just an itch."

Harmony rose like a furious sea nymph and kicked wet sand in his face! "Thickheaded dumb-ass jerk! Scratch your own itch from now on!"

Chapter Forty-one

HARMONY had never moved as fast through the water as she did to get away from King. On the beach, she snatched her robe and put it on while she ran to the castle.

King called to her from a distance, but she didn't look back. Let him crawl out of the water. He deserved to crawl.

"Fool." When they were mak—yes, making love, or getting as close as *she'd* ever gotten—the idiot had lowered his wall long enough to taste passion, which terrified the starch out of him. So he backed off, the jerk. Not that she could read him like she used to, but she *knew* him better now, and he was running scared . . . on the inside.

Fine, go. Run till you're alone and lonely. It won't matter. You'll always want me. And that wasn't magick speaking; it was fact. He didn't know it yet, but she, unfortunately, did.

After she dressed, she went to the kitchen, where everyone was eating a quiet supper—too quiet—except for Jake, who rattled on about the educational video he'd watched before his nap. His rendition of the playmate song not only broke the ice, it melted everyone at the table, especially King, who beamed with pride.

"Tell us about the bonfire," Reggie said.

"Our ancestors built bonfires on midsummer's eve to honor the light of fire, and we'll build ours like theirs. Bonfires are rare these days because most people don't have a private beach, so we're lucky and grateful to King for lending us his. To help celebrate, after supper, anybody who wants can come with us to gather wood to burn. It's part of the fun, but we take only dry branches off the ground. We never hurt a tree."

After a heavily frosted brownie, Jake dragged Reggie to the door. "This is so much fun," he said, though he hadn't started yet, but he stopped to look beyond his mother. "Grampa? Hurry up. We gotta go get branches."

"Grumpy Grampa," Harmony said as he passed.

Within the hour, Harmony placed her branches on the growing pile and stood where she and King had escaped the parlor car, now back in the shed for Aiden to rebuild. Hard to believe, looking at King now, all hard and detached, that they'd been so close, in mind and heart, in this very spot.

She welcomed the joking revelers as they added branches to the pile. "My sisters and I have never had the opportunity to share this holiday with anyone," she said, "and the camaraderie is wonderful. Thank you, Morgan Aiden. Jake, that's such an impressive bundle of wood, I'm gonna ask you to hold some protective blue balloons during the ritual tomorrow. You carried as much wood as a man just now."

"I can carry balloons . . . but I'm only a boy, not a man."

"Nearly three going on sixty, right?"

"No." He giggled. "I'm not sixty. Grampa is sixty."

King pulled the boy against his good leg. "I'm thirty-seven, you little terror. Can you say, 'My grampa is young, and *handsome*, and thirty-seven'?"

"No." Jake giggled and hid his face against King's leg, until he peeked at Harmony.

She turned his little chin. "Repeat after me. My grampa is young, and *dense,* and thirty-seven."

Jake nodded. "My grampa is young, and *dense,* and thirty-seven."

King tickled him. "Her version, you remember?"

Reggie lifted her son so he could hug King, and she ruffled both their heads. "Dense the both of you," she said. "Hey, Harmony, I understand dancing around a bonfire, but what's with the dawn ritual?"

Harmony sat in the sand, and everyone but King did the same. "A midsummer ritual is perfect for protective magick," Harmony said. "We're hoping to cleanse, purify, bless, and protect the castle, replace its negative energy with positive, and send Gussie on her peaceful way. This is a sun holiday, so I'm asking the light of the sun to master Gussie's darkness."

Reggie didn't look convinced. "Suppose Gussie goes nuts first? Couldn't she send your altar flying before you start, like the mural scaffolding?"

"We've been cleansing the negativity in the castle, room by room, in preparation, so there should be enough positive energy for us to get started. And the ritual circle is a sacred place, so Gussie won't be able to break in. We'll wear protective garlands of herbs and flowers. A powerful herb against negativity is chase devil, known to you as Saint-John's-wort."

Harmony didn't want to scare King with the belief that young women would find their significant others at midsummer festivals.

"Hey, Sis, I know this is serious stuff, but you forgot the best part."

"Storm, I don't think—"

"Get this, Reggie," Storm said. "The moon at midsummer is called the honey moon. Unmarried women wearing herb garlands during the festivities expect to find lovers or husbands."

"Cool," Reggie said, but King stood more rigid, his free hand clenched, his eyes broody.

As if the sun matched his mood, dusk descended with Harmony's hopes, and they all went inside.

King's body language said he thought she was trying to trap him, though she knew he was more afraid of his own feelings.

Didn't matter. She didn't need him. She didn't need anybody.

"You know what?" King said, when they got inside and he saw the Oak King table. "This is nuts. I'm taking Reggie and Jake to Boston for the next couple of days."

"Why?" Harmony and her sisters asked.

"To protect them—"

"And yourself," Harmony said.

"Right." He ushered Reggie and Jake toward the great hall door and turned back to her. "Stay, have your ceremony, then go."

Harmony recovered from her shock and followed them.

"Let's go, Reggie. Get in the helicopter."

"But, Dad, we need to pack our things. And I wanna stay."

"We're going. We'll get everything we need in Boston."

Reggie sighed, and King got her and Jake settled before he went around the helicopter to get in, but he looked back at Harmony, and their eyes met and held.

She raised her chin so he wouldn't see how much she hurt. "You protect them from me," she said, "and I'll protect them from Gussie."

He gave her a half nod and got in the chopper. By the time it lifted off, she turned to find Aiden, Morgan, and her sisters behind her.

Destiny took her arm. "Maybe we shouldn't go through with the ritual. I mean, he doesn't care. We could go home and let him keep Gussie."

Harmony stopped. "Listen to that demented cry. If it were just King, I'd go," she said, "I'm mad enough. But Reggie and Jake love this place. It's their first real home. We need to try and reclaim it for them."

"That's sporting of you," Aiden said. "King doesn't deserve you."

"No, he doesn't." But she'd belong to him forever, whether he wanted her to or not.

Storm took her other arm. "Sending Gussie to a place of peace, and away from here, is your psychic mandate, isn't it?"

"Yes, I believe that bringing peace to Paxton Castle is the reason I was directed here."

"You realize that you may never see King again," Storm said.

Harmony laid her head on the rebel's shoulder. "I don't believe I will."

They sat on the beach, Destiny holding one of her hands and Storm holding the other. "You can't read him like you used to, can you?" Storm asked.

"How did you know? Weird, isn't it?"

Storm shook her head with regret. "Not if you've fallen in love with him."

"You're nuts."

"Well, I am, but I also see the present. You're in love with the tight-assed technocrat. Not only that, you're pretty fond of his off-with-your-head castle, and you adore his daughter and grandson."

"A grandfather? I'm in love with a doddering old grandfather."

Morgan chuckled and bent down in front of her with a glass of something the color of King's eyes.

She sniffed it. "I hope this is *very* strong tea."

"Whiskey. Go ahead. Do you good."

She sipped it, and while she did, she thought about the way she drank King in when his whiskey eyes gazed into hers.

Chapter Forty-two

AS his helicopter rose off the island, King tried to ignore the disappointed look on Reggie's face. He especially tried to ignore Jake's tears, though that was difficult, because that boy could wail louder than Gussie. "I wanna be a dragon," he cried. "I gotta beat the drum."

"I'll buy you a dragon suit and a drum in Boston."

"No. I want *my* dragon suit. Dessie made it for me."

Jake's little bottom lip made for a really good pout, King thought, wishing the boy's sadness didn't tear him up inside. "How about a drum?"

"No."

"Dad, there are some things you can't buy. Happiness and the joy of family celebrations are two of them."

"Those witches are not your family."

"We got nisheeated!" Jake shouted.

"What'd he say?"

"They initiated us into their family when we stayed with them in Salem. Harmony, Destiny, and Storm—even

Vickie and Rory, though you haven't met them, yet—are all part of our family."

"Yeah," Jake said. "And I wanna hold the blue balloons."

"Is this the downside of parenthood?" King asked Reggie.

"What? A crying child? Or making stupid decisions based on your own fears?"

"Ouch! Nice talk." King did a double take his daughter's way.

"Don't think I can't stand up for myself," she said. "I wouldn't have survived on the streets or found you if I couldn't."

"You've learned a lot from Harmony, too." He eyed his daughter's irreverent T-shirt. "Who Are You and Why?" he asked, reading it.

Reggie folded her arms and raised her chin. "I could ask you the same question."

What could he say to that? "I like Harmony," an understatement he wouldn't explore, "but her magick doesn't—"

"Fit in with your belief system?" Reggie asked. "What do you believe in, Dad? I mean do you believe in a higher power?"

"Like the electric company?" He shrugged. "I guess I never thought about it. At military school I went to services because I had to."

"Which denomination?"

"Whichever one had the shortest service. It changed, depending on the preacher/priest/rabbi/monk of the semester."

"Do you know how I got through my year on the road?"

"No," King said turning to her, "but I'd like to."

"You're gonna think this is lame, but my favorite TV show when I left home was *Joan of Arcadia*. And, well, I pretended I was her, doing what God wanted me to do—take care of my son and find you—no matter how hard it got sometimes."

"You did an excellent job. Your son's bright and well-mannered."

"That's him, not me. I put him in a day care preschool in Jersey for a couple of months, and they said he tested like a four and a half to a five-year-old. I think somewhere along the line, he picked up on my struggle, and he tried to make it easier for me, or God tried, and Jake helped." Reggie shrugged.

"The point is," she said turning back to him a minute later, "if I hadn't believed in something greater than myself, I couldn't have done it. So don't get all bent out of shape at Harmony's belief system. At least she has one. She's a good person, Dad. They all are. They took me in so *you* could go to jail in California."

"Low blow."

"I'm feeling low."

Jake had fallen asleep by then, a temporary quiet King appreciated. Reggie turned away to look out her window, though it was too dark to see anything but lights.

Who was he? she'd asked. A man who'd been making mad, passionate love to—no, having sex with—a woman he'd just met. A woman who claimed to be a psychic witch. But since she'd practically read his mind from the first, he figured he might have to give her the psychic part.

What *did* he believe in?

He believed . . . he wanted his birthright, that blasted haunted castle, as much as his daughter did, though he'd been afraid to admit it until Harmony made him hope she could save it from Gussie—or whatever caused the wail, and accidents, and arguing—okay, so maybe it was Gussie. Hell, Jake had *seen* her.

How could he fault Reggie and Jake for falling for Harmony right off, when he'd done the same?

Well, he hadn't fallen for her, precisely. He'd been attracted, and a little in lust, maybe. A lot in lust. He wanted to see her when he opened his eyes mornings, hold her as he fell asleep at night. He wanted to tell her everything that happened at the end of the day.

Like now, he wanted to tell her about Jake crying to be a dragon, and about his grandson's word for *initiated*.

What would life be like if he never saw Harmony again?

King couldn't imagine a lonelier existence . . . so he must be fond of her. He'd never really be lonely with Jake and Reggie around, though Reggie might get married someday, and Jake would go to school, and away to college. Hmm. Maybe he would be lonely.

He loved Harmony for taking Reggie and Jake under her wing. And he adored her for saving their lives. He *almost* had the sense that she'd saved his life, but that was more nonsense.

King didn't remember landing the chopper, but since Ed was opening the door to his limo, he figured he must have. "My apartment, Ed," he told his driver, who got them efficiently out of Beverly and on the highway to Boston.

"After you drop off my Dad," Reggie said leaning forward. "Will you take me and my son back to Salem, please?"

"Get off at the nearest exit, Ed," King said, "and find a place to pull over."

"I'm gonna be a dragon, that's me," Jake sang. "I'm gonna beat on a drum, that's neat. I'm gonna hold a balloon, that's blue."

"You think your kid's gonna take up mind reading or song writing when he grows up?" King asked his daughter.

"He can be anything he wants." Reggie leaned close to whisper in his ear. "Jake can even be a dense, tight-assed technocrat."

King reared back.

"What's a tekkacrat?"

"You see what you did?" King said, indicating his grandson in the car seat facing them.

Reggie laughed. "The apple doesn't fall far from the tree, and he's got your genes written all over him."

"So do you." But that didn't make King happy at the moment, because the only gene that came to mind was the stubborn one. "Damn it, Regg!"

"Damn it, Regg!"

"Jake, cut that out. Ed, you wanna take us back to the Beverly Airport and call ahead so my chopper's ready?"

"Yes, sir."

Reggie threw her arms around him. "I love you, Daddy."

"Me, too, kitten," he said, appalled that he couldn't even use the word *love* with his family. What was *wrong* with him?

Before long, they were back at the Beverly Airport. "We won't need you anymore tonight, Ed. Thanks." King got out of the limo. "Will every dense Paxton in this car please follow me?" If he had one shot at giving these two the home they deserved, then Harmony and her midsummer madness seemed to be his only hope.

Okay, so it might be *his* one shot, too. Who knew?

When the island came into sight, King shivered, deep down, as if he were foolishly happy to be back.

"Now, when we land, Dad," Reggie cautioned. "You're gonna keep an open mind, right? Promise you will. And loosen up, will you? Stop being such a tight—"

"Regg!"

"I'm gonna be a dragon, that's me."

"Stop being dense and unyielding," Reggie said, correcting herself. She saw the beach and whooped. "Jake, there's no fire, yet. We got back in time. You can be a dragon with a drum!"

"Yay, Grampa!"

King chuckled. "Yay, Jake!" He landed and took Jake from his seat.

"Here comes Honey," Jake whispered in his ear, as if he understood there was friction between them. "Be nice," his grandson added.

"Keep it low on the grouch meter, Dad," Reggie said. "Harmony's headed this way."

"Thanks, but your son already gave me my orders," King snapped, and Reggie chuckled.

Harmony looked like a wounded animal, afraid to trust. He'd never seen her shut down like this. He knew, because he . . . he'd done it to her, the way he'd done it to himself. Damn, he didn't like grasping that fine point. He wanted to blame her for helping him grasp it, which pretty much meant that *he* still had the mentality of a two-year-old. Why not cry and sing his woes? Maybe Jake would teach him how. And maybe Reggie would teach him to grow up.

Harmony ran to meet them, and King's heart lifted, but she passed him to welcome Reggie and Jake.

The three of them walked around him and passed him by without a word, Harmony carrying Jake, who was chattering away, happy as a clam.

King leaned more heavily on his cane and shoved his other hand in his pocket to follow them home—to the castle. He stopped to look up at the monster. When had he stopped thinking of it as an albatross and started thinking of it as home?

By the time he got inside, Jake was already dressed like a dragon. Cute little barefooted green thing.

"If he isn't the most adorable midsummer dragon I've ever seen," Harmony said, "I'll eat—"

"Your words," Destiny said. "You've never seen a midsummer dragon, like we've never been able to celebrate with a bonfire."

Harmony shrugged. "I forgot." Her feet bare, her toe ring glistening, and her black robe flowing around her, she handed everybody a candle, except for Jake. To his grandson, she gave the drum, which Jake started drumming immediately, off beat and nonstop.

"Something tells me you're gonna be sorry," Reggie yelled over the din.

"Nah." Harmony grinned. "This is a fun celebration. That's the point. Have fun. Everybody get in line, and

Destiny will put a wreath on your head. Flowers for the ladies and greenery for the gentlemen. I'll light your candles, then we'll parade out to our soon-to-be-glorious midsummer bonfire."

"Why isn't anyone wearing shoes?" King asked.

"Because we're not uptight like you," Storm answered.

Destiny chuckled. "We're communing with the elements of nature tonight—earth, air, fire, and water. Communing works better without clothes. I should think *you'd* know that."

King swore inwardly and pulled off his shoes.

When all the candles were lit, Harmony hooked a duffel bag over her shoulder, lit her candle on Destiny's, and took Jake by the hand. "I'll chant, and Jake will drum, and everybody, follow us."

She led them in a serpentine parade through the kitchen and out the door, but before they cleared the castle's shadow, King's bare feet were killing him, plus he felt like an ass, because Morgan and Aiden were enjoying themselves.

So why couldn't he loosen up and enjoy himself?

Because, if the ritual worked, Harmony would leave? Hell no.

He *wanted* her to go.

Of course he did.

Chapter Forty-three

HARMONY'S voice mesmerized King as her chant rose like a prayer:

> *"Oak and Holly vie for rule*
> *Seasons change so fight your duel.*
> *Fall will come, embrace the sight*
> *From shades of green to colors bright."*

Harmony stopped by the unlit bonfire to wait. Someone had set it up like a Boy Scout, kindling perfectly placed. Morgan, King figured.

"This is it," Harmony said. "The big lighting. I'll sing a chant, and when I end it with 'torches to wood,' touch your candles to the kindling and step back. Everybody ready? Good." She stood Jake to the side away from the pyre and began to chant.

> *"Dragon of chaos, eager and sprite,*
> *Drum to summer's endless light.*

Spark fire and wondrous might
Welcome a new twelve month right.
Torches to wood; make it bright!"

Jake laughed louder than he beat the drum. Before long, the fire cracked and snapped, smoke wafting around them. "Blow out your candles," Harmony said, "and give them to Storm." She looked around, not meeting his eyes, and made sure the candles were snuffed and put aside so no one could get burned.

"Jake," she said, bending to him, "you can put your drum down and dance with us, or you can keep drumming."

"I gotta drum."

"Then drum you will. Everybody else clasp hands and do what I do. This is like playing ring around the rosy with a twist of your hips."

King stood to the side and watched, because his ankle wouldn't allow him to dance.

Following Harmony's undulating motion—quite the turn-on—everyone spiraled around the burning pyre, and damned if King didn't enjoy watching them. Aiden looked like a goose, and Storm tripped over her own feet and pulled down Morgan the Miserable, who was enjoying himself.

Their hilarity was contagious, but the more pleasure they took in the festivities, the louder Gussie wailed.

Harmony stopped dancing and looked up at the castle. "The fire needs feeding. I have just the fuel. Come and get it."

"What's this?" King asked when she handed him a picture frame.

"One of Gussie's empty 'negative' picture frames." Harmony handed out a dresser set, buttonhook, gloves, and scarves, and more frames. Taking her turn last, she took out the headless doll that had been in the toy room doll carriage, chanted something to herself, and tossed it in.

The fire flared to life, and Gussie quieted.

Harmony gave them each a paper and pencil. "Write what you wish to receive from our hostess the sun on the eve of her special day. I suggest that you write 'Peace for Paxton Castle.'"

King figured everybody wrote that, so he wrote, "I want Harmony . . ." and stopped. He wanted Harmony *to* understand him, and like him anyway, sleep with him, live with him. He wanted her *to* bring peace to the castle, but he wanted her to stay when she did. He wanted so much from her, he couldn't decide which was most important, so he left, "I want Harmony . . ." and hoped the sun would pick wisely from his many choices, because he couldn't.

After all the paper wishes had been thrown on the fire, Harmony and her sisters started singing "Ring of Fire," people joining in, clasping hands, and walking around the fire, while Jake's drumbeats slowed with the movement.

The lyrics felt personal. King wanted to dance, to drop his cane and join them, but he couldn't. "Bound by fire and desire," all he could do was watch Harmony sway to the music.

They all seemed to stop moving at the same time, perhaps all bound by desire, except for Reggie, who was too young, yet she lifted her child in her arms, nonetheless. She came and kissed his cheek. "Night, Dad. And thanks. See you at dawn."

"Are you going to be all right inside with Gussie?"

"As long I have Jake, I'm safe. Gussie adores him."

King watched his baby girl walk into the dark, unforgiving night toward a haunted castle to put her baby to bed. She'd walked alone through many a dark and unforgiving night. Maybe that's where she got her strength.

Aiden danced alone like a doofus. "I don't wanna stop partying yet. This is fun. What's next on the agenda?"

Storm sat in the sand and pulled him down. "Sit with me and appreciate the majesty of the universe."

Destiny sat and wrapped her arms around her knees to watch the fire, and like a moth to a flame, Morgan sat beside her and watched her.

King saw Harmony opening a cooler to take out cheese, crackers, a bowl of fresh mixed berries, and small bottles with homemade labels of dandelion wine. She offered food and drink to everyone but him.

He didn't know what to say.

Yes, he did. "Harmony, I'm sorry."

She didn't hear him, or she was ignoring him.

"Harmony," he said louder. "I acted like an ass today, and I'm sorry."

She took a half turn his way. "I understand. You are, by nature, an ass."

Chapter Forty-four

HARMONY couldn't believe that the mighty King had apologized.

"I am an ass for hurting you. I know that."

When Morgan and Aiden enthusiastically agreed, King laughed with them . . . at himself, which also surprised her.

Then King put an arm around her and drew her to the fire, though she walked slow to match his pace.

She wasn't sure she wanted to be with him. If Morgan, Aiden, and her sisters weren't there, she'd say no. She would. "I didn't think you'd make it through the procession, never mind the entire celebration," she said, as he pulled her down beside him.

"Neither did I. My feet are killing me after stepping on all those rocks."

"Grow thick soles, why don't you?"

"Plus I felt like an ass."

"For taking part in the revelry, or for being yourself?"

"For being the only one who wasn't *enjoying* himself."

Harmony knocked shoulders with him. "What made you stick with it?"

"You, being such an angel to my grandson."

"Jake's easy to love."

"Not like his Grampa, hey?"

Breaking waves filled the awkward silence.

King cleared his throat. "I didn't mean—"

"I'm sure you didn't."

"How could I not follow along with Jake beating those drums, the sound of his laughter reaching me at the tail end of the parade?"

"So what made you come back from Boston?"

"Reggie practically told me to grow up. Get a life. Get a belief system."

"As in, have faith in *something*?"

"Pretty much. Turns out faith is what got her here."

"She's a smart girl, and she didn't think she needed protecting from all this, huh?"

"All she wanted was to get back here, and she was coming with or without me."

"Maybe you were projecting your own need for emotional protection on her and Jake?"

King tilted his head and gave her a noncommittal shrug. "Crazier things have happened."

"You know, Paxton, you might be growing up. Care to give me a demonstration?"

Harmony caught the sudden stillness of his body, as if all systems went on alert. The intensity of his gaze in firelight made her shiver. "What kind of demonstration?" he asked.

"Stay with me. Hold me by the fire until dawn while I meditate in preparation for the ritual tomorrow. I need to visualize the negativity leaving the castle."

King stared into the fire, dealing with some inner struggle of his own, and though she could no longer discern its nature, she knew she was asking for something a great deal more intimate than sex. She understood his self-protective instinct. She'd never felt about anyone the way she felt about him, and before she fell any deeper in love, she needed to know what King Paxton was really made of.

He stood as if he was leaving, and her hope plummeted, but he put wood on the fire, sat in the sand behind her, and wrapped his arms around her. He nosed her hair aside, let his lips roam from her shoulder to her ear. "You're naked under this robe, aren't you?"

"Mmhmm."

"Is this a test?"

"Mmhmm."

"Visualize," he whispered. "And when you're ready to sleep, use me as your pillow."

Harmony visualized . . . and woke with a start. Use him as her pillow? She'd used him as her mattress. King, Aiden, and Morgan were still asleep, but her sisters had left the fire.

Harmony got up, careful not to wake King, and went inside to prepare the ritual.

"Harmony, wait," King called a minute later.

She stopped. "I thought you'd sleep a little longer."

He took her hand and laced their fingers together. "My front got cold."

She leaned into him. "First time your front ever wakes up cold."

He kissed her neck. "There's a difference between cold and ready."

She pulled his head down and blew into his ear. "I noticed."

Inside, Destiny and Storm were setting up the altar.

"Harmony," Destiny said. "We were just going to wake you. Is our high priestess ready to lead us?"

King stopped. "High priestess?"

Chapter Forty-five

KING woke Aiden and Morgan and found Reggie and Jake waiting for them inside when they got back. The saplings forming the circle each sported a blue balloon, and a bouquet of balloons was tied to the table, er, altar, leg.

Three gorgeous visions came down the stairs, three kittens walking behind them. Harmony—in a red robe that caressed her breasts, hugged her waist, and flowed to wide points at her hands and bare feet—wore silver sea horses on her earrings, pendant, and toe ring. But on her finger, she still wore the Celtic puzzle ring. Destiny wore butterfly jewelry with her yellow gown, and Storm wore dragon jewelry with her orange gown, each different, and beautiful all three, even the spike-haired rebel. But none were as startlingly radiant as Harmony, the high priestess.

King didn't know whether to be scared or turned on.

"I invite you all to take part. If you wish, take off your shoes and step into the circle of trees." Harmony spoke in an ordinary tone, which surprised King. "Remember," she added, "that after I cast the ritual circle, you can't leave until I close it down."

Reggie and Jake joined Destiny and Storm in the circle. He, Aiden, and Morgan looked at each other.

Jake came and grabbed his hand. "Come on, Grampa," he said, pulling uselessly. "Mama," Jake called, "Grampa's scared again." King laughed and let his grandson lead him into the circle, and he felt . . . as if he belonged. The area radiated a kind of peaceful warmth. Or was that Harmony's smile?

Morgan shrugged and joined them.

"If you don't believe in what we're doing," Destiny said, "get out, because anybody who doesn't help bring peace is feeding strife."

Morgan slipped his hands into his pockets. "Want me to go, King?"

"This isn't my ceremony," King said. "I have to respect the girls' wishes."

Morgan chuckled. "You never let anyone tell you what to do, but you're letting a woman take control? You've changed, buddy. I guess black magick wins. Or is it sex magick?"

"You don't believe in any kind of magick," Destiny snapped. "But for the record, we work white magick."

Morgan scoffed, and Aiden steered him toward the door. "King, I think Morgan needs me more than you do."

"That's probably true," King said. "Come back later."

"You don't have a ghost of a chance," Morgan yelled as Aiden shut the door.

Harmony tied the balloons to Jake's wrist. "You have an important job. Bright blue is for protection, and we chose *you* to protect us."

Jake beamed.

God, how he loved that boy, King thought, though he'd never actually said so to Jake or Reggie. He *had* been scared.

Harmony stood before the altar to face them. "We're dressed in the colors of midsummer to honor the sun. Close your eyes and imagine sending roots into the earth like a tree."

Jake smiled. "My tree grows balloons instead of leaves."

King knew the drill.

The girls walked the circle: "Three times around, I cleanse the circle with salt," Storm said as she sprinkled salt while Warlock sat on her shoulder and followed a dangling earring with his eyes.

"Three times, I cleanse the circle with water." Destiny sprinkled water from a scallop shell, Caramello hitching a ride on her gown's train.

"Three times, I cleanse the circle with incense," Harmony said, Gingertigger hopping around her skirts to catch its points.

Jake giggled, and Reggie tried to quiet him.

"Let him laugh," Harmony said. "Joy makes the circle stronger." She and her sisters began to chant:

> *"We gather at the tree*
> *The root and crown so tall*
> *Together we make our call*
> *In hope, with a plea for all."*

After making three full clockwise circles, Harmony stepped to the altar, her sisters behind her.

> *"Divine light, enter this sacred sphere.*
> *Ban negativity from entering here.*
> *Peace and love, grow and adhere."*

The mother cat jumped on King's shoulder, and he shouted his surprise.

"Relax, King," Harmony said, her breath at his ear and her hand at his back, infusing him with peace. "Let her stay. I'm glad she's joining us. She has a powerful protective energy, don't you Star?" Harmony petted the cat, then she combed her fingers through King's hair, raising a shiver of awareness between them, before returning to the altar.

His peacemaker became a dagger-bearing high priestess then, and she wielded her dagger to construct a circle around them. "For a future of peace and love, this circle is cast." She placed the dagger on the table and lit the corner candles.

> *"At the dawn of the solstice sun,*
> *Ancient elements join as one,*
> *Air, fire, water, and earth*
> *East, south, west, and north*
> *With your strength let peace be won."*

Gussie's whimper echoed, weak but rising, the first they had heard from her with Harmony *inside* the castle.

Harmony lit four tall candles in the center of the altar. "I light this candle for peace . . . this for protection . . . this for positive energy . . . this for harmony."

Gussie's wail gained momentum and volume. The triplets hummed together, and the objects on the altar trembled:

> *"Father God, Mother Goddess,*
> *For this island, aid in our resolve*
> *All negativity to absolve.*
> *Free its people, land, and shores,*
> *Sweep the evil from its doors.*
> *This is our will; set Paxton Castle free.*
> *And it harm none, so mote it be."*

Lightning flashed, and with it, Gussie's wail grew strong.

Harmony looked at her sisters, and concern passed between them.

King's protective instincts went on alert. He knew from his stint in the parlor car that lightning was Gussie's ally.

"Lightning is a powerful energy," Harmony said. "Gussie is gaining strength, so we have to grow stronger, as well."

Chapter Forty-six

HARMONY hadn't told King that in fighting such a powerful witch, her psychic and physical energy could be compromised. Yet she'd never felt more alive, more focused or determined, lightning and all. Nothing was more important to her than giving King, Reggie, and Jake a safe home.

She rang the bell three times to halt the storm and evoke good energies, and she turned to face the circle. "The storm is forcing an unplanned addition to the ritual." She handed a sprig of holly to each of them. "Holly protects against lightning and negative witchcraft," she said, arranging holly branches on the altar to form a star.

> *"Holly King soon to reign,*
> *Protect this home from lightning's bane.*
> *Oak King, raise your staff;*
> *Cut lightning's energy thrice in half."*

Feeling a bit dizzy, Harmony rang the bell again as Gussie's fighting wail became otherworldly.

"Let the Paxton family thrive
Joyful, calm, free, and alive.
Peace and love in this home bloom,
Safe from she who plots its doom."

Gussie's howl radiated fear in the people around her. "Positive thoughts," Harmony said. "The power of three as one will prevail."

She took a red velvet pouch. "Inside, I place angelica, thistle, holly, mistletoe, a hair from Gussie's brush, and her dolphin brooch."

Gussie's scream became shrill as their royal battle of wills gained momentum.

"In your mind," Harmony said, "add to this pouch: Gussie's cry, Paxton home and family troubles, accidents, worry, hurt, negativity, pain, and sorrow." She tied the pouch with a red ribbon. "Red heals, protects, and combats evil." She set the pouch aflame with a red candle and placed it in the cauldron. "As smoke rises from the cauldron, so castle negativity rises and dissipates like smoke up a chimney."

The timbre of Gussie's wail changed to distress.

Destiny and Storm aligned themselves beside Harmony:

"Augusta Paxton, this spell we cast:
In this place, your time has passed.
No more will you fill this air
With wailing energy to ensnare.
The vindication you sought for years
Is freely given by Paxton heirs.
And it harm none, they set you free.
This is our will, so mote it be."

The lightning reenergized Gussie, so her cry came from beside the circle. The cats arched and hissed as they guarded the perimeters, and Harmony's energy waned. She rang the bell, grasped the altar for support, and fell into a black pit.

"Gussie! Enough!" King's voice reached Harmony as if through a tunnel, and she knew *he* cradled her. "If you hurt the people I love," he shouted, "I'll take the castle down stone by stone and plow it under. I swear I will. Peace, Gussie! It's time. Harmony, sunshine, wake up."

Someone smoothed her hair and stroked her cheek. "Des! Storm!" King shouted. "I can't wake her!"

Her sisters clasped her hands, and Harmony accepted the life energy they passed to her. She opened her eyes. "What happened?"

Storm chuckled. "Gussie sucked you under, and Bomb Diggity, over here, took over the ritual. Pretty touching and resourceful, for a detached hunk with no belief system."

"You scared me to death," King said, pulling her close, his heart beating double time against hers. He captured her gaze. "Harmony, I know you can do this, but do you feel well enough?"

"You believe in me? But not in witches, psychics, or angels, right?"

He chuckled. "I figure you have aspects of all three—though, rarely, the angel—but yes, I believe in you." His loving kiss helped replenish her well of strength, and she leaned on him to stand.

"I'm ready," she said. "Hold hands and imagine that Gussie is a spiral of smoke going up the chimney." She took King's cane and placed it on the altar. "You don't need the cane for this. We'll hold you up." The six of them formed an inner circle.

"Can the purple lady play ring around the rosy with us?" Jake asked.

Harmony looked around. "Is she here, Jake?"

"She's watching us, and she's sad."

"Gussie," Harmony said. "Lisette sent me to help you find peace."

Brahms's "Lullaby" wafted into the room, while *inside* the circle, someone hummed. Harmony looked at each of them, all shocked by the sound, all denying the source.

Had Lisette joined the circle to lend her strength from the beginning? "Jake, is there a girl in the circle wearing a faded gown?"

Jake nodded. "She cares about Gussie."

Harmony nodded toward her sisters. "Now!"

"With the grace of the angels and elements, we bless you, Augusta 'Gussie' Paxton, and free you from the negative forces empowering you, so you may find eternal peace and rest.
We bless and free you with the power of the God and Goddess!
We bless and free you with the power of the sun, moon, and stars!
We bless and free you with the power of the angels!
We bless and free you with the power of earth, air, fire, water!
With the grace of the angels and elements, we bless you, Augusta 'Gussie' Paxton, and free you from the negative forces empowering you, so you may find eternal peace and rest."

Gussie wept quietly.

"I honestly feel bad for her," King said, and at his words, his cane flew from the altar, into the air, hit the rafters, and shattered. Debris rained down on them, and the cane's gold tip bounced at his feet. King picked it up, took a tiny leather box from inside, opened it, and looked up. "The female half of the ring." He took it out and read the band. "What does your half say?"

"Love eternal," Harmony whispered.

King took her hand, removed her half, snapped the two pieces together, and held it for them to see. "The Paxton Celtic lovers' ring, at last." He took her hand, again, and Harmony bit her lip against hope as he slipped the coupled ring on her finger. Still holding her hand, he gazed into her eyes. "Love eternal . . . when bound we be," he said, revealing the full engraving, then he bent to kiss her, the most gentle and . . . loving . . . kiss imaginable. "Hold that thought," he said, straightening.

Harmony trembled inside, while Gussie wept, and the cats stopped hissing.

"The purple lady is sorry," Jake said. "She's gonna go with the girl, so we can have the castle." Jake hugged King's legs. "I love you, Grampa. Can we live here forever?"

"Yes," King said. "We can. I love you, Jake, and I love you, Reggie." He drew his daughter close. "Welcome home."

Gussie's last, unexpected sob burst like a glass ball into a million echoing shards of . . . joy.

Then . . . silence. Blessed silence.

The cats did a psycho-cat dance of joy, backflipping, altar-hopping, and running up pants legs. Jake giggled and went psycho with them.

Still trembling inside at the implications of the Paxton ring on her finger, Harmony continued the ritual. She broke and shared a warm loaf of honey-drizzled bread among them, leaving a plate on the altar to honor and thank the Goddess.

She and King kissed between bites. "We still have to give thanks," she whispered against his lips.

He winked. "We certainly do."

She returned to the altar.

"God and Goddess, angels fair,
Earth, fire, water, and air,

Thank you for our bountiful fare
Especially for this peace so rare."

"Amen," King said.

"Des and Storm, extinguish the candles, if you will."

Harmony closed her eyes, bowed her head, and raised it. "The circle is open."

King winked. "Are we free to move about the cabin?"

Jake stood on his toes to look around. "Is the purple lady gone?"

Harmony picked him up so he could check the room. "I feel peace all around us. I hope she's gone and at peace, Jake."

King touched her arm. "You hope? How will we know for sure?"

Harmony touched a finger to her lips, then to his. "Live here."

Chapter Forty-seven

"KING," Harmony said after their ritual, "this is Gussie's scrying mirror. We sealed it in one of your metal toolboxes, so Gussie couldn't access it during the ritual. It's the last piece of her magick in the house. I have a plan to dispose of it. Let's go."

"Scrying?" he asked, as they left.

"You read it like you read a crystal ball. Do you need another cane? There are at least a dozen upstairs."

"A dozen? And you gave me the one with the ring inside?"

"I had no idea, but no wonder I got a sense of the ring near the cane stand. Guess I must be psychic or something."

"You're something, all right, and I'd rather lean on you than a cane."

Harmony's heart tripped. "I never thought *you'd* lean on anyone."

"Walking alone isn't all it's cracked up to be.

"Especially up this hill." They walked slowly, their arms around each other, toward the edge of the cliff. "This is the place," she said, "looking down to the base of the cliff. Gussie loved the sea. Nicodemus died there. Lisette escaped there, and Gussie's mirror belongs there."

"This is Mermaid Cliff," King said.

"Appropriate, since we're both fond of mermaids."

King brought her as close as he could with the mirror between them. "You're the only mermaid I want."

"I'm glad." She accepted his kiss but didn't push for more than he was willing to give. "I promised to explain the meaning of the sea horse after the ritual. Are you ready? The ancient Celts believed that the sea horse was a transporter to the otherworld."

"Blessed peaceful ghost! What made you choose a sea horse tattoo?"

"It was cute. We were thirteen when we got our tattoos. We didn't understand the symbolism. You named your boat *The Sea Horse*. Why? Because you wanted to cross somebody over? I don't think so. Yet I believe that your compassion, when you felt sorry for Gussie, is what made Lisette give you the other half of the ring."

"I think she did it for you." He looked out over the cliff. "How did you know about this place?"

"I came for a walk last night . . . when I never thought I'd see you again."

He winced. "I was a fool. Have you forgiven me?"

"I'm thinking about it."

"Think harder." He grazed her neck with his lips to persuade her.

Looking down, she eyed his interest . . . with interest. "I see *you're* thinking harder."

"Ignore that. I have a sock in my pants." He turned the mirror so she could look into it. "Tell me what you see."

Harmony gasped. "Lisette! She's wearing my gown, saying, 'Thank you.' Ah, she's gone, but I did it, King!"

She threw her arms around him. "I completed my psychic mandate."

"Somehow, I knew you would. I'm glad you saw proof. I didn't expect it, but I'm glad. I showed you the mirror so I could tell you what I see when I look at you . . . at us."

Harmony's radar went up, and she stepped back. "I'm listening."

"During the ritual, I realized that I'd entrusted you with my family's future, and my thoughts crystallized. You and I are polar opposites. "I'm broody, skeptical, controlling."

Harmony nodded. "Single-minded, uptight, impatient, bossy . . ."

King frowned, such an endearing frown. "I'm trying to make a point."

She slid an arm to his waist via his tush. "Please continue."

He raised a brow. "I'm all the things you said, while you're unconventional, willful, impulsive, stubborn, and scary/thrilling . . . everything I've been missing in my life. You stir my heart, Harmony, the way you stir that cauldron, arousing fire and peace, magick and love."

"I do?" Harmony stilled and felt herself coming back to life. "I wanna kiss you, but I can't get close enough with the mirror between us. Throw it, now, as far as you can, so it doesn't break on the rocks."

King tossed it in a sweeping arc, and the mirror slid clean into the sea.

"Yay team!" Harmony cheered. "Give me an *O*."

King crushed her in his embrace and kissed her senseless. When he broke the kiss, he looked up and turned her in his arms to face the sea. Dolphins played where the mirror had landed. "Look, they're celebrating for Gussie."

The sun slipped from behind a feathery white cloud and crowned the dolphin playground with a rainbow.

Harmony's eyes filled. "The dolphin symbolizes the end of an old life and the birth of a new one."

"Speaking of which . . . ," King said. "When my cane shattered, I think the walls around my heart shattered, too, because all manner of emotions poured out. Then there was this ring." He took her hand. "*This* amazing symbol of the missing half of my heart."

"I feel like we're in the lagoon," Harmony said.

"The lagoon," King repeated, "was more than passion. That's why I ran."

"I know."

"You've always known things about me that you shouldn't."

She smiled. "When I got to the castle, I could read you—every sexy move, touch, lick, kiss, and maneuver you imagined—I read your every *fantasy*." She wiggled her brows. "But I can't read your thoughts anymore." She tried to sound wistful.

He raised a knowing brow. "Want me to spell it out for you, do you? Then I will. Remember what I said about getting married once in a blue moon?"

"I remember. Blue moons happen about thirty-seven times a century."

King searched her expression. "Do you know the date of the next blue moon?"

Harmony couldn't stop her smile. "I do, but do you?"

He gave her an enigmatic smile. "Seven days from today. On June thirtieth, there'll be a blue moon."

"I found Lisette's half of the ring with the first full moon of the month, June first," Harmony said.

King's laugh lines crinkled to the breaking point. Her heart about stopped with his all-out grin. "And with the second full moon of the month, the blue moon, we can split the ring so *we* become two halves of a whole, each of us wearing half. Romantic, huh?"

"I could faint from the romance—that *was* a proposal, right?"

"There's that smart mouth, but I love you, anyway."

"Get out!" She pushed from his arms. "You don't know what you're saying. You *love* me?"

"Didn't I say so during the ritual when I gave you the ring?"

"Uh, no, McClueless."

King shook his head. "Smart mouth and all, I love you," he whispered against her lips, and his words touched her in amazing places, especially her heart.

He pulled her down to the wet, lavender- and thyme-scented grass.

Harmony touched his face, his dear, dear face, traced those wonderful laugh lines, gazed into his deep whiskey eyes, his emotions there for her to see, including . . . love. The man she loved . . . loved her in return. Bless the stars, how had she gotten so lucky? Her psychic mandate had turned a handful of unwanted misfits and an off-with-their-heads castle into a home and a family. "I love you, King." She cupped his cheek. "I love you, but I never thought I'd get to tell you."

"Harmony Cartwright, will you marry me? In sickness and health, grandchildren and castle renovations—not to mention great times in the sack with multiple multiples—for as long as we both shall live? How's that for a proposal? Spontaneous *and* romantic, heh?"

She laughed. "I'll marry you in sickness and health, lust, passion, peace, and love—in spite of your fractured tries at spontaneous romantic sentiment—for as long as we both shall live . . . *and beyond.*"

Despite his exaggerated wince and the quirky half smile that accompanied it, Harmony could see that King's emotions sat close to the surface. He cleared his throat. "I love your laugh, you witchy woman. And I love that you're a smart, sexy, sassy high priestess. I noticed the first day that you have a great rack, a fine ass, and legs that go on forever—but I didn't know about the tattoos." King began his nibbling way down her cleavage, toward the triquetra hidden there, but he stopped, looked up, and grinned, an easy, no-holds-barred grin that overflowed her heart with love. "How can a man not love a woman with tattoos?" he said.

"All this sweet talk is going to my head, McBullseye. Good thing you're aces in the sack."

"How do witches get married?" he asked, raising his head. "Do we have to fly in a high priest on a broom?"

Turn the page for a preview of
Annette Blair's next novel featuring

Storm Cartwright.

Coming soon from Berkley Sensation!

BENEATH a rare blue moon in June, Storm Cartwright, bridesmaid, her black hair streaked blue to match her gown, accepted the arm of Aiden McCloud, the stud man she planned to kidnap after her sister's wedding—unless he decided to cooperate, in which case, hell was bound to freeze over by midnight.

"Are you sure you won't come with me to find the baby I hear crying in my mind when I'm near you?" she asked one last time, just to be fair.

Aiden shook his head, his long dark hair shifting in the breeze, the sexy quirk of his lips was beguiling " 'In your mind,' being the operative phrase," he said. "Yes, I'm sure. Strong instincts of self-preservation compel me to say no. Chasing the voices in *your* head scares even this tough out-law biker."

Storm gave him a flirty wink. "I'm so proud." Since meeting Aiden—a case of electromagnetic attraction at first sight—her clairaudience had kicked into overdrive. Audible only to her and only when she was near him, that crying baby's telekinetic plea put all her instincts on high alert. And her plan to follow the sound and find the child—his child, she believed, but he denied—meant taking him on a journey with no destination, a concept he found understandably ludicrous.

He stroked the soft flesh of her wrist with his thumb, demonstrating his ability to turn her to jelly, which did not come as a surprise. "Drop the agenda," he said, "and it's a hot-date road trip in a luxury motor home that could pamper you prissy."

"Hah! Me, prissy?" She bit her lip. Could she accept the hot date and let the sound in her mind direct the trip without him realizing? She'd planned to take his motor home, anyway.

"Forget it," Aiden said, reclaiming his hand. "No road trip, and no wands or spells to get your witchy way. Your body language alone is beginning to make me twitch. We'll stay in Salem. You can give me a"—he leaned close—"*personal* tour." He eyed the triquetra tattoo revealed by her gown, low on her right breast, then he forcefully shifted his hungry gaze to her lips. "I could make a meal of those blackberry lips," he whispered.

Good. The stage for her plan was set: A horny hunk, a wedding beneath the stars, soft music wafting over Paxton Island, waves breaking against the shore, fairy lights in the trees, and rose-scented air. A scene teeming with allure.

For weeks, they'd been playing a sexual version of chicken, a bit like juggling fireballs, but almost hoping to get burned. As far as she was concerned, tonight was more than her sister's wedding. It was an opportunity for some preforeplay foreplay that pointed to a premeditated coed inferno, which might—or might not—take the top spot on her agenda at the end of the day.

She'd make it work and she didn't need magic to pull it off. She had a plan going for her, a choreographed seduction . . . and celibacy, three weeks' worth. Abstinence, as in the lack of, as in they'd never had sex—with each other—a rather mystically mutual state of affairs that fit her scheme so well, she hadn't questioned it, though perhaps she should have.

After the reception, if she and her sisters played their parts right, she and Aiden would drive off alone together on a psychic quest that just happened to include sex as a bonus. Multiple bonuses, and multiple multiples, she hoped. It was a matter of fate, providence, and a spiritual directive of discovery and rescue.

Storm beamed, and judging by Aiden's quick physical reaction, her anticipation hit him square in the libido. Oh yeah, they were on the same wave length, all right, both hot as a lightning bolt. They had sexual chemistry stockpiled in gigawatts.

"Cut that out," Aiden snapped in a whisper as he faced her, turning his back on the wedding guests. "We're standing, literally, in the spotlight. People are watching."

"Hah," she whispered, glancing down. "*You're* certainly giving them something to see. You cut it out. This is the bride's day. Don't go shortchanging my sister." On the outside, her scowl matched Aiden's. On the inside, she rubbed her hands together in glee with tingly, warm sexberry gel. Judging by her mark's insta-boner, the role of seducer was "up" for grabs.

Aiden leaned in, his nearness tickling her skin and invading her senses like whipped cream and rose petals. "I'm gonna get you for this," he promised.

Dragon's blood, he looked hot in a tux. "Finally," she quipped, tossing down the proverbial gauntlet to speed her plan on its merry way. "You'll excuse me if I have my doubts about your libido going the distance?"

"Are you kidding me?" He straightened, forgetting to whisper.

"Shh!" Storm faced forward as the musicians began to play "By the Light of the Silvery Moon," in lieu of the wedding march, and she and Aiden began their trek down the garden path toward the gazebo. There they separated as Aiden went to his side, and she went to hers to witness the marriage of her sister Harmony to Aiden's best friend, King.

In the center of the gazebo, wearing the beautifully restored gold linen day gown that led her sister to King Paxton in the first place, the bride as high priestess cast a ritual circle that encompassed the bridal couple, the wedding party, the justice of the peace, and four cats.

Harmony—with her clone attendants, triplets extraordinaire—had also chosen her future step-daughter as a bridesmaid, and their pregnant half sister, Vickie, who positively bloomed.

Beside King stood his three-year-old grandson, as ring bearer, his two best friends, and the Scot who'd knocked up the bride's half sister and married her shortly afterward.

After a romantic and emotional ceremony, utilizing portions of both Celtic and traditional weddings, Harmony and King kissed as husband and wife for the first time. Applause and a hearty rendition of "Blue Moon" followed them into Paxton Castle for the wedding reception.

The constellations winked, and the moon smiled wide as Storm imagined taking Badass McMagic prisoner, likely in shackles. And later—once he willingly joined the quest—she anticipated having her very wicked way with him.

For **Annette Blair**, writing comedy started with a root canal and a reluctant trip to Salem, Massachusetts. Though she had once said she'd never write a contemporary, she stumbled into the serendipitous role of "Accidental Witch Writer" on that trip. Funny how she managed to eat her words, even with an aching jaw. After she turned to writing bewitching romantic comedies, a magic new world opened up to her. She loves her new home at Berkley Sensation.

Contact her through her website at www.annette blair.com.